Jack Crane's Secret World

David & Pooraka
Primary

Dedicated to my late father, Joe Stone, for all his love and support throughout my life.

A CHP production

Published in Australia by
Crawford House Publishing (Australia) Pty Ltd
34 Kingdon Place
Goolwa SA 5214
www.crawfordhouse.com.au

National Library of Australia
Cataloguing-in-Publication entry:

Burnell, Suzanne, Lee, author
Title: Jack Crane's Secret World / by Suzanne Lee Burnell
ISBN: 9781863333382 (paperback)
Target Audience: For primary school age.
Subjects: Gardens--Juvenile fiction
Magic--Juvenile fiction.
Friendship--Juvenile fiction.
Dewey Number: A823.4

Printed in China

19 18 17 16 15 14 13 7 6 5 4 3 2 1

Jack Crane's Secret World

Suzanne Burnell

Crawford House Publishing Adelaide

Prologue

Ten year old Jack Crane woke up with a start. He had never heard a scream so intense. He didn't have time to think as he jumped out of bed, grabbed the torch from his bedside table, and raced into his parents' bedroom. He expected to see his mother sitting up, waiting to comfort him, but there was nothing: no loving arms to greet him, or soothing voice to tell him it would be all right. There was nothing but his father's loud snoring. Jack couldn't believe it. How could they? How could his parents sleep through all this noise? The storm was far worse now than when he went to bed, and that scream; how could anyone sleep through that scream?

He wanted to wake them and tell them about the screams. He wanted to tell them how scared he was, and how much he hated the thunder, but he didn't dare. Shivering, he closed the door behind him, and called out to his dogs, but there was no sign of them. They hated storms even more than he did. He wanted to go downstairs, and find out where the screams came from, but that was scary. It meant going out into the garden in this storm, and there was something about the garden, something that worried him.

Jack's hand was shaking as he fumbled to switch

on the torch. He saw the staircase ahead. He walked towards it. It was the strangest feeling; like he was being led there. Shining the torch onto each step he crept down, gripping the rail for support, but the closer he got to the bottom the more anxious he became. He was starting to lose his nerve. The thunder rumbled above him, as heavy rain battered the windows. Even the banging of the pet door in the wind gave him the creeps. He tip-toed past the grandfather clock, jumping with fright as it struck three o'clock.

With some trepidation Jack entered the family room. It was creepy; dark, cold and creepy. The bushes outside looked frightening, like angry monsters with long swaying tentacles. The wind howled around them. He didn't want to move any closer, but some force was pulling him, pulling him towards the door.

He moved slowly, as if in a trance. He was nearly there, only a few more steps. Jack turned the handle, and slowly opened the door. He reached out..., and there, right in front of him, was the most amazing sight. The garden was bathed in the brightest light he had ever seen. He expected it to be scary. He expected to see something horrible, but it was beautiful. It was like fairyland.

A sense of calm had returned. The wind had died down and the rain had nearly stopped. Jack felt excited. He could see the brick wall and the cobblestone path winding its way to the green shed. The lower branches of the gum tree were swaying above it, and he could see... Jack rubbed his eyes. It couldn't be. It wasn't possible. He looked again. Something was standing right in front of the green shed: something unbelievable.

Jack couldn't take his eyes off it as the thing stared

down the cobblestone path. It looked straight past him as if he didn't exist. He could swear the creature was wearing a red dress. He could see it billowing around its feet. He could also see two small ears poking out from beneath the red bonnet. What was it? It was the weirdest thing he had ever seen. Jack blinked. He must be imagining things, this just couldn't be real. It was too weird. It looked like a small animal, but it was dressed from head to foot. The whole thing was crazy.

Jack screwed his eyes tight to get a better look. He could just make out something long beneath the dress. Was it a tail? And beneath that red bonnet could he see a furry head? He couldn't tell what it was. It was so frustrating. He kept focusing on the small creature. Should he help it? Did it want his help? However, it was too late. The garden was suddenly plunged into darkness as an almighty clap of thunder shook the house.

Jack dropped the torch in fright and raced back inside, slamming the door behind him. The storm was back with a vengeance. He flew up the stairs. He just wanted the safety of his room. He just wanted to get out of the garden. None of this had happened, none of it. He hadn't seen that animal. He hadn't heard those screams. It was in his head, all of it was in his head.

He flung himself onto the bed and pulled the covers over him. He could hear the dogs panting as the wind tore through the garden. The branches of the old gum tree groaned and moaned above the house.

There was a sound; he heard it through the wind. It was that scream. He was sure of it: that same piercing scream. Jack felt sick. Something was wrong. Something bad had happened out in the garden. He thought of the creature. He was scared for it, but he had to stop worrying. The creature wasn't real. It couldn't be.

Jack shuddered as the grandfather clock struck, the chimes echoing throughout the house. He closed his eyes and counted them. It was four o'clock in the morning, and suddenly there was silence. No screams, no storms: nothing but silence.

Twenty years later.

Jack opened the back door of the old house. He had loved this place. He had grown up here. All his memories were locked up within its walls. All his memories were locked up within its garden. He could still remember the pain he felt the day his parents said they were leaving. He was sixteen years old, and he thought he would die. He couldn't imagine his life ever being the same again, and now, thought Jack, all these years later he had found this house again. He and Bella were now the proud owners of their very first home.

Stepping onto the verandah, Jack felt overwhelmed. It was all so familiar yet somehow so much smaller than he remembered. The garden had seemed so big when he was ten years old but now it looked just like any other garden. As a child his world had changed in this garden and, like that ten year old child, he felt excited again. He had found friendship and love here at a time when his real world was so awful. Even though he was grown up now, his thoughts were always with this place. In fact, he had even written two books about his adventures here, and now he was back. Twenty years after the storm he was back.

'Daddy, Daddy!' Jack's six year old daughter, Mia, raced up the path towards him, her dark curls flying behind. 'I've found some of them, Daddy. They are just like in your book. They are in the same places too. I've found Daisy, the mouse, Felicity, the little girl, and Ben, the dog. The only one that's not under the wrought iron seat is Annie, the mushroom. Come and have a look, Daddy, come quickly.'

With some trepidation Jack followed his daughter to the place where she had made her discovery. He stared down at Daisy, Felicity and Ben. They all looked the same. He wanted to be with them. He needed to be with them.

'Come on Daddy,' said Mia, impatiently. 'I want to find the others.' He followed her again, this time up the narrow pathway towards the cubby. It used to be his secret path. It used to be his and their secret path.

'Wow,' said his daughter as they reached the cubby. 'It's so pretty. It even has flower pots on the balcony. Just like the book.' Jack couldn't help groaning. Mia comparing everything with the book was getting a bit annoying. He had to admit though, the cubby still looked good.

'And look,' cried Mia, excitedly, pointing to the top of the garden. 'There's the big statue of the girl. There's Theresa, but where's her long, dark hair? In your book she has long dark hair.' His daughter looked disappointed.

'Well,' said her father, staring up at Theresa, 'in the book, the ornaments don't come to life until after sunset. At the moment they are just ordinary ornaments. Also,' said Jack, 'it is just a book. You know it's not real.' He looked down at his daughter's pale face, and gently ruffled her black curls.

'I know,' said Mia, 'but it makes me feel sad. I want them to be real, so badly. Just like in your book Daddy. I just want them to be real!'

'Come on,' said Jack, grabbing her hand, 'let's see if we can find Annie, and also your brother. He might have found some of the others. Who knows,' he said, grinning, 'maybe they are real. Maybe they do come to life after sunset. What do you think?'

Mia chuckled, her dark eyes dancing with delight. Sometimes her dad said some really silly things, but she'd go along with it. It could be fun. She could imagine they did come to life. Yes! She'd come out into the garden after sunset, and imagine.

'Yes, Daddy, let's say they are real.' She reached out towards him and smiled. 'But now, let's look for Annie.'

Hand in hand, they wandered around the garden. For Jack, it was like Memory Lane, and for Mia it was as if the book had come to life. Every time she recognised something she would squeal with excitement. First, she found the vegetable garden that Mr Tom, the big cat, worked in, then she spotted Maggie, the magpie, and Katie, the kookaburra. 'I can't believe it.,' she cried, 'they all look the same as the pictures in your book. They look exactly the same....'

Mia suddenly stopped and pointed. 'But what are those?' Standing side by side, under the spreading fig tree, were two small wooden crosses: one with the name, 'Scarlet', engraved on it; the other, 'Maxine'. 'Oh No!' she cried. 'It's the two little dogs from the book. I didn't know they were real dogs. Oh, Daddy, it's so sad.' She squeezed her father's hand. 'When did they die?'

Jack looked down at the graves. He had loved those

little dogs. They were always there for him. Always. 'Just before we sold the house,' he said quietly. 'But now they are happy. They've gone to a much better place. So we mustn't be sad.'

'No,' said Mia, gently touching the wooden sticks. 'Now they have gone to live with the angels.' She had thought about asking her dad for a dog. Especially now they were settled in their very own house, but looking at the little graves in front of her, and watching her father wipe away a tear, she didn't think that now was a very good time.

A shout nearby made Jack look up. His eight year old son Peter was running down the cobblestone path to meet them. 'Dad, Dad! I love this garden. I love the cubby. I love everything. I've even found some of the ornaments. Come and have a look, and would you believe that they are in the exact same spot as in your book. I even found the Indian boy in the vegetable garden. It's awesome.' Jack looked at his son. He looked happier than he had seen him in ages. He looked alive. Peter was just like he had been at the same age. A quiet sensitive child, not able to make friends easily; a child who found life difficult.

'Look,' cried Peter. 'There's Mr Tom, the big cat, against the wall, and by the blue pot is Reggie, the gnome, and Herbert, the wombat. 'Isn't it exciting.'

It is exciting, thought Jack, looking around at his old friends again. After all this time they hadn't changed, but he had changed. Life had changed. His parents now lived in a little cottage by the sea, and his grandparents, who were in their seventies, lived in a retirement village in the city. Jack sighed. He, himself, was thirty years old. He wasn't ten any more. He had aged, but sadly, the ornaments hadn't.

'... and there's Annie the mushroom,' yelled Mia, breaking into his thoughts. 'Can I take her back to her proper home? She must be lonely here. She's meant to live near Daisy and Felicity.'

Jack felt sad as he looked down into Annie's face. He felt sad that he had had to leave them all those years ago. He felt sad that he had caused them pain, and he had missed them. Oh!, how he had missed them. Smiling, he watched his children carry Annie back to her normal spot, and carefully place her under the lavender bush. He knew then that the ornaments were in good hands. With his children, they'd be safe. Jack was glad that he had decided to bring his children home. Back to the valley. Back to where his memories were. Not just for him, but for his wife, Bella too. They were both glad to be home.

After the evening meal, Bella and the children sat together in the lounge room. The grandfather clock chimed. 'Ok, you two,' she said patiently. 'Go upstairs and get ready for bed. You've both had a big day. I'll come up later and tuck you in.'

'But I'm not tired,' wailed Mia. 'I'm too excited. Now that I've seen the ornaments, couldn't Daddy read us his book?' It was strange, thought Bella, how books had come back into fashion again. Unlike the children, she had struggled with all the new ways of reading. They were meant to make reading easier, but it was never the same as reading a book; touching it and smelling the richness of the cover, and it was great for Jack; books coming back. Suddenly being an author meant something.

'Come here, Mia,' said Bella, brushing a black curl

out of her daughter's dark brown eyes. 'Dad's read you that book lots of times. Look darling, it's seven o'clock. Why don't you let him read his second book. He hasn't finished writing it yet, but it's still about the garden. It's still about the ornaments.' Bella was tired, even if her children weren't. It had been a long day; an emotional day. Just like Jack, she had felt excited from the moment she stepped into the old house, and she couldn't wait to go out into the garden. She couldn't wait to see them again, but right now all she could think of was bed, and the prospect of a good night's sleep.

'No,' said her daughter, stubbornly. 'Daddy hasn't finished writing that book yet. It would be stupid to start reading it before it's finished. I want Daddy to read this book.' She pointed to the novel lying on the table. 'I want him to read *Jack Crane's Secret World*. Please Mummy.'

'Yes, Mum,' piped up Peter. 'I want Dad to read it too. Right from the beginning. Right from the time Daisy the mouse is watching the house. Before the storm. Before the boy Jack discovers their secret. Please Mum.'

Bella sighed. All of her ached, and she was honestly too tired to argue. 'Okay then, ask your father. If he says he will, make sure you are both ready for bed first. Now give me a hug, because believe it or not, I am tired.' Mia squeezed her mother tightly then ran from the room in search of her father.

Peter watched his mother walk slowly up the stairs. She had shaken her hair loose; black curls falling down around her shoulders. He couldn't get over how much his sister looked like their mother. Just a smaller version. He, however, didn't look like anyone. Sometimes he wondered if he was adopted. His mother turned around and blew him a kiss from the top of the stairs, then disappeared into the bathroom. He adored his mother. Without her, he didn't think he could survive. Without her, life wouldn't be worth living.

Mia rushed back into the room. 'Peter, we've got to hurry. Daddy said if we are in bed by half past seven, he'll read the book. Hurry, we have to clean our teeth and get into our pyjamas. Quick! I'll race you up the stairs.'

'You only just made it,' said their father, puffing slightly as he entered the bedroom. The old grandfather clock chimed in the hall. Peter thought that it had to be the oldest clock in the world. It was even older than his great grandparents, and they were ancient. He loved the clock though. Its sound was comforting.

'Now.' said Jack, sitting on the edge of Mia's bed. 'Are you two sure you want to hear this again from the beginning? As you know, it's a long story.'

'Yes,' cried Mia. 'I know where the ornaments live now, and I know what the garden looks like. When you read it, I can see it properly in my head.'

'Me, too,' said her brother. He looked up at his father. 'Dad. This story is about real things that happened to you as a little boy, isn't it?

Jack nodded. 'Mostly. Some things I might have exaggerated a little. Like Grandma Mary meeting Theresa.' Although Jack did wonder sometimes. He did wonder if his mother had known. It was something Daisy had said. Something she had let slip.

'Well, how come,' continued Peter, 'how come the storm was real and everything else was real. Like Grandma Mary and Grandpa Alan, and the garden. Everything in the garden is exactly how it is in your book. Everything, except the ornaments.' He looked directly at his father. 'They don't really come to life, do they, Dad? That's all make believe isn't it?'

Jack opened the book to Chapter One. He studied his son's face before he answered him. Peter looked troubled. He wanted to make him feel better. He almost wanted him to believe.

'It depends,' said Jack, finally. 'The ornaments can be whatever you want them to be. They can be real in your mind. They can be as real as you want them to be. Or maybe,' he said, winking at Mia, 'maybe they really do exist. Maybe they really do come alive after sunset. Who knows.'

'I'd like them to be real,' said Peter, softly. 'I'd like to be in their world.' He flicked a strand of blonde hair out of his eyes. 'I don't like this world much Dad. It sucks.'

Jack stared at his son. He felt sick for him. It was like going back in time. Jack knew what it was like to be Peter's age. Life had sucked for him too, but this was his son. He wanted things to be better for him.

'Is it that bad, Peter? Is your world that bad? You know we can talk about it. Right now, if you want.'
Peter shook his head. 'Don't worry about it, Dad. I just want to hear the book. Then I will be in their world.'

'Me, too,' said Mia, clutching her doll. Me, too.'

'Okay,' said Jack. 'Let's do it then. Let's go deep into their world.' He turned the page. 'Chapter One - A Problem In The Garden...'

1

A Problem in the Garden

Daisy, the grey mouse, stood by the birdbath, lost in pleasant thought. She loved the garden this time of day. The sun was setting behind the hills on the other side of the valley, casting large shadows over the lawn. A soft breeze floated through the garden, brushing past her face and stroking her long whiskers. She sniffed. Even the strong smell of jasmine made her feel happy. Daisy decided that spring was the very best time of the year. It was perfect.

She squeezed her brown eyes shut to concentrate on the sounds around her, but there was nothing. Not a bee, not a sparrow, not even those loud-mouthed parrots that came to feed this time of night. There was absolutely nothing. She opened her eyes: she couldn't see anything that explained the silence. It was very strange. Still, thought Daisy, shrugging her shoulders, that was spring. Things changed all the time in spring.

Daisy's mind turned to less puzzling things. Like the special place she had found to stand each day. It was near the birdbath, and was surrounded by the branches of two bright yellow daisy bushes. She was able to wedge herself comfortably between the bushes without being seen. It was wonderful. Nobody could find her there, not even her friends. The bushes protected her from bad things like cats and snakes, and best of all, gave her a clear view right down the garden path to the big house. That's where the humans lived, and, chuckled Daisy, they didn't even know she existed.

She felt a bit put out today because the boy who lived in the big house hadn't come out to play. His name was Jack and he always came out this time of the day. Well, thought the mouse, nearly always, but so far there was no sign of him, and she had waited all day to have some fun. Daisy loved it when Jack came outside and played with the dogs. She especially loved it when one of the tennis balls they were playing with came close to her. She would kick it back onto the lawn, leaving the dogs and Jack looking very puzzled. Other times she would hide the ball under her bush and watch the dogs go mad trying to find it. The little black dog could be a pain because she would come up to her bush and try to get in. It did make her giggle though.

Her best friend, Felicity, said she was mean and should stop teasing them. Daisy didn't think she was mean. It was fun. Anyway she liked the dogs, and she liked Jack. She even felt sorry for him. He always seemed to be on his own. Sometimes, it was all she could do not to talk to him. One day she was that close to speaking to him, but when she told Annie and Felicity their eyes opened wide with alarm. Annie, the old mushroom, got quite cross.

'How many times must you be told, pet?' said Annie, wagging her thin finger. 'You know the rules. None of us is allowed to talk to humans. I'm sorry pet, it just can't happen.'

Felicity didn't get cross exactly, but when she

shook her red curly hair and put her hands on her hips, she didn't look very happy. Even the freckles on her face seemed to stand out more as she stressed how wrong it was to talk to Jack. 'You mustn't do it, Daisy. It would ruin everything. You just mustn't do it.'

Daisy was always getting into trouble. Like the time she found Jack's scarf and hat. She loved them. The scarf made a beautiful rug and the hat was perfect to sit on. She was furious when Annie told her to put them back. She always made her do that when she found something special. Annie said it was stealing, but Daisy preferred to think of it as borrowing. She sighed. Life could be very unfair sometimes.

Suddenly a gang of raucous black crows screeched over the valley, bringing Daisy back to the present. She squirmed. The sound of crows always sent a shiver down her spine. Their cries made it seem as if something terrible was about to happen. They gave her the creeps.

Anyway, thought Daisy, once it's dark everything will feel normal again. She smiled, her small black nose twitching in anticipation. Today was Saturday, the best day in the whole week. This Saturday was story night and Theresa was going to read her favourite book. It was called Peter Pan, about a little boy who never got old. Imagine, thought Daisy, imagine never getting old.

She had to admit though; the rest of the week was so boring. Take last week. The only hint of excitement was when Reggie, the chubby gnome, lost his hat. The garden was plunged into chaos as they all searched high and low for the red cap. Reggie was in a terrible state, huffing and puffing and yelling at people to look harder, but the novelty of the search was short-lived for Daisy. She was sick of it after the first ten minutes and ended up telling Reggie to look for it himself. She yawned at the memory.

Feeling bored, she pushed back her head and took a long hard sniff. Her fine whiskers quivered. She could smell a barbecue. 'Yum.' Maybe that's what Maggie and Katie were getting for their tea. She sniffed again. There was another smell, a damp heavy smell. Something was definitely up; something was different. Daisy raised a paw to the side of her head. She always scratched her left ear when she was anxious or had a problem, but she knew that if Annie spotted her she would tell her off. It seemed everything she did annoyed the old mushroom: absolutely everything.

Daisy drew some more air into her lungs. I don't know, maybe I am imagining things. Maybe I am trying to make something exciting out of nothing. However, she knew she wasn't imagining the changing sky. She really could see the clouds thickening right before her eyes. It looked all wrong.

She began to feel edgy. She didn't want to be stuck between two daisy bushes any more. Branches and twigs scratched at her arms while her apron flapped dangerously around her feet. She found it hard to think. The blasts of air pushed her bonnet backwards and she felt unsteady on her feet. The wind was scary. She wanted to be home with Felicity and Annie. She just wanted to be home under her wrought iron seat. This special place no longer felt safe.

Daisy held down her bonnet so she could think. There was nothing for it. She would have to go to Theresa. She would know what was going on, but she had to move quickly, she had to get there before dark.

Yuk! thought Daisy, as she trekked up the hill to where Theresa lived. This is horrible. She had to force her way through a forest of shrubs and bushes and, about halfway, had to flop down on a pile of leaves to rest and catch her breath. She knew if she could just make it to the garden path things would become easier. She just had to get there. Head down to protect her face from the shrubbery, Daisy leaned into the wind once again. She trudged across the lawn towards the cubby house: it was all she could do to stay on her feet.

'I say!' yelled a voice from in front of her. 'Watch it, young lady. Take some care.'

Daisy jumped. 'Reggie! You scared me half to death. Why do you always have to shout? Do all gnomes shout all the time, like you? It's most unnerving.'

Reggie glared back. He was still upset with the mouse for refusing to keep searching for his hat. In fact there were a lot of things about Daisy that made him mad. He hated the way she hid balls from Jack when he was playing in the garden, or the way she took things that didn't belong to her. One day she was going to get caught. One day she was going to put them all in danger. Reggie thought she was a selfish little miss, and how dare she accuse him of shouting!

'Well, if I didn't shout,' retorted Reggie, 'you would have walked straight into me. You might be small, but you could still hurt me, and right at this moment I don't feel like being hurt.'

'I'm on my way to see Theresa,' said Daisy, ignoring his rather rude behaviour. 'There is something odd about the garden. I can't hear the bees, or the insects .

or any birds, for that matter. Even the air smells weird and the sky looks scary. What do you think?'

With hands on hips, Reggie looked around. 'Everything looks fine to me. So what if the sky looks different and you can't hear those annoying birds and bees? I'd enjoy the peace and quiet if I were you.'

'Well you're not me,' said Daisy, crossly, fed up with Reggie's attitude towards her. 'I know what I feel and I say we have a problem: a big problem.'

'Problem my foot,' retorted Reggie. 'I've just been through all this rubbish with Theresa. She thinks something is going on and wants us all to meet at her place. She's even asked me to go and get Herbert. It's absolutely ridiculous. You know how slow wombats are. I can't see why we can't just stay home.'

Daisy was shocked. Why wasn't she told about this meeting? And what about Annie and Felicity?

'Anyway,' said Reggie, rocking from side to side in the wind. 'I suppose I'd better get moving. It's just so stupid: so absolutely stupid.'

As much as Reggie annoyed Daisy, she had to agree. It was stupid. Still, she was nearly there, she would just have to keep going.

Finally Daisy reached the path and the old cubby house. She stood in front of it, trying to catch her breath. She felt so tired. Even her long tail ached. She rested her body against the rails and surveyed the cubby. It was so dirty and ugly. The ivy almost covered it completely. It was hard to imagine that Jack ever played in it, but Theresa said he was in it all the time: he loved it. Daisy waited for a few more minutes, took a deep breath, and kept moving. She was on the last stage of her journey.

Entering Theresa's home, Daisy wasn't surprised to see everyone gathered around: especially after her conversation with Reggie. She was just annoyed that no one had bothered to tell her about the meeting.

Looking around she spotted a space on the ground next to Ben the dog, and plonked herself down, still annoyed.

'Why wasn't I told about the meeting, Ben? I'm not very happy.'

'I'm sorry old girl,' whispered Ben. 'Theresa sent me to tell everybody to come here as soon as possible for an urgent meeting. I did try to find you, but you were not in your usual spot. I didn't have time to get Annie or Felicity either. I feel bad about that.'

Daisy softened. She loved Ben, he was so sweet, and it wasn't his fault that she couldn't be found. 'That's okay,' she said, leaning over and patting the little dog reassuringly. 'I've found another special spot where nobody can see me but I can see everything. I can watch the humans without them even knowing. I love it, and because I like you so much I might even show it to you one day '

'Be quiet, you two!' came a raucous cry from behind them. 'Theresa is about to speak, and some of us want to hear what she's got to say.'

Daisy knew it was Maggie the magpie. She thought it was pathetic. Maggie telling her to be quiet when all the magpie ever seemed to do was jabber on in that loud grating voice of hers. Poor Katie the kookaburra lived next to her and was stuck with Maggie day and night. That voice, thought Daisy, it would drive you mad, but Katie was nice and never once complained. Annie said she was a saint; a real saint.

And Theresa too, thought the little mouse, was completely different from Maggie. She was kind, patient and a very willing listener. Theresa was special; she even had her own pedestal to stand on. On a clear day she could see right across the valley to the distant hills and, if something exciting happened, she would tell them all about it over the evening meal.
Daisy couldn't help smiling as she spotted Herbert the wombat. Poor Herbert, he hated being dragged away from his home at the best of times, but on a night like this he must be wondering what he was doing here. Daisy felt a bit sorry for Herbert. Maggie and Reggie were particularly mean to him just because he was slow, but she liked Herbert. In fact if it wasn't for the rumour of snakes and cats near his home, she would visit him more often, she was sure she would.

'Oy!' squawked a voice behind her. Daisy was quickly brought back to reality. 'Are you two listening? Theresa is about to speak, and you,' said the annoyed bird, pushing her sharp beak into Ben's back. 'Stop panting like that. It's driving me mad.'

Daisy leaned over and squeezed Ben's paw. He was panting rather loudly. Maybe he was sick.

'Are you okay?' whispered Daisy. 'I've never seen you like this.'

'I don't know old girl. I've never been like this. I keep sensing something bad is about to happen, and I can't stop panting. I'd give anything for a drink. This wind is giving me the creeps. I hate it.'

'I know. So do I,' said Daisy, scratching behind her left ear. 'So do I.'

Theresa looked down on the small group. She felt sick in the stomach. She knew she had made a mistake bringing them here. They should have stayed close to their homes, but she had to tell them. She had to tell them about the storm. She flicked her long dark hair behind her ears and held on tight to her skirt. The wind was driving her crazy; her long dress billowing around her, making it hard to stand still. She didn't know how to begin, but she had to try. She cleared her throat as the group fell silent.

'I'm so sorry,' yelled Theresa over the strengthening wind. I'm so sorry that I've dragged you all out on a night like this.'

'Not as sorry as we are,' interrupted Reggie. 'Do you realise how much effort it took to get Herbert here? Do you?'

'Of course I do.' Theresa was slightly irritated at this interruption. 'But it is very important, Reggie, so I want you to listen. I want all of you to listen.' She looked up at the darkening sky and shivered. It gave her the creeps.

'Ten years ago,' continued Theresa, 'there was a massive storm. It tore bushes up from the ground and uprooted trees, and the rain: I have never seen anything like it. Nobody was safe.' Theresa hesitated. 'It was that night I lost a very special friend. I shall never forget it, and tonight, I fear, we are going to have another terrible storm. It terrifies me that one of you could be lost forever. So I have brought you all here to give you some ideas on how to stay safe.'

'The first thing is to go and prepare your homes. Surround your homes with twigs and small branches. If you can't do that find a snug place away from the wind and rain, especially the wind, and don't, whatever you do, leave until the storm is over. You have to keep safe. Now go, so that you reach them before the grandfather clock in the big house strikes four bells. If that's not possible, find somewhere safe to hide. Remember,' said Theresa, lowering her voice. 'Remember, if any of you are found too far away from your homes questions will be asked; and that could be dangerous. The storm must not let us be vulnerable. We must be aware. It is important that our secret is never discovered. The humans must never discover our secret. Never!'

2

Chaos in the Garden

The group was silent as each one of them thought about what to do. Herbert let out a low groan. He knew he could never get home in time. Maggie and Katie began to chatter in nervous excitement as they tried to work out the safest way to travel. Should they fly? Or should they walk? Daisy was also worried. Her stomach was churning and her nose was twitching. She looked up at the sky. The clouds were now pitch black, except for long yellow flashes in the distance. She couldn't understand it. Why did the sky keep changing? And why did it light up with those scary bright lights? She just wanted to go home. Was that too much to ask?

'I don't understand,' yelled Reggie, glaring at Theresa. 'Why didn't you just let us stay where we were? How is someone like Herbert going to get home in time? And what if we are discovered? The whole thing is ridiculous. Herbert and I were already at home, and then we were told to come here, and now we have to go back again. It's absolutely ridicu ' But, before Reggie could finish his sentence a huge gust of wind came out of nowhere. The noise was deafening and tore through the bushes with such strength that it lifted the sturdy gnome high into the air. Daisy watched in horror as Reggie landed with a thud amongst the glory vine. The poor gnome lay there motionless.

Daisy could hardly believe her eyes. She looked around to see if anyone else had been injured. She could hear Maggie squawking, but couldn't see her. There was no sound coming from Katie. She tried to go to them, but the wind was so strong she could barely stand up herself. It was horrible.

She turned to see Theresa kneeling over Reggie. His red hat was pushed to the side of his face, and his body was covered in mud and leaves. Theresa gently lifted him up and started to carry him back to her home. Daisy couldn't take her eyes off him. A terrible thought crossed her mind. What if Reggie was dead? What if Maggie and Katie were trapped or injured? And where were Herbert and Ben? It was like a bad dream, a terrible, terrible dream.

Somewhere in her brain she heard Theresa. She was screaming over the wind. She was holding Reggie and screaming. 'Go home Daisy. It isn't safe. Just go before the storm hits us.'

However, Daisy didn't know how to get home. She was confused and frightened. She just stood there trying to remember, when something stirred in her memory. A tunnel? A path? Yes! That was it. A path! Somewhere in there was a secret path: a shortcut to home, but she hadn't used it in ages. Perhaps now it was overgrown or had disappeared completely. She had to find it. She just had to.

Despite the darkness and the wind Daisy searched frantically. After several minutes she found it; a half-hidden entrance. She pushed forward. The bushes had grown a lot since she was last there, but the pathway still existed: just. The wind sent branches waving in her face and twigs pricked at her hands and arms like needles. It was horrible.

She was halfway through when she heard something. It sounded like someone crying out, but she couldn't be sure. She headed towards the noise, pushing through the tangle of bushes. The cries were getting louder and more desperate. Daisy pulled up her dress and ran. She raced past a huge daisy bush, tripping over a branch. She picked herself up, wiping the mud off her apron. The crying was getting louder. She could see something. It was just past the daisy bush. It looked big and furry; its four thick legs waving about wildly. She edged closer.

'Herbert,' cried Daisy. 'What have you done? How did this happen?' She couldn't help thinking how ridiculous the poor wombat looked.

'Daisy.' said Herbert, weakly. 'I seem to have got myself into a bit of a pickle. I tripped over a branch, and well, here I am. Ben's gone to find some rope.' He shook his head. 'I don't know. I always seem to cause problems.'

Daisy knelt down beside him. 'That's okay Herbert. I'll wait until Ben comes back. Are you hurt anywhere?'

The wombat shook his head. 'No. Just very embarrassed, and I must confess a little scared. That storm Theresa warned us about sounds close. I don't like it Daisy. I don't like it at all.'

Daisy shivered. She could hear something rumbling in the distance, and yellow flashes were all around her. She felt anxious. What if there were snakes nearby? What if there was a cat waiting to eat her? The wind was picking up. She could hear twigs breaking and heavy breathing. Something was coming to get her. Something was coming to eat her. She screamed. She had to get away. She couldn't help Herbert, she had to run.

'Daisy, it's only me,' said a familiar voice. 'Daisy, it's Ben. I've come back to help Herbert. I didn't mean to scare you, old girl. Come on. Take a few deep breaths. Remember how Annie tells you to do that when you're anxious.'

She nodded. Sucking in the cool air, Daisy could hear the clock chiming in the big house. She counted three bells. Now she had another problem. She only had an hour to get home.

'Ben, can you get Herbert on his feet on your own? I have to get going. Annie and Felicity will be worrying, and knowing Annie, she'll tell me off. She does that when she's worried.'

Ben looked across at Herbert. He was very big, but he'd just have to manage. 'I'll be fine Daisy. You go, and go quickly. It won't be long now before the storm really hits, and the last thing you want is to be discovered. Once I've helped Herbert, we'll hide under this bush. Go, old girl, and stay safe.'

Rain started to fall as the little mouse began her long journey home. She hitched up her flowing skirt and tucked in her tail. The last thing she wanted was to trip again. She certainly didn't want to end up like Herbert. Poor Ben and Herbert, thought Daisy, flicking wet leaves from her face. I just hope they are safe under that bush.

Her legs were beginning to ache as she dragged her feet across the sodden ground. Everything was dark and creepy. She strained her eyes to see if she was near anything familiar, but everything looked different. The rain dripped into her eyes and she felt cold. The thunder was so loud, rumbling endlessly over the pitch black sky. Daisy shuddered. She wasn't even half way home. She could feel tears welling up in her eyes, and her throat felt dry and sore. She kept thinking of Ben, and wishing she had stayed with him. She wanted Annie. She wanted Felicity.

Daisy stumbled through the maze of bushes and tangled undergrowth. Surely she would see something familiar soon. Surely she was nearly home. She was drenched. Her dress felt heavy, making it hard to walk. Maybe she should just find a bush to hide under, maybe she should give up. Trying to think, she squeezed her eyes tight. Through the bushes she saw something. Daisy could just make out a shape. It looked familiar.

'It's the shed!' squealed the mouse ecstatically. 'It's the shed. I've nearly reached the cobblestone path, and then I am home. I'm so close, so very close. Nothing else can happen now. I'm nearly home.' Clapping her cold hands with joy, Daisy leant against the shed door and tried to work out what to do next.

She knew that she had to be very careful for the next few metres. The cobblestones would be very slippery and she certainly didn't want to slip and fall over the dreaded brick wall. Theresa had told them awful stories about the brick wall. If someone fell they disappeared and were never seen again. Daisy cringed. She certainly didn't want to disappear and never be seen again.

She pulled her bonnet further over her ears as the wind blew into her cold face. She would have to move sometime, and now was as good as any. She put her right foot forward and, as if by magic, the whole garden lit up. Those strange yellow lights in the sky showed her everything: the cobblestone path, the brick wall and, in the distance, her home. She thought she saw something else, a large shadow by the big house. She thought it moved, but she couldn't worry about that now. She was nearly home; finally she would be safe.

Then suddenly the light disappeared, and the loudest sound she had ever heard boomed above her. The whole garden shook and the shed window rattled so hard she thought it would break. She heard a door slam. The boughs of the trees creaked and groaned as the wind roared through them. She was so frightened. Her heart was racing but she couldn't move. She looked up. The branches looked like giant ghostly arms reaching out to get her. Daisy couldn't believe it, she was nearly home; but the arms were getting closer, they were getting closer. Terrified, she screamed: a loud piercing scream. She had to get away. She had to move, but she couldn't. Her feet were stuck like glue to the cobblestones. Sobbing loud harrowing sobs, she just stood there. What was she going to do? Whatever was she going to do?

Daisy didn't hear the loud crack, nor did she see the huge branch breaking off from the tree. All she saw was long waving arms bearing down on her. All she heard was the clock chiming four bells, and then there was nothing.

3

After the Storm

Jack crawled out from beneath the covers. He was exhausted. Last night had been the worst night of his life. It wasn't just the storm that was so terrible, but that weird dream. It seemed to be with him nearly all night. In his dream he had heard screams; terrible screams. He had gone out to the garden to investigate: out into the storm. It was frightening. He tried to get back inside, but he couldn't. Something was standing by the shed, but he couldn't remember what it was. He just remembered being terrified, and racing back inside. It was so ridiculous.

And now, as he looked out of his bedroom window, it was as if nothing had happened. It was a beautiful sunny spring day; white fluffy clouds floating across the blue sky. How could it be so different?

He could hear sounds of movement below. The comforting noise of the kettle singing and the clatter of dishes drifted up the stairs. He heard the bathroom door slam, and the shower being turned on. Everything sounded so normal.

Jack smiled. There wasn't a sign of his dogs. They were too busy getting stuck into their breakfast to worry about him. Nothing was going to make them miss out on crispy bacon. They obviously hadn't suffered any lasting effects from last night's storm, thought Jack. However, he had. It was all a horrible jumble in his head. He couldn't work out what was the storm and what was his dream. It was confusing. It didn't make any sense. He needed to do something enjoyable today, something that would get this jumble out of his head.

Maybe his dad could take him and the dogs down to the river. That would take his mind off things. He needed something, and the dogs loved a walk to the river. Next to playing in the back yard, or chasing cats, it was their favourite thing.

Jack yawned and waited for his mother to call him for breakfast. He was proud of his mum. His friend Sam thought she was the best looking mum around, and Jack had to admit, that with her long dark hair and beautiful smile, she was very pretty. She even had a nice name: Mary. Like Princess Mary of Denmark.

Both Jack's parents worked, and life was always busy, but they were good parents and he knew he was lucky to have them. Half the kids in his class came from broken homes.

His grandma said it was the curse of the 21st century, and people didn't try hard enough. 'All they want are things,' his grandma would say crossly. 'All they want are mobile phones, plasma television sets and everything else technical. What about their children? What about spending more time together as a family?'

Jack didn't really understand what his grandma was on about. It would be a terrible world without computers and plasma television sets, but he did know that if his parents ever split up, he would find it absolutely unbearable. He just couldn't imagine it. Contemplating this terrible thought, he was suddenly brought back to reality as his father called out to him from downstairs.

'Put on your work clothes, Jack, and don't bother to have a shower. After breakfast I want you to help me clean up outside. That storm's made a real mess. You can start on the back garden by yourself and when I've finished with the front, I'll come around and help you finish off.'

Typical, thought Jack, there goes my walk to the river. I was even going to take my tadpole net: absolutely typical. There was always something that stopped him doing fun things with just his dad. Life was really quite boring sometimes.

'Thank goodness for Sam,' mumbled Jack, slowly stretching. He was his one and only true friend. They would hang around together most weekends, often riding their bikes to the local shop to get chips or ice-cream. Other times they would ride to the reserve. In winter, when the creek was full, they would make boats out of bark and race one another. Then they would ride home, as fast as their legs would take them. It was exhilarating, he thought, feeling the wind in your face as the houses and fields flew past. It was the only time Jack felt like a grown-up. It was the only time he felt really free. They were fun days, thought Jack. Not like the awful days he had at school. Not like the days he felt like running away. Those days were terrible.

Climbing out of bed, Jack grabbed his glasses. He hated them. It wasn't until Harry Potter became popular, that the kids at school stopped teasing him about them. When Harry Potter wore them it was cool!

Trying to get a brush through his unruly hair, Jack couldn't help grinning. He and Sam spent hours some days working out what they would do if they had magical powers. They had planned great things to do to Brian Madison and his gang of dorks. It usually involved being captured and sent to some evil island, where nobody would ever find them: a place where they could never bully him or Sam again. It never stopped though. Now he got teased for supposedly being stupid.

Jack didn't think he was stupid. It was just that he found it difficult to fit in. Just because he didn't like sport, thought Jack, throwing on some old clothes in disgust. It wasn't always his fault that he stuffed things up, and as for schoolwork.... Jack sighed. Reluctantly, he had to admit that it was sort of his fault that he found the work difficult. He had this terrible problem. He couldn't stop day dreaming. He preferred to make up stories in his head rather than listen to his teacher. Still, Mr. Jones never explained anything, and on the rare occasions that he did, Jack's mind would go completely blank. Then he did look stupid.

Putting on his sneakers, Jack suddenly remembered something about last night, something about the storm. The thunder had become so loud it was frightening. He couldn't stand it so he went to his parents' room for company, but they were asleep. He knew he had really been there, because his dad was snoring, but what happened next was a mystery. He knew he had done something else, but what? It was bugging him. He had definitely done something else.

As Jack walked down the stairs he was suddenly brought back to the present. Scarlet, his toy poodle, was standing in front of him, her feathery tail wagging expectantly. She had her favourite white ball in her mouth and wanted Jack to throw it down the stairs.

The aim was to reach the ball before it got to the bottom. Jack shook his head. 'No, Scarlet, I haven't got time for games today. You'll have to play with Maxine.' He grinned as the tail went down, and those black spindly legs of hers made their way slowly back to the kitchen.

Jack took a deep breath as he entered the family room. The delicious smell of bacon and eggs wafted his way. He felt a slight shiver as he walked through to the spacious kitchen. He sat himself down next to his father, and looked out the huge bay window. He looked at the bushes. There was something about them. His dream flashed into his mind. He remembered them in his dream. They were scary, like monsters trying to break through the window. Jack sighed. He had to stop doing this. It was only a dream.

However, his eyes wandered around the room, looking for more clues. Jack couldn't help smiling when he spotted Maxine. His white Maltese cross was lying happily in front of the fire. A bit different from last night, thought Jack. Last night she was a panting mess. Scarlet was also back in her basket, cuddling into her white ball. Sometimes he envied the dogs. They lived for the moment. As long as they had food, drink and a warm bed they were happy.

Looking across at his father, Jack thought he looked tired, even though the last time he saw him, he was snoring his head off.

'Did you get through last night okay, Jack?' said his dad, putting down the paper. 'It was a shocking storm. It woke us up, and we couldn't get back to sleep for ages. The thunder was unbelievable.'

'Sort of,' said Jack, with some hesitation. 'It was

pretty wild though, even the dogs hid under the bed. It was so loud.' Jack looked at his mother. 'I did come to your room, but you were both asleep.'

'Oh! Jack. You should have woken us,' said his mum, as she placed a plate piled high with bacon, eggs, and tomato in front of him. 'That makes me feel terrible. You must wake us if you are scared like that again. You must.'

Jack was relieved. 'I'm all right now, but I never want to go through a storm like that again, never.'

'None of us would,' said his father. 'But to be honest, this storm was nothing compared with the one we had ten years ago. You were only a baby, but it was the worst storm I've ever known. About eight weeks earlier your mother had gone mad doing up the garden with plants and ornaments. When the storm hit, just about everything was lost or damaged.'

'Yes,' said his mother. 'I was actually fearful for our lives. Trees fell down, bushes were uprooted and worst of all I lost one of my favourite ornaments.' She paused, staring through the window. 'Her name was Rachel,' she whispered, 'and she was the prettiest ornament I had ever seen. She wore a blue ribbon in her hair and carried a basket of flowers.

When I found Rachel smashed to bits at the bottom of the brick wall I felt really sad. I felt like I had lost someone; someone very close.' She sipped her tea. 'Stupid, I know, but even now I feel sad when I think of her.'

Jack stared at his mother. Surely she wasn't upset over a garden ornament? I mean, they couldn't talk or anything, they just stood there. However, as he looked into his mother's eyes, he could have sworn they were misty. She looked like she was going to cry. It was weird. He just hoped he didn't find any smashed up ornaments when he went outside. He didn't think his mother could cope.

Jack felt a little awkward. Normally he loved this time with his parents; his dad reading the paper, and his mum quietly going about her chores. Sunday was always his favourite day, but talking about the storm had made his parents miserable and strangely quiet. Now all he had to look forward to was the rest of today, and he couldn't imagine that was going to be very thrilling. Then of course there was Monday: the absolute worst day in the whole week. Yes, thought Jack, as he headed for the back door. There was always Monday.

4

Jack's Discovery

After breakfast Jack stood on the large verandah breathing in the cool sweet air. The dogs had gone tearing past him like mad things, eager to have a good sniff. He was glad to be out of the house, particularly the way his parents were acting. Out here he could listen to the sound of magpies. Out here he could enjoy the freshness of the garden after rain, and out here he was in his own perfect world, and nobody, not even Mr. Jones, could take that away.

Jack's eyes wandered over the side fence where he could see right across the valley. The houses looked so small, like dolls houses dotted amongst the greenery. Looking at the view always gave him a chance to think, and right now his brain was racing. He couldn't stop thinking about his dream. It felt like he had really been there: out in the garden: out in the storm. He couldn't get it out of his head.

And the really weird thing, thought Jack, was that lots of odd things had been happening: real things. Like when his hat and scarf disappeared. He had left them on the wrought iron seat and the next day they were gone. The creepy thing was that they mysteriously appeared a few weeks later, left in a pile on the verandah. There was even one of Scarlet's soft toys with them.

That had been missing for months. Jack shuddered. It gave him goosebumps.

And then there were all those tennis balls that kept disappearing? What was that all about? Jack decided he didn't want to know. It was just too weird. Anyway, he had too many other things to worry about just now. Like all this! Jack couldn't believe it. The garden was disgusting. He had never seen it in such a shambles. The lawn and paths were covered in leaves, branches and mulch, and some of the pots had been smashed in the wind, large chunks scattered over the lawn. It looked like a disaster zone. Jack felt annoyed. He didn't want to do this. He didn't want to spend the only decent day in the week cleaning up. Tomorrow was Monday. He hated Mondays, and he hated school.

Last Friday had been the absolute pits. Mr. Jones had totally humiliated him in front of everyone. He could hear him now. 'Crane! What's the capital of Burkina Faso?' Jack had just stood there, not moving and not speaking. How was he to know that it was called 'Ouagadougou'? He bet no-one else knew what it was, and now he had to face everyone who had laughed at him tomorrow morning. He hated it.

The whole school thing was an absolute joke, thought Jack, as he turned sharply onto the cobblestone path. Frustrated, he began kicking sticks and bark out of his way. There was so much rubbish. He even found a torch lying on the side of the path, half hidden by the small bushes. Jack picked it up. It was his torch. He vaguely remembered having the torch when he went to his parents' room, but he never came outside. He was sure he hadn't. He stood there for a moment trying to clear his head.

Again, bits of his dream came back to him. He remembered standing here; in this exact spot. He remembered looking up to the shed. There had been a bright light: a strange bright light, but what else? Shaking his head he kept walking, until he finally arrived at the small green shed.

He stared at the huge branches of the gum tree that were sprawled across the shed door and onto the pathway. Bark and small branches were everywhere, completely blocking the entrance. He had heard that tree creaking last night. He knew something like this would happen. Jack cringed. He didn't want to touch anything. He just wanted to go.

He hurried past rows of bright red Japanese bamboo and large yellow daisy bushes. He wanted to get away from the shed. For some reason it was creeping him out. Once in the main garden, he was able to stop and take a breath, but there was something odd here as well. It was so quiet. Strangely quiet. Apart from the odd magpie, there wasn't a sound to be heard. No rustling of bushes, or things moving around in the undergrowth. Sometimes when he was in the garden he felt that he was being watched. Sometimes he sensed he wasn't alone.

Jack had a quick look around, before forcing his way past the overgrown bushes. He heard the dogs barking, and followed their sound. He found Scarlet standing over a small object. She was licking it madly. Maxine was sitting next to it, her white fluffy face towering over the poor thing. She wasn't trying to hurt it though. Usually Jack spent a lot of his time saving small creatures from Maxine, but this time she looked almost protective.

He moved closer to the small object. It was Ben, the little stone dog. Normally the dog sat guarding the urn, just beyond the verandah. So what was he doing here? And why were Maxine and Scarlet acting this way? He patted Maxine and gently picked up Ben. He tucked him under his arm and kept walking.

It took awhile to get past the shrubbery, but finally Jack found the short-cut through the bushes that led him to the top of the garden. It was once his secret path, but was now so overgrown it was hard to find. At the end of the path and next to the large stone slab stood his old cubby house. It was surrounded by trees and looked awful. Jack felt a sense of relief getting to the cubby. This part of the garden didn't feel scary. It was being near the shed that gave him the creeps. He didn't want to go back to it.

Jack glanced up at the cubby. He could hardly tell what it was, there was so much ivy covering the roof, and where was the wooden ladder? Even the red curtains his mother had made were all faded and torn. He dreaded to think what was inside, probably baby snakes and spiders. He felt guilty. His father and grandfather had spent six months building it, just for him. Now it just stood there empty.

Maybe it was worth asking his dad to help him clean it up and paint the parts they could, but deep down he knew his father would be too busy. He always was. Jack thought about his grandpa. His grandparents were moving up in autumn, right across the road. They were having a brand new house built. Jack couldn't wait. He loved his grandparents. He especially loved his grandma's cooking. He could almost smell her chocolate cakes now.

Suddenly, he had a brilliant thought. Maybe he and Grandpa could fix the cubby. His dad didn't even have to be involved if he didn't want to. Every time Grandpa was up visiting he always asked if there was anything he could do, and now there was.

Giving the grubby rails a pat, Jack moved on to the top of the garden. He noticed that the statue of the lady holding the water jug was still in one piece. It was especially good that she hadn't fallen over. According to his dad, it had taken three strong men from the garden centre just to get her up onto the pedestal. Jack stared into her pretty face. Sometimes when he looked at her, he could swear she was smiling at him, but that was stupid; she was just an ornament.

His mother had named her Theresa after her very plump aunt. An odd choice thought Jack, as Theresa was beautiful. There was nothing plump about her. Jack looked around to see if there was any damage here from the storm, but it didn't look too bad. There was nothing for it; he would have to go back to the shed. All this creepy stuff was all in his head.

Jack turned around, ready to head back, when out of the corner of his eye he spotted something shining amongst the leaves. It looked quite large. He bent down to investigate, and there, staring up at him was Reggie, the red-hatted gnome from the side garden. 'This is getting ridiculous,' murmured Jack, as he picked up the rather dirty gnome. He scraped mud and leaves off his face, and cleaned his red hat with a bit of old rag he had found, but something was definitely up. Something wasn't right. The gnome's face looked different. It looked frightened. Like something terrible had happened. This was crazy, thought Jack, absolutely crazy.

He decided to have a hunt around the garden to see what else was missing. Jack found Katie the kookaburra sprawled under the fig tree. She was also covered in leaves and mud, and there was a deep gash under her left eye. He placed the poor bird back under the diosma bush.

In a strange way, he found this whole ornament thing intriguing. Who would he find next and where would he find them? He didn't have to wait long. Not far from where he found Katie, Maggie the stone magpie was stuck firmly into the fence. Her feet were jammed in between the rails. Jack untangled her legs and placed her back amongst the ground cover. It was a mystery how she and Katie had ended up in such odd places. He couldn't understand it.

He tried to think what the other ornaments were, and where they stood in the garden. Of course, thought Jack. There was Herbert the wombat. He lived with Reggie the gnome. Jack ran around to the side garden, out of breath by the time he got there. He stared at the big blue pot. The wombat always sat in front of it, and now he was gone! Jack raced back to the secret path where he had found Ben, and there to his amazement was Herbert. The wombat was squeezed between a large daisy bush and a very prickly bottlebrush. The whole thing was getting more and more insane. He'd come back later and put Reggie and Herbert back around the side. Right now he wanted to find out what had happened to the rest of the ornaments.

Jack called the dogs. He had decided to check the whole garden thoroughly, and maybe they could help him find them. He'd have to go slowly though, the ornaments could be anywhere. Jack went the long way round, following the concrete path down to the vegetable garden. He found a heap of missing balls behind the green gate leading to the vegetable patch, but he couldn't worry about that now; he had to keep moving. He had found seven ornaments, but where were the others?

Walking quickly in the direction of the house, Jack detoured right into the main garden. He followed the strong scent of the lavender bushes where he knew he would find the wrought iron seat. The small seat was almost hidden by the lavender as it nestled snugly in between the two bushes. Thank goodness, thought Jack, looking under the bush. Annie the mushroom was still there. He couldn't help thinking what a funny old thing she was, roughly scooping her up, and shaking dirt from the top of her head.

'You really could do with an overhaul,' said Jack, loudly. 'Including a new paint job,' he added as he stripped off peeling paint from her head, but he would think about that another day: he was anxious to keep moving. He stopped by the seat, and bent down to have a really good look under it. Good, thought Jack. The little girl he had named Felicity was there too.

He had now found nine ornaments, but one was still missing. He felt sure another ornament lived with Felicity under the seat, but who?

Jack stopped abruptly as he came to the cobblestone path, the dogs racing ahead of him. It was stupid, but that feeling of fear crept over him again. He wished Sam was here. They could do this together. Sometimes he felt like telling his best friend about the garden, but he didn't have any proof; only feelings and imaginings, and odd things happening: nothing that he could show him. Until he did, he would say nothing.

Taking a deep breath Jack continued up the path until he reached the shed. His dad would have to move the large branches. He'd start with the smaller ones that were on the garden. Scarlet and Maxine were already there, sniffing madly under the branches. Scarlet seemed particularly interested and had begun scratching. Jack watched her tiny black paws dig faster and faster into the soft soil. She was getting excited, her scruffy tail going berserk.

'What is it?' said Jack, kneeling down amongst the leaves. 'What's under there, Scarlet?' He picked up the branches and threw them into a pile. Working steadily, he removed all the small twigs. The only thing left was mulch, but nothing was there. So why was Scarlet still digging so frantically? Maxine had even joined in, dirt and leaves flying in all directions. Jack took a closer look. He could just see something under the dirt. He brushed away the remainder of the mulch, and there, staring up at him was Daisy, the concrete mouse. He felt a shiver go down his spine as he studied her face. Like Reggie, she looked terrified. He thought of those screams. It just wasn't possible. Those screams were in his dream. This was an ornament, just an ornament. It couldn't be her. It just couldn't.

Shooing Scarlet away, Jack picked Daisy up and carefully brushed some of the dirt and leaves from her mud-splattered dress. He noticed a large gash on the top of her head where her bonnet usually sat. He looked around him. The bonnet lay on the cobblestone path near the shed door. It was still in one piece. He shook his head. The bonnet! There was something about the bonnet, and how did Daisy end up under all this rubbish? How?

He placed the poor mouse back under the wrought iron seat. He had finally found the last one. He had found the ten ornaments, but something was wrong. Jack couldn't understand why they were in these strange positions. Was it to do with last night? Did it have something to do with the storm or had he just discovered something amazing?

Clasping Daisy's bonnet, Jack could hear his mother calling him for lunch, but he didn't want to leave. He wanted to stay. He looked down at the ornaments. Something was going on. Something was odd about this garden, and something was odd about them: all the strange things that had been happening over the past year: all the things that went missing and the funny feeling he got every time he went outside, and the dogs: he had never seen them react this way. Never! Then there were the screams: those terrible screams. Jack headed back to the house deep in thought. He was going to find out. He was going to solve this. He wasn't even going to tell Sam. Not yet. Nobody else was to be involved. Nobody else was to know. His dream had something to do with all this, and he was going to find out what. This was his special secret. This, thought Jack, as he opened the back door, was all his.

5

Daisy's Loss

Daisy sobbed and sobbed, large wet tears running down her cheeks. They caught in her long fine whiskers, and dripped like raindrops from her pointed nose. Her little body heaved with every sob and a sharp pain pierced the top of her head. The ten days since the storm had been the worst the little mouse had experienced in her whole life. She slowly raised her arm, feeling around in the empty space where her bonnet once sat. Nothing, absolutely nothing, could compare to the misery she was feeling right now.

She had been like this for over a week, and Jack had not been back again to check on her. It was horrible. She felt numb with cold, even though the evening was quite warm. She just couldn't stop shaking, and every time she thought of that terrible night her eyes filled with tears. Her old friend Annie said she was in shock. 'You poor little mite,' was all Annie could say as she wiped the mud and leaves off Daisy's wet face. 'You poor little mite.'

Everyone in the garden was concerned about Daisy, and throughout the week brought offerings of food and friendship to cheer her up, but Daisy was in her own little world. Nothing could make her feel better, nothing.

Even Maggie felt sorry for the poor mouse and decided to pick her the first of the season's strawberries from the vegetable garden behind the large gate. It was lucky for Maggie that they were ripe, as all the vegetables and other fruit in the garden were as hard as rocks. She found it difficult collecting strawberries, often complaining that they were very tricky to peck off, 'hiding amongst all the leaves and mulch', and so it was with great pride that she presented Daisy with four beautiful smelling bright red strawberries. However, her joy turned to fury when the glum-looking mouse simply thanked her 'for her trouble' and said that she 'just couldn't stomach a thing at the moment'.

Maggie couldn't believe the cheek. 'You weren't the only one hurt in the storm! Look at me, I was stuck in a fence all night,' she shrieked. 'Try to help a person and all you get is rejection!' With that, she flapped her wings and flew off in a huff, vowing never to help anyone again.

It was a difficult season for food, as the winter crops had finished and, except for Maggie's strawberries, the summer fruit had not yet ripened. The summer vegetables had only recently been planted so they wouldn't be ripe for ages. It made fossicking for food very time consuming, so anything that could be found was precious. Ben had discovered some early cherries that had fallen from the neighbour's tree, but these were still quite small and green. He wished they were ripe. Daisy loved cherries. Ben smiled as he thought of the fun times they had in cherry season.

All through December the tree was loaded, and luckily for the folk, many of the branches hung over their fence. Felicity, Ben and Daisy would wait until there was a full moon, then creep around to the side garden and collect as many cherries as they could carry. Daisy and Felicity would open their aprons as wide as possible, stuffing the cherries into them until they could hardly move. Ben would wander behind them with an old disused basket in his mouth so the girls could tip their cherries into it.

The cherries were stored in a safe place and, in summer, Saturday nights became cherry nights. It was so much fun, thought Ben. Nothing could be better than sitting with friends on a hot night, stuffing yourself silly with cherries, but now, since the storm, things had been awful, and unless something changed, he feared they were in for a miserable time this summer.

Ben looked down at the dried up piece of turnip he was taking Daisy, and just hoped she was hungry. He was a bit nervous about seeing the mouse again, and didn't really know what to say to her. Annie said he would be good for Daisy, but he was a little unsure. I mean, how do you cheer up your best friend when she has a big crack in her head? How do you? You can't tell her she looks well. You can't lie.

When he finally reached Daisy he couldn't stop himself from staring. She looked awful. Gone was the pretty bonnet, and a nasty gash stretched from the back of her head to the front. Ben was devastated.

'How are you going, old girl?' he said, gently touching her on the arm, afraid to go anywhere near her head. 'I've brought you something to eat,' he said, holding out the turnip. 'It's not very thrilling, but there's not much around at the moment. Would you like to try some?'

Daisy slowly shook her head, looking at Ben through sad vacant eyes. 'Thanks Ben, but I don't feel hungry and I don't want to be mean, but I don't feel much like talking either. Thanks for coming though. Maybe later I'll feel hungry. I might even feel like talking, but right now I just want to be on my own.'

'Okay old girl, if you say so,' said Ben, feeling a bit put out. He'd never seen Daisy like this. 'But can I come back later to see how you are?' Daisy nodded and closed her eyes. Ben felt terrible, absolutely terrible, and he had no idea what to do next.

Felicity felt awful for Daisy, too, and spent the early evenings brushing the dust off her friend's torn dress, but she was getting sick of it. She felt tired and her head hurt. It was all the bending down to clean Daisy's dress. She just wished her friend would snap out of it. It had been ten days now, thought Felicity, rubbing her sore eyes, and she still wasn't talking. She sighed. Daisy was almost a full time job sometimes. If something bad was going to happen then it would usually happen to Daisy. Still, she did love the little mouse, and she did try to be understanding.

She looked across at Daisy. The poor thing looked terrible. Felicity hated to admit it, but the only person who could help Daisy now was Jack. He was the only one who could fix her bonnet. He was the only one who could make her happy again. Maybe, thought Felicity. Maybe they didn't have a choice but to tell him their secret. It was so hard to know what to do.

However, Annie would have none of it. She was very much against involving Jack, particularly as in her opinion he had treated her 'in a manner not becoming an older lady'. She was still furious at his behaviour, lifting her roughly into the air, shaking her until her head hurt, peeling off her paint, and above all informing the whole garden that she needed 'a good sprucing up'. She thought she was in perfect order and was often told what a happy face she had, with her cheeky smile and sparkling eyes. So what if she had some flaky paint? She would like him to name one ornament in the garden that didn't have flaky paint! In fact, if young Jack stood in the garden day after day in all weathers, he would start flaking off somewhere! For an old fat mushroom, Annie could get quite fiery at times. 'How humiliating,' was all she could say over and over again, shaking her little arms in Maggie's face.

It wasn't long though before an impatient Maggie had had enough and with a loud flap of her wings bluntly told Annie to 'put a sock in it' and get on with her life. Annie never confided in Maggie again.

The garden folk had to be very careful that no one discovered their secret life after dark, so it was important that the humans in the big house never had cause to question the things that happened in the garden. During the day the garden folk were stone ornaments. They could still see and hear things and smile, but it wasn't until the sun set that they came to life and went about their business as if they were human. Each one had a job to do and in winter these had to be done quickly before darkness set in.

Maggie and Katie were responsible for finding food outside the garden while the others foraged in the vegetable patch and underneath the fruit trees for their evening meal. Summer was the best time, as food was plentiful and far more enjoyable to eat. In winter the food was bland, but it was better than going hungry. Once collected, all the food was placed on the large slate block where Theresa stood. It was then shared, each person having contributed to the evening meal. Some summer nights they had all sorts of interesting things. They might have figs, apricots, cucumbers, carrots, and sweet corn, and if they were really lucky, such delicious treats as strawberries, cherries and mulberries. They could only eat what was in season, but they never went hungry.

Theresa was in charge: mainly because none of the others had a clue about leadership. Even Reggie was hopeless. He spent all his time arguing. Theresa was only eighteen, but she was very capable. She had to sort out the food, stop squabbles and organise roles in the garden, but her most important role was to listen, and that was what she loved the most. She had all the time in the world to just listen.

One very important rule, that Theresa was constantly reminding them of, was to be back in their homes before the clock in the big house struck four bells. For some reason, unknown even to Theresa, at four o'clock in the morning they all turned back into stone. It was dangerous to be found too far away, but on the night of the storm they had had no choice. Especially Reggie, Katie, Maggie and Daisy, who were all injured. Felicity knew that they had to keep their secret, but how was Daisy ever going to have a life again unless Jack was told? He really was the only one who could help her. She would speak to Theresa. They must have an urgent meeting and it had to happen tonight.

Jack sat up and looked longingly out of his bedroom window. The sky was bright blue, with not a cloud to be seen. It was a perfect spring day, and there he was stuck in bed with the measles. He had come down with them a week ago and still had the spots to prove it. In fact, as far as Jack could tell, nothing had gone right for him since the night of the storm. His grades at school had slipped right back and he had failed the last two spelling tests. He couldn't concentrate and he found the work difficult. Some days it was as if he was drowning and there was nobody around to save him. It was horrible. His lack of ability was perfect ammunition for the group of boys who continued to bully him. They called him 'no-brains-Crane' and took much delight in taunting him. Brian Madison was the worst. He egged the others on, making school life unbearable. They threw rubbers at him from the back of the class, and sent notes around to one another, laughing out loud. Jack knew the notes were about him because Sam accidentally got one and told Jack about it.

If only I could play soccer, thought Jack. If only I was good at sport. It seemed to him that anyone who was good at sport was treated like a hero. He was just too scared to try. What if he was hopeless at it? Jack knew he should tell his teacher about being bullied, but he never had the courage to go and see him. Anyway, his teacher was hopeless and didn't seem to have a clue about keeping discipline, or teaching for that matter. Sometimes, thought Jack, I just want to run away. I want to find somewhere safe.

The last straw was on Tuesday afternoon when he noticed a group of boys hanging around his bike. As soon as they saw him they ran off, but Jack recognised Brian Madison. When Jack got to his bike he found both tyres had been slashed and the new bell he got for his tenth birthday had been ripped off. It was all he could do not to cry and if his best friend, Sam, hadn't been with him he didn't know what he would have done.

When Sam saw the state of Jack's bike his face went white. 'This is terrible, Jack. I mean really terrible. What will your dad say? Mine would be furious, absolutely furious. I can't understand why they pick on you,' said Sam, seriously. 'You've done nothing to upset them. I just can't understand it.'

'I don't know either,' said Jack, miserably. 'They are all idiots. That's what they are: idiots. Anyway, they give you a hard time too, so that proves they are idiots.' Poor old Sam, thought Jack with affection. His friend was always getting teased for being overweight, and his mother didn't help matters by always putting him on diets. She was obsessed. Sam's mother would have been furious if she had known what Sam ate last month at 'sweets day.' The school had it to raise money for new computers. Jack could still see Sam gazing longingly at the rows of glass jars full to the brim with delicious lollies. There were red and green frogs, chocolates, all sorts of jellied sweets, and the longest snakes Jack had ever seen. It was mind-blowing.

'I think I've died and gone to heaven,' said Sam, almost in a trance. 'Leave me, Jack. Please leave me. I could be a while.' Sam didn't think that this sort of stuff would be part of his mother's diet plan though, so Jack had to promise not to tell her. Jack laughed. He didn't think it would be part of the plan either. So he promised never, ever, to tell.

Yes, thought Jack, Sam was a very good friend and, on the day that his tyres were slashed, had happily helped Jack drag his bike home without a single word of complaint.

Jack kept looking out the window. He longed to get back to the garden. It was ten days since the night of the storm and he still thought about the dream. It still felt so real. He longed to find out what was going on, and it annoyed him that all he could do was sit here and do nothing. It was totally boring. His thoughts also kept wandering back to school. According to Sam, when Jack got back the class would have a new teacher: a lady called Miss Newman. Apparently Mr Jones left because he was stressed. That's a laugh, thought Jack bitterly. I should be the one on stress leave, not Mr. Jones. Anyway, it made life a bit more interesting. It almost made the thought of going back to school bearable. He rather liked the idea of a lady teacher. He just hoped she was a better teacher than Mr Jones. He just hoped she was nice.

Jack was so busy thinking about things, that he had no idea that his mother had entered the room, and had been watching him for the past five minutes.

'Hi, darling,' said Mary, quietly resisting the urge to rush over and hug her son. He looked so unhappy. She wished he would confide in her and Alan more. As far as they could tell he was happy at home, but what about school? How did he feel about school? He never told them anything. She wondered whether things might have been different if he had had a brother or a sister. Maybe life would have been easier for him, but that was now something they would never know, thought Mary sadly.

She kept staring at him, wishing she could magically make all his pain disappear. However, life wasn't like that. Life wasn't always fair. All she could do was be there for him and hope that things would get better, and anyway, thought Mary, sometimes life doesn't get better, just sometimes it gets worse.

It was so hard not to nag Jack into telling them how he felt, because she had a terrible feeling that he was getting bullied at school. On one of the few occasions she was able to pick him up she saw a group of boys nearby yelling at him. She caught the words, 'no-brains-Crane', and her heart sank. She had tried to speak to Jack about it, but he was a closed book on the subject. Even his grandfather, in whom Jack often confided, could not prise out of him his reasons for disliking school so much, but enough of this gloom, thought Mary. For Jack's sake she must put on a happy face.

Flopping down on the bed next to him, Mary touched his warm forehead and smiled. 'I'm going up to the shops to get you something nice to eat, and buy a few things for tea. Do you think you will be okay on your own? I promise I won't be gone long.'

Jack looked into his mother's worried eyes. 'I'll be fine, but I'll be even better if I could have some strawberry icecream and the biggest chocolate bar you can find. Much better,' said Jack, smiling.

'Agreed,' said Mary, giving him a quick kiss on the top of his head. She chuckled as she got up, stretching her long legs, and giving her hair a final brush. 'You must be feeling better Jack to want strawberry icecream and chocolate. On a more serious note, you have to promise me that you will only get out of bed if you really have to, and if the doorbell rings do not open it unless you know who it is. Understood?'

'Understood,' said her son, quietly.

'Good,' said Mary, blowing him a kiss from the doorway. 'Oh! That reminds me,' said his mother, coming back into the room. 'Grandpa and Grandma are coming up today, so you'd better let them in if they get here before I get back, but only open the door if it's them. Anyway I'll be off. Love you darling.' And with that, his mum was gone.

He heard the front door slam and the faint whine of his mother's car as she reversed out of the driveway. He strained to hear more, but all was silent as the old bomb disappeared out of earshot. Suddenly, the house felt very empty without the sound of his mother clattering about in the kitchen. Jack wished she had never left. He called out to Maxine and Scarlet, but their absence meant they were waiting faithfully at the lounge room window for his mother's return.

He looked up at the shelf above his dressing table, to make sure it was still there. His mum had a habit of tidying things up all the time, but thankfully there it was, in the exact place he had put it after the storm. The bonnet looked odd sitting on its own. It looked odd not being attached to the mouse. He felt awful that it was still sitting there after all this time. He had meant to reattach it to the mouse, and then he got sick.

Jack knew Daisy wasn't a real living animal but somehow he felt he had betrayed her. He'd never forget for as long as he lived, that weird feeling that had come over him the day he had discovered her. He couldn't explain it. It was just weird. Anyway, he would do something about fixing her now.

Jack gingerly climbed out of bed and put on his slippers. He still felt a bit odd. His head still ached and he felt hot. Maybe, thought Jack hopefully, he wouldn't be able to go to school next week either.

Standing on a stool, Jack was finally able to grab hold of the bonnet. He stroked it absentmindedly, his mother popping into his thoughts. She had named the little mouse Daisy after her grandmother, his great-grandmother. Jack had really liked his great-grandmother, even though she was very old and wrinkly. His mother said she was ninety one when she died. Jack couldn't begin to imagine what it was like to be that old.

The only thing he could remember about her was her wonderful stories. She had lived in England as a little girl, and the stories of her life were so vivid. However, his very favourite stories were about man-eating army ants in South America. They were so scary. Nevertheless, he would happily sit for hours revelling in the gory details until he felt physically ill, but Great-Grandma never seemed to notice his discomfort. She just ploughed on regardless. Jack was secretly pleased that there weren't any army ants where he lived. That would have been horrible because according to Great-Grandma they ate every single bit of you.

It was funny, thought Jack, how his mother always named her ornaments after members of the family. He wondered who she had named Rachel after. It must have been someone special. She only ever named them after someone special.

Still thinking about the problem of fixing Daisy,

Jack was interrupted by the sound of a car coming up the driveway and the dogs barking madly. Grandma and Grandpa thought Jack, throwing the bonnet onto his bed. It has to be. He raced down the stairs and waited for the doorbell to ring. He opened the door and flung his arms around his grandmother.

'Wow!' said Grandma. 'What a welcome. We're a bit early darling, but Mum said to start lunch without her. So how does chicken soup and apricot muffins sound?'

'It sounds great,' said Jack, leading them into the kitchen. 'It sounds better than great.'

'Good,' said his grandmother, touching his flushed cheek. 'Let's get started.'

'What can I do to help?' said Grandpa, placing the soup and muffins on the bench. 'Your grandmother always seems to have things under control, but I'd like to help if I can.'

'Well, there is something,' Jack began hesitantly. 'On the night of the storm lots of things were smashed. One of them was a stone mouse. Luckily she's still in one piece, but her bonnet was ripped off. I promised Mum I would fix it, and I sort of promised the mouse.' He looked across at his grandpa. 'Do you think you can help me? I need to do this, Grandpa. I really need to. Not just for me, but for Mum. She said that she still thinks of the statue Rachel, and now Daisy is broken too.'

Grandpa looked at Grandma, and then at the boy's worried face. A feeling of sadness crept over him. Mary was never going to let go of Rachel. It broke his heart, and now her only child was worrying about a broken mouse.

'All right, Jack,' said Grandpa, ruffling his hair. 'What are Grandpas good for if they can't fix things? Let's go outside and we'll work out how to fix your mouse, but you mustn't linger. When you've shown me what you want me to do, you'll have to go straight back inside and sit with Grandma. Is that okay by you?

Jack nodded, silently overjoyed that this particular worry had now been solved. However, little did the boy know that this was the beginning of a brand new problem.

6

Daisy's Adventure

Daisy shivered inwardly as the old man with his big head and shock of white hair loomed over her. His shadow blocked out the morning sun as she stared up into the lined face. Who was this person? She had never seen anyone so ancient before. Even Annie wasn't as old as this! She wondered what Annie and Felicity would be thinking, particularly Felicity. Daisy was a little afraid as the man reached out to touch the top of her head, but he had a kind face, and when she saw that Jack was with him, she knew she had nothing to fear.

She couldn't help thinking how terrible Jack looked. His face was white with funny red spots all over it, and his thick curly hair was a mess. He looked so miserable that Daisy felt guilty for only worrying about herself. She just wished she could talk to him. He seemed so lonely when he came out into the garden. She knew she could be his friend, she just knew she could and Felicity frequently discussed the boy and how he was often alone. Sometimes he had one special friend come round to visit. His name was Sam. He was a big boy for his age, and always seemed to be eating something. Whenever he was over he didn't run around much or play games like Jack; he just ate!

'It's not right' said Annie. 'That child lives on that stuff found in those packets. I think I've heard him call them 'chips'. I haven't seen him eat an apple yet, and another thing, he never gets a scrap of exercise when he is here; he just sits. All little boys should play in a garden of this size. Poor little blighter; what are the parents thinking, just letting the boy eat and not exercise.' Annie believed a garden was to be played in, not just to sit in and do nothing. 'That boy may as well be like us, for all the movement he makes in this garden.'

Maggie, on the other hand, was less sympathetic. When the subject was brought up around her, she promptly stated that quite simply the boy was too fat and therefore was unable to run around. 'Imagine if a magpie was that fat. It would never be able to get off the ground!' No one could disagree, but sometimes Maggie could be too direct and therefore quite hurtful. Daisy felt sorry for Sam. He couldn't help it if he liked food. She understood perfectly because she loved food. She couldn't imagine life without it.

Daisy was so engrossed in her thoughts that she didn't notice the old man's large hand reach out towards her. He tenderly picked her up, cradled her in his arms, and started walking. She felt the warmth of his body as he held her close, and a feeling of exhilaration. It seemed as if she was flying through the air with every step he took. It was all a bit exciting really. Maybe, squealed Daisy to herself, just maybe this is going to be the beginning of a really good adventure, not a bad one, like the storm.

Bewildered, Felicity and Annie watched in horror as their friend was carried away. The old man headed down the concrete path, onto the large verandah and towards the back door of the big house. Felicity watched his every move until eventually he disappeared out of sight. She felt sick as she heard the back door slam behind them, and then there was silence.

Daisy was gone, and there wasn't a single thing she could do to help her. She would just have to wait, and hope that her friend would be back before the sun went down. Felicity shuddered. What would happen to the mouse if she wasn't home by then? What would happen if the real Daisy was discovered by the humans? Oh! Please Daisy, thought Felicity angrily. Please come home before the sun sets, please.

Daisy looked around the room. It felt as if she had been sitting on this hard piece of wood forever and it was getting very uncomfortable. The only good thing about the long wait was that she had a chance to work out who the old people were. The old man who brought her into the house was called Grandpa, and the old lady was called Grandma. Very strange names, thought Daisy, even for humans. Anyway, she didn't really care how long she stayed in the room; it was fun watching all these strange things happening.

Her eyes watched the old man's every move and it was all she could do not to squeal with delight when she saw him carry her beautiful bonnet from the kitchen table and place it carefully next to her. He got out an odd-looking bottle and squeezed something onto the base of the bonnet and then fixed it firmly onto her head. Grandpa pushed the bonnet down as hard as he could. Daisy winced inwardly. It was painful, but the little mouse knew she had to stay still. Finally it was over, and she could relax. Grandpa stood back and had a good look at his handiwork. He looked pleased with the result. She was so glad; her bonnet meant everything to her. Without it she felt lost.

'Well, what do you think?' said Grandpa, proudly. 'Are you happy with this, Jack?'

'It's fantastic, Grandpa,' said Jack, staring into Daisy's eyes. Mum will be rapt. Thankyou so much.'

Daisy stood perfectly still. She couldn't afford to move a muscle, she especially couldn't blink, but what she did feel like doing was letting out a long loud squeal, she was so excited. She couldn't believe what had just happened. It was amazing. The old man called Grandpa had fixed her bonnet; he'd actually fixed her bonnet. She felt whole again and wanted to cry out thank you, Grandpa, but she knew she couldn't. She would just think it instead.

She smiled. It certainly had been exciting. From the minute she was carried into the big house and placed on the piece of wood she knew something good was going to happen. She loved the room she was in now. It was enormous, and so bright and cosy. There were no cold strong winds here. There were huge windows on three sides and her beautiful garden could be seen through every one of them. She had never seen anything like it. She was fascinated by everything, particularly the old people. She was intrigued with them and wished someone would worry about her, like Grandma worried about Jack.

'Come on Jack,' said Grandma, encouragingly. 'Eat some more chicken soup. It will make you feel better.'

'Actually Grandma, I think I'll go back to bed. I really don't feel very well. Thanks anyway for the soup. I hope you don't mind.'

'Of course I don't mind. Sleep is the best cure when you're feeling unwell. Anyway,' said Grandma, 'your mum will be back soon, and there will be lots of boring chatter. Off you go, and have a good sleep.'

'Before I do,' said Jack, slowly. 'I'd like to ask you and Grandpa something. It's important to me. I'd like to ask if either of you have ever had a dream that felt so real that you were sure that it had really happened?'

There was a moment's silence before Grandma spoke. 'I've had lots of dreams Jack, but none that worried me. What about you Ted?'

Grandpa shook his head. 'Not anything that I can remember. What was your dream about? Do you feel like telling us?'

Jack hesitated. He couldn't tell them everything, but he really needed to tell someone about his dream, and Grandpa and Grandma always had time to listen. 'On the night of the storm,' began Jack, 'I had this awful dream that someone was hurt out in the garden. There were these terrible screams. In my dream I grabbed the torch and walked downstairs. It was awful, everything was so scary: the wind, the thunder, the lightning, but something was pulling me towards the door. I couldn't stop walking. It was horrible.'

Jack took a breath. 'I ended up outside. The storm had almost stopped, and there was this light, this beautiful light.' He looked at his grandparents. 'It was then I saw something. It was small and looked frightened. It was standing by the shed, staring right past me, but it's so frustrating Grandpa, because as hard as I try, I can't remember anything else. Do you think I'm going mad?'

It was a few minutes before Grandpa answered. 'Of course you're not going mad. You have just had a very vivid dream, and don't forget there really was a storm, so you would have heard all sorts of things. Isn't that right, Grace?' Grandma nodded, but didn't say a word.

'But the weird thing was,' continued Jack, 'the next morning when I was cleaning up, I found my torch: in the exact spot where I was standing in my dream. How did it get there if I didn't go outside?'

'That is strange, darling,' said Grandma, squeezing his hand, 'but there must be a perfectly simple explanation for your torch being there. Ask your dad when he comes home. I bet Dad will have the answer! Now my boy, let's stop worrying about dreams, and get you to bed. You are starting to look tired.'

Daisy watched Grandma lead Jack up the stairs. The mouse couldn't believe what she was hearing. He had seen her. Jack had been that shadow. It was Jack who had slammed the door. She wanted to tell him. She really wanted to tell him that he wasn't dreaming; to tell him that it was real. That she was real. Oh! If only she could tell him.

It wasn't long before Grandma was back in the kitchen. She came over and looked at Daisy with kind grey eyes. She gently touched the mouse's newly fixed bonnet and brushed the remaining leaves off her dress. She was so nice, thought Daisy, but she looked so sad.

Still staring at the little mouse, Grandma finally spoke. 'I worry about that child, Ted. I keep telling Mary to encourage him to play more sport, or even to do more with them. These young parents today are just too busy; they don't have time to be a family. It makes me cross. Jack's got such a vivid imagination, but he needs to do other things. I mean this dream, Ted. What do you think about that?'

Grandpa shook his head. 'I honestly don't know. It is strange that he found his torch outside. Maybe he was sleepwalking. I think,' said Grandpa, eating the last of the bread, 'I think that when we come up across the road to live, we must spend more time with the boy. I think the poor kid is lonely. This dream is probably part of it. Anyway, we mustn't worry about him, and we mustn't blame Alan and Mary. They are loving parents and they do care, and that's all we can ask for.'

Grandma reached over and squeezed Grandpa's hand. 'You're right dear. As usual you make perfect sense. I don't know, it's everything lately: shifting house has been a huge upheaval, Jack's problems and Mary; particularly Mary. I don't think she will ever get over losing Rachel. Sometimes I feel so helpless, but, don't worry about me,' said Grandma, wiping away a tear. 'I'm just a bit emotional at present. I'll get over it. Once we are in our new house and settled I know things will be better. It might even be fun.'

Grandpa came over and hugged his wife. 'You're a good woman, Grace. Everything will fall into place. Life somehow manages to sort itself out. You just wait and see.'

Daisy listened carefully to the conversation and thought what terrible lives human beings had. There seemed to be nothing but problems. It was odd that Grandma talked about Mary losing someone called Rachel. Very odd, thought Daisy, because Theresa had also lost someone called Rachel, ten years ago in the last big storm. It surely couldn't be the same one. Rachel was one of them. Rachel had been one of the folk.

Daisy was starting to get restless. It was a long time since the mouse had seen Jack and she wondered when he would come back downstairs. It was also a bit boring now because the old people were sleeping and everything was deathly quiet. Mary had come home briefly, and then gone out again. It was something to do with meeting Jack's new teacher. All Daisy could hear now was the ticking of the grandfather clock. It chimed two bells. Her eyelids felt heavy as the afternoon sun streamed into the room. It was so relaxing, and she was so tired. As hard as she tried, she couldn't stay awake. She just couldn't.

Daisy must have slept for hours, because when she finally woke she was shocked to find herself in a different room. It was a very small dark room, and much higher up than the big room she had previously been in. There was a window that looked down onto a view she had never seen before. It was so beautiful. She could see every coloured rose imaginable. There was a red brick wall similar to the one out the back, but much bigger. It was covered with big yellow and white daisies that spilled over the edge. Daisy was spellbound.

The only place it could possibly be, thought the mouse with a touch of excitement, was the front garden. It had to be, but it was nothing like she had imagined. Daisy felt quite important, as she was the first of the folk to really see what the front garden looked like. It was a mystery to them, and over the years such horror stories had been told about the front garden that no one was ever game to venture into it, but to Daisy, it didn't look sinister at all. She couldn't wait to tell everyone what it was really like.

Daisy was beginning to feel very hungry, and this room gave her the creeps. It was so dull. She had been placed on top of a type of bench that faced the window. She couldn't see much else in the room except a long, flat piece of furniture that lay underneath the window, and a large square thing that leaned against the far wall. Next to it was a torn picture of some odd looking green creature. It certainly wasn't human. She slowly read out the words on the picture. It said 'Shrek'. How odd, thought the mouse. She couldn't help thinking that apart from that green monster on the wall it was a very boring room.

From her perch she could see that the long shadows on the lawn had disappeared, and realised that the sun was setting. This was a bit worrying. She should be home by now. This could be dangerous. What if she was discovered? Daisy shivered. She'd had enough of this adventure; she wanted to go. She wanted Felicity and Annie. She wanted to go home.

7

The Introduction

Jack lay there thinking. Grandma and Grandpa hadn't been very helpful. They didn't seem to think his dream meant anything. They actually made him feel a bit stupid. Still, thought Jack, what's new? He was going back to school on Monday. He was always made to feel stupid there. He thought about Brian Madison and shuddered. The last time he ran into him, it was awful. Brian had cornered him in the toilets. Jack could still see the mean look on his face; and his voice! It was so loud. It was as if he was yelling at him.

'Got any money on you Crane? 'Cos I'm dying for a pie with sauce, and I haven't got no money.' Jack had just stood there like an idiot, shaking his head.

'Wrong, Crane,' said Brian, smugly. 'I saw you order your lunch. So don't go shaking your head at me. Cough it up.'

Jack couldn't believe it. They thought he was stupid. He spoke slowly. 'Yes! I did order my lunch, but I needed the money to pay for it, and now I've no money left. Simple.'

Brian stared at him. 'Don't talk to me like I'm stupid. Pay up next week or that brand new bike of yours will be on the scrap heap. I'll do a real good job of it this time, if you don't do what I want. Get what I mean?'

At the time Jack had felt quite brave. He had stood up to Brian Madison, but now he felt scared. He never wanted to face him again. Everything was such a mess. He knew he should tell his parents, but how would that help? It would probably make things worse. Jack could feel his eyes welling up with tears. He didn't know what to do. He just didn't know.

As Daisy stood there wondering what was going to happen to her, she heard something strange. It sounded like someone crying. It appeared to be coming from the long, flat piece of furniture, but what was it? She screwed her eyes tight to get a better look. She could just make out a shape. Daisy squealed in surprise. The shape was Jack, and this dull room was his. Poor Jack, thought Daisy. I wonder what has made him cry. She hated seeing someone cry: especially someone like Jack. He had helped her, and now he needed help. He needed a friend.

Daisy swallowed hard. What was she to do? Betray her friends by speaking to a human, or help Jack? This was the hardest decision she had ever had to make. She wondered what Annie would do. The old mushroom was always so practical. If she tried hard enough, Daisy could hear Annie's voice going over and over in her head. She was always calling Jack 'a poor little blighter,' or 'a poor little soul': always. She would want Daisy to help. She was sure she would.

Daisy could hear the big clock chime four bells. She had run out of time. She was no longer an ornament, but that didn't matter. For Jack's sake, the little mouse knew exactly what she had to do.

She took a deep breath and spoke. 'Please don't cry, Jack, please don't cry.' Daisy could hear her voice echoing around the quiet room. It sounded funny. It didn't sound like her at all.

Jack sat up, his tears coming to an abrupt end. He looked around him. He felt sure he had heard someone call him, not once, but twice. This was weird. He couldn't see anyone, but the words were so clear.

'I'm up here Jack, on the bench, overlooking your bed,' continued the voice. 'It's Daisy, the concrete mouse.'

There was a moment's silence before Jack spoke. He couldn't believe what he was hearing. 'Daisy, the grey mouse that Grandpa had left to dry? Daisy the concrete mouse I found under the branches? That Daisy? I mean who is this really? I'm not in the mood for stupid games. Tell me who you are.'

'It really is me,' continued the voice. 'It really is Daisy, the mouse, and I don't like being told that I'm playing stupid games, when for once I'm not. I'm only concerned about you.' There was complete silence except for the quiet ticking of the bedside clock.

It seemed forever before Jack replied. 'You really are Daisy, the concrete mouse? The little ornament that sits under the wrought iron seat?'

'Yes,' said Daisy. 'How many more times do I have to tell you?'

Jack stared in disbelief. 'But how can it be possible? How can you talk? You're not real. You're made of concrete, aren't you?'

Daisy sighed. This was going to be so difficult. The mouse had a terrible feeling that Jack was a bit slow like Herbert. The wombat needed to be told things over and over again before they sank in, and Jack seemed exactly the same.

'It's hard to explain,' said Daisy, slowly. 'I don't know how I can talk, and why I can talk, but I just can. We all can,' said the mouse, in a very matter of fact way. 'We can do all sorts of things and are very self-sufficient; in fact we have never needed to involve humans in our lives until now.'

Jack sat quietly, almost in a state of shock. Was he really having a conversation with a concrete mouse, or was his mind playing tricks? However, Daisy was still talking and he was still listening. Jack just hoped he wasn't going crazy. Maybe he had stress, like Mr Jones. With everything that had happened to him lately, it was enough to make anyone go mad.

However, he found himself wanting to know more. There were so many questions he wanted to ask. He moved closer towards the voice. He still couldn't see her properly. He turned on the light, and stared up at the shelf.

'It's you! I don't believe it. It's you!' cried Jack. He remembered now. He remembered her from his dream. It was Daisy standing by the shed. Jack couldn't take his eyes off her. He couldn't stop looking at her bright red bonnet and dress. Beneath her bonnet were two pointy ears. She had a small furry face, and two beady brown eyes. Her black nose and whiskers were twitching. He had never seen anything so cute. 'But you were just a dream,' cried Jack. 'You're not real. You can't be. You were only ever a dream.'

There was a brief lull in the conversation before Daisy spoke. 'It was me, Jack, standing by the shed that horrible night, and I am real. All the ornaments are. We call ourselves the "folk," and the garden is our home.'

'Why are you called "folk"?' interrupted Jack. 'It's a very strange name and sounds old-fashioned to me.'

'I don't know,' said Daisy, a little miffed at being called strange. 'We just are, and I'd much rather be a "folk" than a "human" any day. That really is a strange name. Anyway,' said the mouse, a little annoyed. 'What does old-fashioned mean? It doesn't sound very nice.'

'It's sort of a compliment,' said Jack, hoping he could get back into Daisy's good books. He looked up at her. She did look cross. 'I'm sorry if I've hurt your feelings. Sometimes I say stupid things, but I do want to know more. I'm just finding it hard to believe, that's all. I mean, I know you can talk, but what else can you do?'

Daisy took a deep breath before she spoke. She always found it hard to stay cross for very long. 'Well, we can all walk and run, and we all have homes. I live with Felicity under the wrought iron seat. She is my very best friend. You can't miss her; she has lots of red curls and is covered in freckles. Annie, the old mushroom, lives nearby under the lavender bush. She is like a mother to us; a very cross mother sometimes.' Daisy chuckled. 'I usually don't take much notice of her, which makes her even madder, and you should see how her legs and arms work. They aren't very long, and when it's time to return to stone they somehow go back into her body. It's really amazing. We have no idea how it happens.'

'How can they do that?' asked Jack.

'Don't you listen, Jack? I just told you; we don't know,' said Daisy. 'It's very rude to interrupt, you know. We are never allowed to do that and already you have done it twice. Now where was I? Oh! Yes.

Reggie the gnome. He is bright blue, and wears a red hat. He has a long white beard, and is the most annoying gnome I have ever met. Reggie lives with Herbert the wombat around in the side garden. Herbert is very sweet and lovable, but doesn't come into the main garden very often.'

Daisy took another breath. All this explaining was tiring. 'And then there is Ben. He is a beautiful, kind dog. We all love him. He never says anything bad about anyone, unlike Maggie the magpie who says bad things about everyone. She even said something nasty about your friend Sam. She said he was very overweight and couldn't run because of it.'

Jack was a bit put out that his friend should be spoken about like this. 'That's not very nice,' he interrupted again. 'Sam is trying very hard to lose weight. His mother has put him on a diet, and he rides his bike to school with me now.'

Daisy smiled. It was nice to know that some humans cared about each other. According to Theresa, that didn't seem to happen very often. Some humans weren't very nice. She was so glad Jack was different. Now, pondered Daisy, have I left anyone out?

It was the first time she had actually stopped talking, thought Jack. The only person who could talk as much as Daisy was Laura Bell, a tall skinny girl with long plaits and an annoying voice. She was in his class for music and no one would sit with her because she always got them into trouble. He felt Daisy could give her a run for her money.

'I know who I forgot', squealed Daisy, jolting him out of his thoughts. 'Theresa and Katie. Theresa is the tall pretty girl who lives at the top of the garden. She is very intelligent and is sort of in charge of all of us. We love Theresa, and everyone goes to her for a chat. She's so pretty,' said Daisy, quietly. 'Sometimes I really wish I was like her. Finally, there is dear sweet Katie. She is a lovely old kookaburra who never interferes with anyone. Sometimes when she is very happy Katie has the most amazing laugh. You want to laugh yourself.' Daisy yawned. She was starting to feel tired, but there was so much more to tell.

'After the sun goes down', continued Daisy, 'we all go about our business. We collect food, have meals together, and read stories. We have a lot of fun. Well most of the time we do,' said Daisy. 'But sometimes garden life can be very boring. We can read very well though,' she said, proudly. 'I read heaps. It takes me to another place, a fun place. Theresa taught us from the old readers and books your mother threw out years ago. The only one still struggling is Herbert, but then Theresa says that Herbert is a bit slow. He certainly is slow at moving, so I guess he has a slower brain than ours!'

Poor Herbert, thought Jack. He knew exactly how he felt. He wondered if Daisy's constant chatter made Herbert quiet. The wombat probably didn't have a choice. Jack wanted to meet Herbert.

He studied Daisy as she chattered on. It really was unbelievable. He wondered what his grandparents would think if he told them about this!'And,' continued Daisy, hardly drawing breath, 'Maggie the magpie and Katie the kookaburra can fly, and they often get interesting food for us from outside the garden. We had sausages last week from four houses down. They were having a barbecue. The sausages were absolutely delicious. They are always having barbecues. There,' said the mouse. 'Now I have told you everything. I have told you our secret.'

Finally there was silence as Daisy suddenly remembered how hungry she was. Maybe if she asked nicely the boy would get her something to eat. She could even offer to introduce him to the rest of the garden folk once she was back home again. That was going to be the next hurdle; telling the folk!

Jack cleared his throat. 'Why have you told me your secret after all this time? Why now? And why me?'

Again there was silence as Daisy tried to find the right words. 'We all care about you, Jack, and for a long time have wanted to talk to you, but we are banned from talking to humans. Your grandpa fixed my bonnet, and I am so grateful to you both. When I saw you crying, I just had to speak. I had to make you feel better, but now I will be in trouble. Still,' said Daisy, scratching her left ear. 'I'm always in trouble.'

She stared into Jack's dark eyes. 'When you take me back outside would you like to meet everyone?'

Jack nodded. It still felt like a dream, but his eyes were glued to Daisy as she rambled on and on. He'd never been able to concentrate so well in his whole life.

'We do have very strict rules though,' said Daisy. 'And they must be obeyed.' She was being very serious now: it was important that Jack knew the rules properly.

'Number one. This secret must never be told to anyone else. It must only be between you and us: nobody else. Not even your best friend.'

'Number two. You must never speak to us during daytime hours. It is not only dangerous, but we do not move or talk between four o'clock in the morning and when the sun sets. We can hear things, and move our eyes and mouths slightly, but that's all.'

'Number three. Don't introduce yourself to any of the garden folk until I have had a meeting with Theresa.' Daisy took a deep breath. She was feeling tired again and so hungry.

'And finally,' squealed the little mouse, 'I'm starving! Is there any way you can get me something to eat? I'm absolutely starving.'

It was all so ridiculous that Jack couldn't help laughing. 'What would you like? What do concrete mice eat? I might not have anything you like.'

Daisy sighed. 'I'm not concrete now, Jack, I'm a real mouse. Can't you see that? Can't you see my grey fur and colourful clothes?'

'Yes,' said Jack, 'but it's so hard to get my head around it. You're not exactly like your average mouse. I don't know any other mice that walk, talk, and wear clothes. It's just going to take a while to get used to.'

'I guess,' said Daisy, not really seeing the problem. 'Anyway,' said the mouse, with some urgency, 'let's get back to what food I like. I'll eat anything that's nice. Mice are not at all fussy, although I mainly eat fruit and vegetables. I really love my food, and I trust you to bring something nice.'

Making his way slowly down the stairs after placing Daisy on the bed, Jack was relieved that the kitchen was empty. He looked in the fridge, but there wasn't much of interest there. He finally found some fresh bread and homemade strawberry jam. He felt sure Daisy would like this. He grabbed two apricot muffins and a glass of lemonade and very carefully made his way back up the stairs. Funnily enough he was feeling much better; he didn't even mind the thought of going back to school. He didn't even mind facing Brian Madison. His head was in such a spin.

'Boy, you can eat', commented Jack, as Daisy demolished the food in record time. 'Even my father doesn't eat that fast.'

'He would if he hadn't eaten for a week. I'm just so hungry, Jack. I've never enjoyed food so much.' Drinking the lemonade was interesting; the bubbles kept going up Daisy's nose, making her giggle uncontrollably. She had never tasted anything like it! She would never for the rest of her life forget Jack and Grandpa for their kindness. Never!

Jack studied Daisy while she ate the last of her food. He was fascinated by her small hands. They were like human hands, but had fine fingers, and pointy nails. She had a long nose with a black tip, and five fine whiskers protruded from either side of her face. Daisy's brown eyes radiated such joy that you couldn't help feeling happy around her. A long apron was attached to the skirt, nearly reaching the floor. He could only just see her feet and tail peeking beneath it. The whole outfit was very old-fashioned, but suited the little mouse perfectly. She looked exactly like she did the night of the storm.

'Tell me Daisy,' said Jack, as he watched her wipe the remaining muffin crumbs off her whiskers. 'On the night of the storm, that was you I heard screaming, wasn't it?'

'You heard me scream over all that wind and rain? You heard me? I didn't think it was possible.' She suddenly shivered. 'That storm was horrible. I never want to think about that night again. Can we talk about something happy, Jack? Can we talk about taking me home? I miss Felicity and Annie. I miss my friends. Can you please take me home; right now.'

Jack secretly wished the little mouse would tell

him everything about that night. He wanted to know how all the ornaments got injured. He wanted to know about Daisy. He wanted to know everything, but he couldn't force her. He would just have to wait.

'Okay,' said Jack, 'but we'll have to work out how to do this. We can't get caught. We'll have to hide you in something, and sneak you outside in it.' He looked at Daisy's worried face. 'It will have to be big enough to fit you in comfortably.' He looked quickly around the room, spotting something in the corner. 'I know,' said Jack, excitedly. 'The box I was going to use to collect all the balls in. That will be perfect.

'What balls?' said Daisy, innocently, as she poked her nose into the box.

'Just lots of lost balls I found,' said Jack. 'Do you know anything about them?' Daisy shook her head, still staring into the box.

'This box is horrible, Jack. It's all dusty and it's got spider webs in it. I don't want to go in it. My dress will get dirty. I won't go in it.'

'Daisy you're kidding. You live in a garden. There's dirt everywhere. Now don't argue.'

Daisy was just about to tell Jack that being in the garden was different, when she heard footsteps. She was going to get discovered, she just knew she was.

'Someone's coming up the stairs,' yelled Jack. 'You don't have a choice Daisy. Get into the box. Don't argue. Get into the box, now!'

8

Going Home

Daisy crouched into the corner of the box and waited. Jack had pushed the box right into the wall so no one could see her, but it made the box so hot, and at times Daisy found it hard to breathe. She heard Jack open the door. She heard him speak in a loud slow voice. He sounded odd.

'Mum! What are you doing here? I thought you were getting tea.'

Daisy heard the bed creak as Mary sat down. She heard her sigh. A long tired sigh.

'I will be soon,' said Mary. 'I just wanted to see how you are, and to ask you what you want for tea. Grandpa and your dad want steak and chips and Grandma wants chicken and vegetables. As you have been sick I thought I would let you choose. Anyway, I'm pleased to see you've eaten something. Do you want me to take the tray downstairs?'

Daisy could hardly stand it. Here she was in this horrible dark, dirty box, and all she could hear was humans talking about food. She wanted to scream out 'get me out of here, and give me chicken and vegetables'. She wanted Mary to go, and more than anything else, she wanted her home.

'I'd like chicken and vegetables,' said Jack, finally,

'and do you mind if I go outside to look for my missing tennis balls until tea is ready? I've got this box to put them in.'

'That will be fine,' said Mary, quietly. 'But be back inside before it gets too cold.' Daisy gave a sigh of relief as she heard Mary's footsteps head towards the door, and then they stopped. The little mouse couldn't believe it. Was she ever going to leave? It was so frustrating.

'Oh! By the way,' said Mary, 'I met your new teacher. She seems very nice, and she's looking forward to meeting you on Monday. I think you will like her. Anyway darling, I'd better get tea started otherwise Grandpa will start moaning. Don't stay out too long Jack, and stay warm.'

Thank goodness, thought Daisy, as she heard the door close. Thank goodness she has finally gone. Now I can go home. Soon I'll be with my friends.

After Jack had taken her into the garden, Daisy crawled out of the dirty box and sucked in the cool fresh air. At last I can breathe properly, thought the mouse. It's fantastic. Better than that horrible box. Standing up, she brushed some dust and cobwebs off her dress. Yuk! She hated cobwebs. Cautiously she made her way to the main garden. Daisy couldn't help feeling a tingle of excitement as the strong smell of lavender wafted around her. She wasn't far from home now; she wasn't far from her friends, but she was also a bit worried. She knew they would be angry that she had told Jack their secret. She knew it was against the rules. Jack was worried too. He had told her how scared he was that they would all hate him: because of a human knowing the secret.

'Not if you have food on you,' Daisy had told him. 'They will love you if you bring food.' She had told him not to come up to the slate block until the big clock chimed eight bells. He wasn't allowed to come before then. Anyway, thought Daisy. It was done now. She couldn't take it back. Jack knew, so they would have to live with it.

So engrossed with her thoughts, Daisy didn't hear the twigs breaking behind her; and she certainly didn't hear the loud scream, until her friend was nearly on top of her.

'Daisy, I can't believe it's you. You're home, you're actually home!' Before the little mouse had a chance to catch her breath, there was a flash of red hair and two white arms hugging her so tightly she could hardly breathe. Felicity had run out from behind a bush, almost in tears, as she wrapped herself around the little mouse. Before she knew it, Daisy was surrounded. Even Annie had tears of joy running down her weathered face.

'What did I say, pet?' she said, looking at Felicity, 'I told you our little Daisy would come home, and here she is, complete with her old bonnet. It looks brand new.'

Felicity clapped her hands with joy and gently touched Daisy's head. As far as she could tell the mouse was now perfect. 'Everyone will want to see you,' said Felicity, gleefully. 'So is it okay with you if I arrange a get-together in about half an hour at Theresa's place? We have all been so worried Daisy, especially Ben and Herbert.'

Daisy nodded. 'That's a good idea. I can't wait to see everyone, and I have something very important to tell you all.' She looked across at her friend. How was she going to tell her what she had done? 'When I tell you this important thing,' continued Daisy, 'please Felicity, please don't hate me afterwards. You are my best friend, and I just couldn't stand it.'

Felicity squeezed her hand. 'I could never hate you, Daisy. What an odd thing to say. You are my very best friend and I will care about you forever. I don't care what you have to tell us. Now let's get moving. Everyone is waiting.'

Daisy took a deep breath. Her friends sat silently around Theresa's slate block anxious to see the little mouse properly and hear all about her adventures. No one had ever left the garden before, so this was all very exciting. One of the folk had been on an adventure! Daisy looked down at their expectant faces. How on earth was she going to tell them about Jack?

'Wonderful to see you, old girl,' said Ben, admiring her bonnet. 'You look as pretty as ever. I'm so pleased you are all fixed; so pleased old girl.'

Daisy blushed. She wasn't used to having so many compliments, especially from Ben. He always kept his thoughts to himself. She was especially amazed that Reggie was so nice.

Squeezing her hand, Reggie coughed a few times and began to speak. 'On behalf of Herbert and myself, we are grateful and pleased for your return. Herbert sends all his love, but is still unable to make the journey through the garden since the storm. You know what a nervous character he is. He hopes you will understand, and go and visit him very soon.' With that, Reggie cleared his throat and sat down.

Daisy smiled. 'Tell Herbert I would love to visit

him, and I do understand,' she said, sincerely. 'He is a very dear friend. You are all dear friends,' continued Daisy, 'and that is why what I am about to tell you is so hard.'

'Come on, old girl,' called out Ben, 'tell us about your adventure. We all want to hear about it.'

They listened in wonderment as Daisy described the big house and the huge kitchen she was placed in. She talked about the large table, and the beautiful view through the windows that looked out onto their garden.

'I could see the lawn, the bottlebrush, and even some of the roses,' said Daisy, quietly. 'It was magical. After quite a long while the old man they call Grandpa took me upstairs to dry. I must have been asleep, because I don't remember any of that, but when I woke up I was in a smaller and much darker room. It was quite depressing compared to the huge family room, but the view out of the window was amazing.'

'Tell us what you saw,' said Felicity, excitedly. 'Tell us, Daisy.'

Daisy hesitated. She just wanted to tell them about Jack, but they all looked so excited. 'Well, there were all sorts of different roses, and there was a brick wall like ours, but much bigger. Lots of colourful flowers hung over the wall. It was beautiful, and not the least bit scary. Maybe we could all visit the front one night.'

'Did you see Roger?' piped up Maggie. 'Remember, he went out the front two years ago. It was a wet, cold winter's night, and we never saw him again.'

Daisy shook her head. 'No, I didn't see Roger.'

'Pity,' said Maggie. 'Katie and I liked Roger. For a

rabbit he was very sensible.'

'Maybe he was hiding behind a bush,' suggested Felicity.

'Rubbish' squawked Maggie. 'Roger went out the front and now he's dead. You won't get me going out there. Anyway,' said Maggie, impatiently, not giving Felicity a chance to reply. 'What happened then?'

Daisy swallowed hard. She couldn't put it off any longer. She would have to tell them about Jack: she would just have to. She stood there quietly, trying to decide exactly what to say to her friends.

However, it was Theresa who broke the silence. 'Is there anything else you wish to tell us Daisy? You seem worried.' The mouse looked at Theresa, then at the other inquisitive faces gazing up at her. There was nothing for it. She had to tell them.

'Yes, I have something very important to say; something that is going to affect all of us forever. When I was up in the smaller room, I heard someone crying. At first I couldn't see anyone, but the sound got louder and louder. I strained to see where it was coming from until eventually I was able to make out a lump on the bed. That lump was Jack.'

A gasp went through the group. 'The poor little mite,' called out Annie. 'I knew he was unhappy; poor little devil. What did you do then, pet? Whatever did you do?'

Daisy looked around at the small group. They were completely still, waiting for her to answer. 'I watched him for a while, and then ... and then I spoke to him.' She flung open her arms. 'I couldn't help it! He was so unhappy; I had to speak to him: I just had to!'

9

The Golden Key

The silence was deafening. Even Theresa was in shock. 'You told a human?' roared Reggie, his furious voice booming through the quiet. 'You told the boy our secret? I can't believe anyone could be so stupid.'

Daisy could feel herself shaking. She had never been spoken to like that before.

'You can say that again,' squawked Maggie. 'Stupid, stupid, stupid! Have you a brain, girl, or is it just that you don't ever bother to use it?' Maggie was furious, and when Maggie got angry she could be very hurtful.

'Please let me explain.' Daisy was nearly in tears. She kept hoping Annie or Felicity or even Ben would come to her defence, but all three remained silent. Felicity had promised not to hate her whatever Daisy said, but now her friend was just staring down at the ground. It made the mouse feel terrible, but she had to explain. They had to understand.

'The boy saved me from a terrible life,' continued Daisy. 'He fixed my bonnet and made me feel whole again. I was very grateful to him. He helped all of you after the storm, wiping the muck off you and taking you back to your homes. Aren't any of you grateful to Jack for helping?'

'No need to talk to him,' interrupted Reggie, still angry. 'You didn't need to talk!'

'I had to,' persisted Daisy. 'He was very upset and needed a friend. I know deep down you have all wanted to befriend the boy. I know you have.' Daisy was struggling now, and prayed that someone, anyone, would speak out on her behalf.

'That may be the case, child,' spoke a sweet voice from the back of the group, 'but you have told him, and I for one am glad. It had to happen sometime, as we need a friend to help us when things get rough. I think in time we will all be pleased about what has happened. It will be seen as a very good thing.'

There was a collective gasp, as they turned to face Katie. Everyone was shocked that this quiet bird, who rarely said anything, did so now when there was a crisis. Even Theresa was still silent, but Reggie wasn't about to give up, and had turned his attention to Katie, ready to give her a mouthful, when Theresa eventually spoke.

'Are we going to meet Jack? And if so what time will he be with us?'

Daisy turned to face Theresa, tears streaming down her face, and dripping off her whiskers. Everyone had been so mean to her since she had told them about Jack. Maggie and Reggie had been particularly horrible. 'I told him to come when the clock chimes eight bells,' sniffed Daisy. 'I told him not to come before that time.'

Theresa sighed. 'Well, before the boy arrives there is something very important I need to tell you all. Something I should have told you years ago. I want each of you to listen carefully, and to try to forget about what Daisy has done. She didn't deliberately set out to disobey us, so we must try and move forward.' There was not a sound; all eyes were on Theresa, intrigued as to what was so important.

'Long ago,' said Theresa, quietly, 'when the garden folk first began, a very important rule was put in place.'

'We know that rule,' interrupted Reggie rudely. 'That's the rule a certain stupid mouse has just broken. That's the rule that states no human is ever to know that the garden folk have secret lives. We all know that rule!'

'I realise that', continued Theresa, annoyed at Reggie's interruption, 'but there is more to it than just knowing about the rule. You all need to know why it is so important to never break it. We all know that it is dangerous for humans to ever find out about us, but we all need to know why.

'One of the main reasons for this is that humans are very powerful and extremely greedy. If some humans discovered our secret we would be at their mercy. They could easily destroy us out of sheer ignorance or mistreat us for their own gain. Look at what they are doing to some of the animals in the wild, and how they are destroying many of the great forests in the world. Do you remember some of the books I read to you about these things?' The folk nodded.

'I don't understand,' piped up Daisy, wiping away the last of her tears. 'Jack and his family are the kindest people I've ever met, and they are humans. They would never kill anyone, never.'

Theresa sighed. This was more difficult to explain than she thought. 'I was just getting to that, Daisy. You are quite right, not all humans are bad. There are some very good ones, but we need to be sure they are good; very sure indeed.'

'How can we be sure Jack can be trusted?' squawked Maggie on top note. 'We don't really know the boy; no one has ever talked to him until now. How do we know he will keep our secret safe?'

'We don't know,' said Theresa, with some hesitation, 'but what I do know is that we have all watched Jack over the years and he doesn't seem to be the sort of child who will rush off and tell people about us. He appears to be a kind boy with a good heart. We have to trust him. Anyway it's too late now. The deed has been done, and we must get on with our lives.

'Now that Jack has been told about us, there is something else of great importance that you all need to know. Something I had forgotten about until now.' Theresa found this story very hard to tell and had deliberately kept it at the back of her mind, but now the folk had to be told. She had little choice. Taking a deep breath she started her story to a sea of fascinated faces all focused on her.

'In the event of a trustworthy human, like Jack, wanting to befriend us, a special golden key exists to enable them to interact with us. This key has been handed down over the years to a chosen member of the folk. That member is responsible for keeping the key safe, and therefore the inhabitants of the garden safe. Once the key is handed over to a human it allows them to become part of life in the garden, unlocking all our secrets. It also binds that human to secrecy. The key has never been handed over to a human before, but this evening I will have no choice but to hand it over to the boy.'

'Thanks to that little fool,' blurted out Reggie,

pointing to Daisy. 'It wouldn't be happening if it wasn't for her. Anyway,' he continued crossly, 'why weren't we informed about this key before now? Why haven't we been told? If this key is so special, why haven't we been able to use it? It's just not good enough!'

Theresa stood quietly. She was unsure about how to explain the history of the key. It was such a complicated story to tell. 'I'm sorry, Reggie, but it all happened such a long time ago, and somehow there has never been the need to tell you. It is quite difficult to explain.'

'Try, pet,' said Annie's comforting voice, from the back of the group. 'Try and explain it to us. We all need to know. After all, it is our history and it is important.'

Theresa nodded and continued. 'Many years ago when I was very young, the garden had a terrible storm. It was not unlike the one we had two weeks ago. The main difference was that someone very close to me died in that storm. It was horrible. After that I blocked out that part of my life. I just didn't want to remember anything that happened that night, including the key. My friend had some sort of connection with the key. I only found out about its existence that night.'

'What was your friend's name?' said Felicity, quietly. She felt sad for Theresa. She couldn't imagine how devastated she would have been if Daisy had been killed in the storm they had two weeks ago. It would have been unbearable.

'My friend was called Rachel,' said Theresa, quietly. 'She was such a happy person, always wanting to have fun. You all would have loved her, but on the night of the storm she was in a very strange mood.

She was very quiet, almost sad. It wasn't like her at all. As she was about to leave for home she hugged me so tight I could hardly breathe. It was as if she never wanted to let me go.' Theresa smiled as the memories came flooding back. 'Rachel told me to take care, and that I would always be her best friend no matter what happened. I can see her now, standing there, her blonde hair blowing in the wind; her favourite blue ribbon barely able to control it.' Theresa stopped to take a breath.

'She took my hand, and pressed something cold and hard into it. It was this golden key.' There was complete silence from the folk as she held up the golden key. 'She told me that it was a symbol of something more powerful. Something I would discover when the time was right.'

Theresa continued in a whisper. 'Rachel told me to guard it with my life in case something happened to her. It was as if she had had a premonition of something awful. It was as if she knew.' Theresa sighed. 'That was the last time I ever saw Rachel.'

The folk remained silent. They felt great sadness for Theresa. Annie knew Rachel, but she didn't know about the key. Annie just wished she could have been there for the girl more during those dark days. Daisy couldn't help thinking how that name 'Rachel' kept coming up in the conversation. It was all very strange.

Reggie finally broke the silence. 'Was there any reason why you and only you had been given responsibility for the key?' he said, looking straight at Theresa. 'What about Annie? Surely someone older and wiser would have been best suited to the task.

A more mature person might have even remembered to tell the rest of us!'

Theresa turned to face him. He was now standing right next to her, making her feel very uncomfortable. Reggie was becoming quite annoying. It was times like these that she wished she had the power to banish folk to their homes when they were being disagreeable, but unfortunately she couldn't.

'It's not that simple, Reggie. I asked Rachel the same question. I asked her, "why me?" All she could tell me was that I was the "chosen one" and that I had the symbol on my person to prove it. Not everyone is born with the symbol.' Slowly Theresa lifted up her long skirt, and there, in perfect form, were three small black circles above her right knee. The folk were fascinated, and couldn't stop staring.

'The symbols are the same as those imprinted on the key,' continued Theresa. 'Only folk who carry the symbol of the key somewhere on their body are chosen to guard it. That's why I have been given this task until the next "chosen one" enters the garden.'

'What happens to the key now?' piped up Daisy. 'It's so exciting. What happens to it now?'

Theresa smiled. 'As I have previously said, Jack will now need to be "keeper of the key" to enable him to move amongst us freely. If he doesn't have the key, we still have all the power. Jack can only talk to us if we initiate it. He certainly cannot be part of our lives or unlock the secrets of the garden without it. He will always be an outsider. I therefore need your blessing to give Jack temporary guardianship of the key.

'Please raise your hands if you are happy for Jack to become part of our lives.' One by one all the group slowly raised their hands; all except Reggie.

'I'm sorry, Reggie,' said Theresa, quietly, 'but the majority has spoken; the boy is to receive the key.' Reggie looked as if he was about to explode with rage when, across the garden, came the sound of a clock chiming. There was a hushed silence among the group as they counted: one, two, three, four... eight chimes in all. Soon the boy would be with them. They heard the back door slam, and the sound of Maxine and Scarlet running through the bushes. They heard footsteps on the concrete path and, before they knew it, the boy was standing quietly before them holding a large box.

No one spoke. Jack shuffled from side to side. He glanced over at Daisy for support, but she remained quiet. He looked down at the row of inquisitive faces; all of them staring straight at him. Nobody moved and nobody spoke. His legs felt like jelly and his throat was so dry it hurt. Jack thought that if he had to stand much longer he would faint. The silence was unbearable, and he wished he had never come, until finally Theresa spoke.

'Come up here, Jack, and stand by me. Put your box down and let me introduce you to everyone. My name is Theresa and I am more or less in charge of things.' Theresa watched Jack carefully. He looked frightened and unsure. 'It's not your fault that you have been told,' said Theresa, kindly, 'but we are pleased that you have been. Now we will have a human friend who will be able to help us in our times of need.'

Jack nodded, but still felt slightly faint. Worst of all, nothing would come out of his mouth. He felt absolutely stupid.

'Actually,' continued Theresa, 'we have something

to give you, Jack: something that has never been given to a human before. It allows you to become one of us. It is very special.'

Everyone remained perfectly still as they waited for Theresa to hand over the key. It seemed to take forever, until finally Theresa spoke.

'Jack, on behalf of the folk, I have decided to make you Keeper Of The Golden Key. Only you will have knowledge of the garden and us. Because of this key, you are the first human ever that will be able to interact with us, and, to a point, live amongst us. If you take this key, in return we expect your loyalty, your respect and, when we need it, your help. The key I am about to give you is only on loan,' explained Theresa. 'If you ever leave the garden it must be returned to me, as I am still the official holder of the key. Do you understand, Jack? And do you want to become one of us?' Theresa held out the key.

Jack stood there, still unable to speak. He turned to Theresa and stared into her hazel eyes. Her dark hair hung loosely around her shoulders, and her long flowing dress fluttered in the breeze. Daisy was right. She was very beautiful. He nodded and slowly held out his hand.

Theresa smiled, and gently placed the key in his hand. She felt a sense of relief. She was almost pleased that a human knew about them: pleased that someone else was there to help them.

Jack held onto the key tightly, as it was surprisingly heavy. A gold ribbon hung from the end of it, and in the middle were three perfectly formed small black circles. The key glowed a bright gold in the moonlight. He thought it was the most beautiful thing he had ever seen.

Looking down upon the folk, Jack knew he had to say something. They were all waiting silently for him to speak, their eager faces staring up. He felt wet, cold tears spilling down his face. He could hardly see because his glasses were getting so fogged up. Never before had he felt so special, never. It was something that would stay with him forever.

'Now for introductions,' said Theresa, aware of Jack's emotional state. Maybe meeting the folk would make him feel better. She looked down at her friends. 'Who would like to meet Jack first?'

Felicity put up her hand, and made her way onto the slate block. She looked up at Jack and smiled. She couldn't believe that she was finally meeting him. All those years she had so desperately wanted to speak to him, and now she felt nervous. She didn't know what to say. It was silly. 'Hello Jack,' said Felicity, finally. 'I'm so pleased to meet you.'

'So am I pleased to meet you,' said Jack, staring into her huge blue eyes, 'and I do love those bright red curls of yours. You look very pretty.'

Giggling with embarrassment Felicity made her way back to the group. No one had ever told her she was pretty before. Imagine, thought Felicity, someone thinks I'm pretty.

Jack smiled as one by one the other folk were introduced. Some were a little hesitant at meeting him, but all seemed to accept that he was now part of the garden.

All that is, except Reggie. He refused to shake Jack's hand or talk to the boy. Looking up at Theresa, he made his excuses for having to leave early.

'I'm afraid I need to get back to Herbert,' he said,

gruffly. 'I'm sure he'll be wondering where I am.' With that he stood up, said goodnight, and left.

Jack felt awful. Now he had upset the folk. It wasn't a very good start.

'Don't worry about Reggie,' piped up Daisy. 'He'll come round, he always does.' Her eyes had been on Jack's box the whole time, and she just couldn't hold back any longer. She knew he was going to bring food, but what sort. 'Have you something nice in that box, Jack? Is it something nice for us?'

'Where are your manners, pet?' said Annie. 'Let the boy tell us in his own good time.' Annie hated bad manners, and was always pulling up Daisy for being too pushy. The little mouse needed constant scolding. It was hard work sometimes, thought Annie, a lot of hard work.

Jack smiled at Annie. He could tell he was going to like her, but he did feel a little awkward around the others, even Daisy. He just hoped this food thing worked.

'I thought that as this was a special occasion,' said Jack, shyly, 'we could celebrate with some food, so I have brought some nice things for you all to eat. I hope you like them.'

'Show us, Jack,' squawked Maggie. 'Let us have a look.'

Annie held her tongue. The manners of the garden folk tonight were appalling. She was quite embarrassed. Whatever would the boy think of them?

Jack slowly opened the box, making sure not to crush anything. Suddenly he was surrounded by eager little faces peering excitedly into it.

Felicity and Daisy squealed with delight as they

looked at the cakes, biscuits and chocolate piled to the top of a large tin. They had never seen such delicious looking food, and wondered what it would taste like. Daisy knew Jack was going to bring food but she never dreamt it was going to be like this!

All pairs of eyes lit up in the moonlight, as each of the folk was able to choose something to eat. Jack gave everyone a plastic cup and straw and explained as best he could how to drink lemonade. Even Theresa chuckled as the bubbles tickled her nose. It was a wonderful moment and one that Jack would never forget for the rest of his life.

'These chocolate cakes are so yummy,' cried Felicity. 'I can't stop eating them.'

'You can say that again, old girl,' said Ben, as he pushed another cake down his throat.

Jack watched fascinated, until finally all the food was eaten.

'We feel sick,' wailed Daisy and Felicity. 'Why did we eat so much?'

'Because you are both greedy,' said Annie, grabbing their hands. 'Now, thank Jack for the food, and let's go home. It's been a long night, and the moon will be disappearing behind the clouds soon.'

'I think I'll stay a bit longer,' said Daisy, releasing Annie's hand. 'But I won't be long, I promise.'

Groaning a little, Ben, Maggie and Katie also decided to go. After thanking Jack they slowly got up, and started the long walk home.

'I'm so full,' complained Maggie. 'There is no way I can fly home.' The last thing Jack heard was Maggie asking Katie why Jack had to bring such rich food, and didn't he know what delicate stomachs birds had.

Daisy giggled as she watched them disappear into the night. She glanced at Jack's worried face. 'Don't worry about Maggie, she's always moaning. You will get used to her; she's just a bit different.' Daisy took Jack's hand and squeezed it. 'I'm glad I spoke to you Jack. I'm glad you are one of us. Welcome to our garden. Welcome to your new home.' With that she picked up her skirt, pushed down her bonnet, and silently made her way through the bushes.

Suddenly they were gone and Jack was left on his own. All was quiet, not a sound was to be heard, and he wondered if any of this had happened at all.

10

Was It Just A Dream?

The next morning, Jack was almost convinced his night adventure had all been a dream. It was just so amazing. Had he really been at a party with garden ornaments and been named Keeper Of The Golden Key? It was just so fantastic, and what about Reggie the gnome? Boy, was he an angry one. Jack couldn't help chuckling as he remembered the day he bought him, and the reason he did.

It had been a Saturday afternoon in the middle of winter. His friend Sam had come over, but they were both bored. His mother suggested they went to the school fete with her; that it was better to do something than lie around moaning. So, after much debate, they went, and were so glad they did.

There were colourful stalls everywhere. Sam spotted the food stall in the first five minutes, and decided to sample the sausages, hot dogs and hot chips. He told Jack that he was 'blissfully happy in the knowledge that his mother was nowhere in sight.'

Bored with eating, Jack went searching for something else. There, two stalls down was a huge sign. It read in large print 'Garden Ornaments For Sale,' and it was here among the stone dogs, snails and pigs that he found a very colourful and serious looking gnome.

The gnome wore a red hat and bright blue trousers. He had a little green spade tucked into the pocket, but best of all, thought Jack, was the long white beard. It was amazing. He had to have him, and from that exact moment the gnome with the red hat and blue trousers became known as Reggie, after his uncle Reginald.

That seemed such a long time ago, thought Jack, as he sat on the edge of his bed. Boy, if he knew how rude Reggie was he never would have bought him, and now here he was; part of their amazing world. It was mind blowing.

Jack suddenly remembered the key. Where did he put the key? He slid his hand under the pillow, but there was nothing. He found his trousers dumped in the corner of his room and searched in the pockets; they were empty. He even looked under his bed. Jack began to feel flustered. Theresa had told him never to lose the key. She had told him to always keep it in a safe place, and he had lost it already.

He heard his mother calling him to get ready, but he didn't want to know. He wanted to find the key. A terrible thought struck him. What if this really had been a dream? What if the folk didn't exist? And what if there had never been a golden key? He felt sick as he made his way downstairs. It all had to be real: it just had to be.

'Finally', said Mary, placing a huge bowl of cornflakes in front of him. 'I've been calling you for ages.' She looked at her son. 'Please make an effort today, Jack. You have a new teacher who is very nice. Just try to make an effort.'

'I don't feel hungry,' mumbled Jack, pushing away his bowl, 'and I don't want to go to school. I'm not properly well yet, and I don't want to meet the new teacher. I want to stay home.'

Mary gave an exasperated sigh. 'You are going to school, Jack. You are going to meet your new teacher, and you are going to lose this attitude. We love you Jack, but sometimes you make it harder for yourself. Now, the sooner you eat your breakfast and get ready for school, the sooner you can play out in the garden with the dogs. So let's get cracking.'

At last breakfast was over. All his mother could talk about was school and the new teacher, and all he could think about was last night and the golden key. Jack knew he had to go out to the garden some time. The dogs had already raced through the pet door and were waiting outside for a play, but he felt funny about facing the ornaments. If only he had the key. He would feel different if he had that. He would know then if it was real. Now he just felt sad: lonely and sad.

He cautiously stepped down into the garden. Everything looked the same. Ben the dog was under the urn, and Daisy and Felicity were under the seat. He spotted Annie near the lavender bush. It all looked so normal. It was hard to imagine that last night did happen. I mean if you really thought about it, how could it possibly be true?

Sighing, Jack threw one tennis ball for Scarlet, and another for Maxine. He walked towards the big yellow daisy bush, thinking about his situation. He had to be realistic. The whole thing had just been a dream, a fantastic, weird dream. Nothing had changed, and now he had to face school, knowing nothing had changed. It was horrible.

He bent down by the bush to pick up Maxine's ball

and give it one last throw, when from the corner of his eye he spotted something glistening in the early morning sunlight. It lay on the secret path just beyond the bush. He walked towards it. The palms of his hands were cold and sweaty. He had used the secret path to get home last night. What if, thought Jack. What if it's the key? Jack knelt down, removing some of the leaves that had blown across the path. He couldn't believe it. There it was; shining so brightly it nearly blinded him. There, right in front of him was the golden key.

Jack took a deep breath, and stared down at it. He felt nervous as he picked it up and held it tightly to his chest. His hand was shaking as he touched the gold ribbon with his fingers. He traced around the three circles on the middle of the key and wondered what they meant. He must ask next time he was in the garden. The garden, thought Jack: no longer was it just an ordinary garden. It had all changed last night. Gazing at the key, he knew that from this day on his life would never be the same. He was being led into a new world and the key would be with him forever, allowing him into this magical place.

It hadn't been a dream after all; it was real. He had solved the mystery. The garden folk were real, the key was real, and now he was the keeper of a secret that no other person in the whole world would ever know about, and, thought Jack, clasping the key tightly, he was part of it. He was really part of it.

It was a strange feeling. Jack now had people depending on him and needing him. All of a sudden he was the person they would begin to trust and rely on. Jack smiled. All those times when his world felt dark and hopeless, he wished more than anything that he could blink his eyes and be suddenly taken to another place: a place where he was the brainy one, and where everyone loved him. A place where there were no teachers or bullies. A place that was full of magic. He had wondered if such a place could ever exist, and now he knew it did.

Jack felt weird as he opened the back door. His world was about to change beyond his wildest dreams. He was in for the adventure of a lifetime. There was certainly no going back now, ever.

11

Life in the Garden

Life in the garden had almost returned to normal for the folk since the storm and the arrival of Jack in their lives. It would never be quite the same, but the boy had settled in very nicely and the folk couldn't imagine their lives without him. Jack had already become an important part of the garden and was always there to listen to any worries or problems they might have. One such problem had been what the folk were to do on very hot days. It was stifling and almost unbearable just standing there in the heat, particularly if one's home didn't have much shade.

'It gets so hot,' wailed Daisy and Felicity, together. 'We hate it, Jack, we really hate it!'

'I don't think it's too good for me either, pet,' said Annie, softly. 'I don't think this stinking hot weather is any good for my paintwork.'

Jack smiled as he reached down and gently peeled a bit of flaky paint off the top of her head. This time Annie didn't complain. 'I tend to agree with you, Annie, and I promise I will do something about it.'

Jack was true to his word, and from that day every time the temperature was over twenty eight degrees he would put the smaller folk under the pergola. Each ornament was placed next to a cool moist fern and he could almost see the relief on their small faces. On weekdays he would do this before he went to school, always taking time to say a quick goodbye.

'What did I tell you,' said Reggie, smugly. 'I told you the boy would be good for the garden. I told you, didn't I?' He said this every time they were shifted, causing the rest of the group to inwardly groan. Reggie must have an awfully short memory, thought Felicity. It was Reggie who was so mean to Jack. She had to agree though; life was wonderful with Jack in it, and she couldn't imagine anything ever going wrong again. Their lives were sheer bliss.

For Jack, meeting the folk had been the best thing that could ever have happened. He felt that his life was slowly getting better and, thanks to their encouragement, he was game to try new things. School had even improved. Jack really liked Miss Newman. She was strict, but was also fun. She even made things like maths enjoyable.

One thing Miss Newman did in maths was put the students into groups of four. Jack was horrified when he was put into the same group as Brian Madison. He couldn't believe it. They were even put into a special maths class together. Every Thursday morning they would trudge down to the Special Education Unit with three other kids from their class.

Last Thursday morning Brian even apologised to Jack for his bad behaviour towards him. Well, he sort of apologised, thought Jack. He was on his way to his special maths class, when he heard heavy footsteps running behind him, and someone calling his name.

'Crane,' yelled the voice. 'Wait up Crane, I need to talk.' Huffing and puffing, Brian was suddenly alongside him. 'Crane, I just want you to know that I won't be hassling you anymore, and I'm real sorry that I did. There's a little nerd in year two who will be perfect for that role.' With that Brian had run on ahead, and said he would save him a seat.

It's weird, thought Jack, as he watched him disappear into the building. It was weird how they had formed this strange friendship after everything that had happened. Apart from his friendship with the ornaments, this was even weirder. Jack did wonder though who the poor little nerd in year two was. He would have to keep a look out, and explain to Brian how wrong it was to bully someone. He felt sorry for any kid who was in Brian Madison's line of fire.

The one thing Jack really wanted to prove to himself was that he could play a sport, but he still had terrible memories of his attempts at playing basketball and cricket, and the nasty comments of his fellow players every time he missed a basket or dropped a catch.

It wasn't until he confided in Theresa one night that he began to think differently. Theresa had been very honest, and didn't try to spare his feelings.

'You have to start taking risks, Jack. It's easy to stand back and say, "I can't do it". How do you know you can't until you try? It's like your schoolwork. Don't keep complaining that you don't understand all the time. You just have to work harder. You have to learn to concentrate. Sport is the same as schoolwork; once you understand what to do, it won't seem so hard. Don't always be the victim Jack. Start proving not only to yourself, but also to everyone else that you can do it. I know you can, so you should too.'

Jack was stunned. No one had ever spoken to him

like that. Not even his parents, but Theresa was right. He was a wimp. Let's face it, thought Jack. If I can become friends with Brian Madison, then surely I can play a sport, but what?

For a whole week he thought about what sport to play, finally deciding to give soccer a go. His father was over the moon and helped Jack sign up with the school's junior soccer team. They would be playing in summer this year to get in some training for the proper winter season. The winning team even got a special award, just like the real season. Sam had even been persuaded to join. His mother was convinced a sport like soccer would help with his weight. Poor Sam, thought Jack. Everything he did revolved around his weight.

The more Jack thought about playing soccer the more nervous he became. Ben had offered to teach him some ball skills. The dog loved playing with the round ball left in the garden for Maxine and Scarlet. He would play with it for hours, using his two front paws and small head to manoeuvre it. He assured Jack that playing with a round ball was 'easy as pie, old chap: couldn't get anything easier'. Jack just hoped Ben was right, as the first practice session wasn't far away at all.

Most evenings, except when Jack had schoolwork to do, he would go out into the garden to play with the dogs and talk with his new friends. One thing he loved to do more than anything else was to help Herbert with his reading, and after that have a chat. Herbert was always so pleased to see him: like he was last night.

'Jack, my boy. How nice to see you. What might we be reading tonight? Is it still the one about the pig and the spider? I like that story. Although one does wonder,' said Herbert, seriously, 'how believable it is that a pig and spider can talk. Still, it is only a story. Carry on my boy; we're nearly up to the exciting part.' Jack couldn't help chuckling to himself as he picked up the book. Obviously Herbert didn't think talking mice, wombats and birds were a problem! Night after night Jack would sit there reading the story, while Herbert closed his eyes and listened. Occasionally Herbert was asked to read a word, but mainly he just listened. Daisy was right, thought Jack, looking down at the wombat. He was a beautiful little creature. It didn't matter that he was a bit slow: it didn't matter a bit.

'How long have you been in the garden, Herbert?' said Jack, taking a break from reading.'

Herbert sighed. He didn't like chatting about himself much but he cared a lot about the boy, so it might be good to finally have a long chat with someone who cared about him.

'Well,' he said, slowly, 'I was the only one in the garden for many years and it was very lonely. I think that's why I don't mind keeping to myself because I am used to being alone. When your parents moved in things got much better. As a matter of fact,' said Herbert, smiling. 'A little girl used to play in the garden. She would come and talk to me. She couldn't say my name properly and would call me "Erbert." She was a pretty little thing,' said the wombat, thoughtfully. 'Had a mass of gold curls, and the biggest blue eyes I have ever seen.'

'A little girl,' said Jack, puzzled. 'Was she one of you?'

'No,' said the wombat, sadly. 'I don't know who she belonged to, but one day she just stopped coming.

I missed that little girl for a long time. So I was rather pleased when Annie was brought into the garden, followed by Theresa a few years later.'

'I remember Dad telling me about that,' said Jack. 'Apparently it was very funny. Theresa was so heavy, or at least her pedestal was, that it took three men to carry her up to the top of the garden. Dad said the men were really cross, because she took so long to get into place.' Jack stopped talking. He had just remembered what Daisy said about butting in. He must stop doing it. It was very rude.

'It wasn't funny for poor Theresa,' continued Herbert, oblivious to Jack's rudeness. 'She was very embarrassed. Poor girl, it took her a long time to recover from that experience. Annie spent the next five nights with Theresa calming her down. It was a very unfortunate experience for her.

Of course she's older now,' said Herbert, scratching his chin. 'She wouldn't worry about that now.'

Jack often wondered how the ornaments aged. I mean, how old was Theresa then? He'd just hate them to get really old. It would be awful. He wondered how old Herbert was, and what his life was really like.

'What about you, Herbert, are you happy that there are more people in the garden to talk to?'

Everything was quiet as Herbert contemplated this question. Finally he cleared his throat and spoke. 'Happy. What exactly is happy?'

'It's when you feel good inside,' prompted Jack. 'It's when everything feels right.'

'Oh!' said Herbert, 'that sort of happy. Well, I'm happy right now, because I love you reading to me and I love having a chat. I'm happy when Daisy and Felicity come to visit, and I'm happy at meal times.' Herbert hesitated. 'But I'm not happy when people laugh at me, and poke fun at me for being slow. I'm not happy when they tell me I'm stupid. I'm not happy at all. So when that happens, I would rather be by myself.'

'That's not fair,' said Jack, looking into the wombat's kind face. 'How could anyone be mean to you? I have a rough idea who it could be, but I want you to tell me. Who's being mean to you? Tell me, Herbert.'

'Well,' said Herbert, unsure about telling on his friends. 'Well, Maggie and Reggie mainly. Sometimes Annie gets impatient with me, but she's never mean.'

'Maggie and Reggie are bullying you Herbert. They have no right to treat you like that! I only thought this sort of thing happened in my human world, not your world.'

'What does "bullying" mean?' asked Herbert. 'You sound cross Jack. Is it something bad?'

'It means,' said Jack, raising his voice, 'that people are horrible to you if you are different or not good at some things, like maths, spelling and sport. It means,' he continued angrily, 'that they think they have some sort of power over you. That's what it means!'

'Oh!' exclaimed Herbert. 'Were you ever bullied Jack?'

'Yes, I was,' said Jack, calming down. 'It was the worst two years of my life, but now it's all sorted. I'm even friends with the bully. Weird, isn't it. Anyway,' said Jack, 'I thought you and Reggie were friends. He lives with you.'

'Oh, he's fine when it's just us. He's very caring really. But when he's with the others, particularly Maggie, he's different. He's very hurtful.'

'That's called peer pressure,' said Jack. Reggie is just trying to big note himself, at your expense. Anyway, I'm going to say something, Herbert. They should not be allowed to get away with it.' He gently patted the wombat's furry head, and turned to the next page of the book. 'Now let's finish this chapter. I have to get back to my maths homework, and it's hard.'

'Really,' said Herbert. 'Believe it or not, I'm rather good at maths. Anytime you need some help let me know, particularly as you have been so kind to me.'

'Did I tell you I have decided to join a soccer team?' said Jack, changing the subject. He was a little unsure about Herbert's maths skills and didn't want to hurt his feelings by refusing his help. 'Ben has promised to teach me some ball skills and my dad is going to take me out for practice sessions. I'm still a bit worried though, but Theresa said I had to try.'

'So you should, my boy. So you should. You won't know until you try, but just remember, if you need any help with maths, you know where to find me. Now, if you don't mind, my boy,' said Herbert, yawning loudly. 'If you don't mind, I need to get my sleep. Concentrating on that book has quite exhausted me.' And with that, the wombat's eyes closed as he fell into a deep noisy slumber.

Jack bent down and kissed the top of his furry head. He loved Herbert, and he hated to see him so miserable. He would talk to Maggie and Reggie, and he would also tell Theresa. She could make the folk more aware of Herbert's feelings.

Picking up the readers, Jack headed into the garden proper, hoping to catch up with one of the others before it became dark. There was usually someone around to have a chat with.

As it turned out he found everyone else at the top of the garden having a meeting with Theresa. They all looked very solemn, and Jack was hesitant to say anything. He still felt a little uncomfortable when he interrupted their meetings, but they didn't seem to mind.

'Here's the boy,' said Reggie, bustling over to Jack and shaking his hand. It had taken a while, but Reggie was a sensible gnome, and had eventually forgiven Jack for 'knowing the secret'. He was particularly grateful when Jack started to help Herbert. Reggie was very fond of Herbert, even though he sometimes teased him unmercifully; it was always only meant to be in fun.

'We have a bit of a problem, boy,' continued Reggie. 'We are getting all sorts of oddballs entering our garden, and it's putting us folk on edge, particularly the ladies. Isn't that so ladies?' Daisy, Felicity and Annie all nodded in agreement.

Jack knew that it wasn't often that they all agreed with Reggie, so this had to be something important. 'What sort of oddballs?' inquired Jack. 'Is it anything I should know about?'

'All sorts,' continued Reggie; 'but the oddball that is causing us the most concern at present is the black wild cat that is roaming the gardens. He's a nasty piece of work, and even the other cats are afraid of him. Trouble is, he likes birds and mice, doesn't he, and so you can imagine how Maggie, Katie and Daisy feel. Scared to move. It's not good enough. Can't roam in your own garden. Just not good enough!'

Jack nodded; he could certainly see the dilemma, but he couldn't be with the folk all night. It was tricky.

'I do try to help, old chap,' piped up Ben, 'but the

blasted animal doesn't seem to take my role as a dog seriously. Keeps showing me its teeth and scratching the tree with its long claws. No sign of fear. Most annoying, old boy, and not too good for the old self esteem either.'

'It's scary,' squealed Daisy. 'I don't want to get eaten, Jack. It's so scary. What should we do?'

This was a problem Jack wasn't sure how to solve. 'Maybe I could send Maxine and Scarlet out on patrol,' he offered. 'They would soon scare the cat off.'

'No offence, old boy,' interrupted Ben, 'but those two animals give us dogs a bad name. They would wake the dead with their constant barking. No, old boy, bringing those two out in the garden would drive us all mad. I'm sorry, but it had to be said.'

'I'd rather get eaten by the cat,' quipped Maggie. Everyone giggled, but Jack felt quite hurt. He didn't realise his beloved dogs were such an annoyance.

Annie sensed his hurt and tried to smooth things over. 'They are dear little souls, Jack, with kind hearts. They're just a bit noisy, pet, that's all. Just a bit noisy.'

Jack looked around at the folk. 'Speaking of Maxine and Scarlet, do any of you folk know where the pet door is?'

They all shook their heads. 'Sorry, old boy,' said Ben, 'we wouldn't have a clue.'

Jack sighed. How was he going to show them without his parents noticing? It was all a bit tricky. He looked down at their worried faces. There was nothing for it, he would just have to risk them getting found out. It was too important. That was what having the golden key meant. It meant that he was now responsible for keeping them safe. The key allowed him into their world, and in return he had to be there for them. He understood that part of the deal, but it worried him. What if something did happen, and he wasn't there to protect them? It was a horrible thought.

'I'll take Daisy, Felicity and Reggie with me and show them where it is. They will need some practice pushing the door, and getting inside the house, so we might be a little while. The pet door can be used in an emergency if you need to get away from the cat or anything else that frightens you. We promise to be back as soon as possible and then Felicity will explain to you all how it works. Okay, Felicity?'

The little girl nodded but was worried that she had so much responsibility. She must listen very carefully.

After saying their goodbyes, Jack, Daisy, Felicity and Reggie carefully made their way through the bushes so they would not be heard or seen. Jack had thought about using the secret path, but it was not as safe, and could be dangerous for the folk. This way was slow going, but finally the house loomed in front of them.

It took a little while for the folk to scramble onto the verandah with their short legs, but at last, huffing and puffing, they managed to clamber up the steep edges of the slate bricks. Jack took them over to a large plastic oval door which sat in a huge glass window.

'Wow,' said Daisy and Felicity together, 'is this the pet door?'

'How on earth are we going to get through?' said Reggie, staring. 'It's so big!'

'I'll show you,' said Jack, pushing the door inwards, then allowing it to swing back into place. 'Now, Reggie, you try and step inside; it won't hurt you. This is how the dogs come in and go out, so you should be able to manage.'

Reggie pushed against the door. It didn't move. He tried again. This time it worked and before he knew what had happened, he had tumbled through to the other side, landing with a soft thud on the carpet.

'Are you all right, Reggie?' yelled Felicity through the gap. She must remember to tell the folk not to push too hard.

Reggie yelled back that he was all right but felt a little overwhelmed at what had happened. He was now in the biggest room he had ever seen, surrounded by large pieces of furniture that absolutely dwarfed him. Why was it that everything connected with humans was so big? Reggie could feel himself shaking; he certainly would be glad when the others arrived. This place felt a little spooky. He didn't have to wait long, as soon both Daisy and Felicity fell onto the carpet laughing and giggling.

'Isn't this fun?' squealed Daisy. 'Isn't this fun, Felicity?' It was the most excitement the little mouse had had for ages, and she intended to make the most of it. 'Can we go again, Jack, can we? It's so much fun.'

Jack spoke from the other side. 'No, Daisy. It's too risky. Once is enough. I'm worried my parents will walk through.' Daisy was being particularly silly and he wanted to get them out before anything happened. Jack explained how to lock the little door from the inside so the cat couldn't get in. 'Now everyone, come back through. I want you all outside, and ready for home.'

'Can't we explore?' pleaded Daisy. 'I'd love to show

Felicity and Reggie the kitchen. Can't we go for a little wander? We've only just got inside and there is so much to see. Please Jack, please...'

Reggie had other ideas. He couldn't wait to get home, and one whining mouse wasn't going to stop that happening. 'No we can't, young Daisy. You heard the boy, now get moving and hold the confounded door open! This is all getting a bit tiresome.'

'Well, I think you are all boring, and I think it's very unfair that I can't take Felicity a little way into the kitchen. I hate you sometimes, Reggie,' said the mouse, stamping her foot. 'Really hate you.'

'Come on, Daisy,' said Felicity, grabbing her hand. 'You don't really hate Reggie. You know Theresa never likes us to use that word. I'm sure Jack will let you show me the kitchen another time.'

Glaring at Reggie, Daisy reluctantly held the door open. However, she knew she would be back. The big house fascinated her and there was so much more to explore. Yes, she would definitely return, and soon.

Back in the garden, a relieved Jack headed towards the cubby house and the rest of the folk. He felt the need to stress again that the pet door should only ever be used in emergencies, but he was especially worried that Daisy wouldn't take this rule seriously. She had been almost defiant inside the house, and sadly, Jack didn't trust her. He didn't trust her at all.

12

Jack's Trust is Betrayed

It had been a week since Daisy and her two friends were shown the pet door, and the garden had been remarkably quiet, with no sign of the dreaded cat. Most of the folk were just relieved they had somewhere to go if they needed to. Daisy, however, felt restless and was itching to get back into the house, so she decided to discuss the idea with Felicity and Annie.

'Not a good idea, pet,' said Annie. 'The boy trusts us and assumes that we would only use the door in an emergency.' Felicity nodded in agreement.

'I know,' said Daisy, 'but it would be such an adventure, and I could show you where all the cakes and biscuits are kept. Won't you change your minds?'

The thought of having some more of those delicious cakes did sound tempting to Felicity, but she knew that going back to the house without Jack was not a good idea. She would have to have a good think about it, and maybe ask Ben and Reggie what they thought about Daisy's idea.

So, that night, without the other garden folk knowing, Daisy, Felicity, Ben and Reggie had a meeting to discuss entering the house. They all agreed that it was just for a quick look around, and could be a practice run in case the cat came back. They would do it at the next full moon.

They told Annie of their decision and promised her faithfully that they would be gone, at the most, thirty minutes. Annie was unconvinced, but what could she do? Daisy always ended up getting her own way, so why waste her breath arguing with her. Only time would tell, thought Annie, if their decision to return to the big house was the right one, and there was nothing a fat old mushroom could do except pray they stayed safe.

Two nights later, the moon sat like an enormous yellow ball in the night sky, its soft glow spreading beams of light over the whole garden. Daisy was so excited she could hardly sit still. Her whiskers were quivering with anticipation, and it was all she could do to keep her long tail under control. 'I can't wait,' squealed the little mouse. 'I just can't wait.' She flung her head right back to get a good look at the moon. It was perfect.

After saying goodbye to Annie, she picked up her skirt, tucked in her tail and set off to round up a reluctant Ben and Reggie.

'I don't know about this, old girl,' said Ben, nervously. Reggie tells me it's a bit scary, and I feel bad doing it without Jack, and worst of all, what if we get caught?'

Daisy sighed. 'Oh, Ben. Where is your sense of adventure? Of course we won't get caught.' She looked at Ben's worried face. 'Come on, it will be fun. Just you wait and see. Now let's go and collect Felicity and Reggie and get going.'

Annie stood silently as her friends slowly made their way through the bushes, the light from the moon almost touching their small bodies. Daisy was leading the group, and Annie could hear her telling them to 'hurry up', as they disappeared into the bushes. Annie sighed. She had a terrible feeling something bad was going to happen. It always did when Daisy was involved, but she couldn't do anything. All she could do was wait.

Daisy and Felicity had nearly made it to the verandah, with Ben and Reggie bringing up the rear. 'Come on, you two,' said Daisy, impatiently. 'Get a move on. Felicity and I will need your help soon to get up these bricks. We haven't got time to waste. Remember we promised Annie we would be back in thirty minutes.'

'Don't tell me to hurry up, young lady,' said Reggie, crossly. Daisy had been doing nothing but bossing him since they left home. 'You mind your manners; otherwise you will get no help from us. Do you understand? No help!'

Felicity hated it when any of them got cross with one another. 'Come on, Reggie.' she said. 'We are very grateful to you and Ben for coming with us. Daisy didn't mean to sound bossy. Let's all help each other and get in and out of this house as quickly as we can.'

Swallowing his pride, Reggie agreed, but was still a little annoyed at Daisy's behaviour. They managed to get onto the verandah more easily this time, especially Ben, who almost skipped up. It didn't seem as tiring, either, and before they knew it they were all facing the oval door. The big room on the other side was glowing in the moonlight, making it look almost welcoming. Ben could not believe the size of it, and was dying to get inside.

'Well, here goes,' murmured Daisy, and pushed her body against the door. In an instant she was on the other side; she even landed on her feet. 'It's easy,' she whispered back through the door, 'and so much fun.'

Felicity was the next one through, followed by Ben and Reggie. It was a new experience for Ben, and he was amazed at how simple it was, managing to land on all fours.

'That was so much fun, old girl,' said Ben. 'I can see why you enjoyed it the first time. 'I say, this room is enormous.'

'I know,' said Daisy, excitedly. 'We are in the big family room. Isn't it fantastic? Now follow me and I'll show you the kitchen I was in when my bonnet was getting fixed. It's very special to me, and luckily we can see most of it in the moonlight.'

They followed Daisy into the kitchen, aware that they were not to make a sound. Felicity could hardly believe her eyes. The room was beautiful. 'Wow,' was the only word she could utter. 'Wow!' All around her were large windows, showing off their garden in the moonlight. The room was full of cupboards, and lovely furniture. She could even see the fireplace and large kitchen table that Daisy had told her about. Everywhere she looked was something interesting. On top of the cupboards stood large blue canisters with labels showing they had flour, sugar, tea and coffee in them. It was fascinating.

'Where are the biscuits and cakes?' whispered Felicity. 'I don't want to eat any; I just want to see what the tin looks like. Can you see the tin?'

Daisy's beady little eyes had been looking for it ever since they had arrived in the kitchen. 'There it is,' she squealed. 'Up on the bench. I can see a tin marked "Cakes".'

'Shh!' muttered Reggie. 'Someone might hear us. Can't you refrain from squealing so loudly? My ears are hurting. Anyway, when are we going to head back?'

'Soon, but I just want to look in this cake tin. We might find something yummy.'

'Are you mad?' blustered Reggie. 'This wasn't the deal. We were going to have a practice and then go. What is wrong with you girl? This is dangerous: absolute madness!'

'Oh hush.' Daisy was starting to get annoyed with Reggie; he was being so boring. 'If I knew you were going to whine all the time, Reggie, I wouldn't have invited you. Now, if I can stand on Ben's back I know I can reach the tin. Come on Felicity; help me onto Ben's back.'

It was a struggle, but finally Daisy was able to grab the tin and pass it to Felicity. The tin was carefully placed on the floor and the lid slowly removed. There, like precious jewels, sat a dozen freshly iced chocolate cakes just waiting to be eaten.

'Oh my goodness,' cried Felicity, her eyes as big as saucers. 'Just look at these beautiful cakes. Do you think we could have some?'

Ben and Reggie looked at her warily, still not happy about the situation. 'I don't know, old girl,' said Ben, with some hesitation. 'I think we should just go home.'

'I agree,' said Reggie. 'This is not what we came inside to do. We didn't come here to steal food. You told us we were having a practice.'

'You two are hopeless,' retorted Daisy. 'One little cake each won't hurt. There are heaps of them. Come on Ben; Jack won't be cross.' Reluctantly, Ben and Reggie each took a cake from Daisy's hand, and placed them into their mouths. They had to admit they were delicious.

'Let's have another one,' whispered Daisy, 'and then I promise I'll put the tin back.'

Five minutes later, the four of them sat around the tin surrounded by empty paper cups. Felicity was rubbing her tummy and wiping the chocolate icing off her apron. 'I feel a bit sick. Maybe we shouldn't have had so many cakes.' She looked into the tin. 'Daisy, there are only two cakes left. I can't believe it. We have eaten nearly all the cakes! Come on, we must get the lid on and put the tin back. I feel so guilty.'

Climbing onto Ben's back once more, Daisy pushed the tin onto the bench, but, in doing so, her long tail knocked over a small bowl filled with eggs. It came crashing to the ground, covering the floor in yellow egg yolks and crunchy egg shells, and scattering fragments of china under the table and next to the refrigerator. Even the cupboard doors were splashed with thick yellow liquid. The whole thing was a disaster. Daisy was mortified.

'What have you done? You stupid girl,' bellowed Reggie. 'Can't you keep that tail of yours under control? Look at the mess, and I bet you've woken the household.'

Daisy put her hand over her mouth in horror. She had totally forgotten about the people living in the house. Please, please, please, thought the mouse. Please, don't let anyone wake up, especially Jack.

'I think we are in luck,' whispered Felicity after a minute had passed. She strained her ears but not a sound could be heard except the ticking of the grandfather clock. 'Let's get going before anything else happens.'

Daisy hesitated. 'I wonder if I could do just one more thing and then, I give you my word, we will go. I thought I'd take Annie some of those nice chocolate biscuits, because I know she loves them. I know where they are kept. Please help me, and then we'll leave straight away.'

'I'm not sure, old girl. This is getting a bit dangerous,' said Ben. 'We were lucky not to be heard when that bowl fell. We might not be so lucky next time. Also I'm not sure that taking things is such a good idea. Isn't that stealing?'

Daisy thought about it then shook her head. 'I'd class it more like borrowing, and that's never as bad as stealing. Now let's get moving.'

'Well, you can count me out!' said Reggie, crossly. 'It's madness. The girl's mad, and for your information,' he said, glaring at the mouse, 'what you're doing is stealing. How can you give something back that is in your stomach? Anyway, I'm going home. I've had enough of this nonsense.' And with that, he headed towards the pet door, stomping through broken shells and egg yolk, unaware of the trail of yellow footprints he was leaving on the carpet. As gnomes went, Reggie was not the most patient of fellows, but he did have good morals. As far as he was concerned, stealing was out of the question, and the others could stew in their own juices if they got caught. It was no longer his problem.

Ben heard the pet door bang as Reggie stormed off. He half wished he had gone too, but felt a certain loyalty towards the girls.

'Come on, Ben,' whispered Felicity. 'Let's not worry about Reggie. I need your help to reach the cupboard. I'm taller than Daisy, and I think I can just make it.' She climbed onto the dog's back, grasped the knob and opened the door.

'She's got it,' cried Daisy. The little mouse could hardly contain herself. 'Can you see the biscuits? Can you, Felicity?'

'Yes, I can, I'm nearly there.' Standing on tiptoe, Felicity reached out. They were so close; she only had to move a can of peas and she had them. Stretching as tall as she could and pushing her feet harder into Ben's back, she clasped the biscuits tightly in her hand. Beneath her, the little dog groaned, then, unable to take the strain any longer, shifted position. With a scream Felicity slipped, losing her balance. She clutched the knob with all her strength, almost pulling it from the cupboard door. Above her, the blue canisters slid one by one off the top of the cupboard and fell to the floor, breaking into large pieces and scattering tea, coffee, flour and sugar as they landed amongst the egg yolk and broken china. Felicity looked down in disbelief. The whole kitchen was swimming in a horrible glutinous mess.

Daisy cried out as Ben grabbed Felicity. The three of them sprinted towards the pet door. As they tumbled through to the other side, they saw lights come on in the house and heard mumbled voices and then a loud scream. Mary's voice rang out as they scrambled down the bricks.

'Alan! The kitchen; it's a mess. There is stuff everywhere. I think we've been robbed. Come quickly!' That was the last thing the threesome heard as they ran back through the bushes. Daisy and Felicity were shaking by the time they got home; it had been an absolutely horrible experience.

'Never again,' said Felicity. 'Never again. Don't you ever ask me to do something like that again. Never.' Ben was too upset to even say goodnight. Felicity hoped that he would be all right tomorrow, and they could have a good talk about it, but for now she just wanted her sleep. She had never felt so emotionally and physically drained in her whole life. She would never listen to any of Daisy's crazy schemes again.

The little mouse watched her friend disappear to the other side of the wrought iron seat. Daisy knew Felicity was upset with her, but it wasn't all her fault. Felicity didn't have to go with them, and it was her fault that the canisters fell off the cupboard, not Daisy's. They made such a terrible noise: really terrible. No wonder everyone woke up.

Anyway, thought Daisy, it wasn't a total disaster. She searched deep into her pockets. Good! They were still there. Despite the panic, she had still managed to pick up the chocolate biscuits, and she was sure that when everything had settled down, Annie would be very grateful to her for getting them. She sighed and looked over at the mushroom sleeping peacefully. She knew Annie would be furious at first, but Daisy couldn't worry about that now, she would worry about that in the morning. All she wanted to do now was to try and forget tonight ever happened.

The tired mouse could feel her eyes closing as the muffled sounds of the garden engulfed her. She could just hear the clock ringing through the night. It chimed four bells, and then all was quiet.

It was a cool grey day for late summer; one of those days that made you feel depressed. Not unlike how Jack was feeling now.

He kept going over and over in his head the unbelievable happenings of the night before, and the look on his poor mother's face when she was confronted with the state of the kitchen. It had been about three o'clock in the morning when they were woken by a loud crash; it almost sounded like a bomb had gone off. Jack's first thoughts had been 'robbers', and this left him with a cold sick feeling. He knew people got robbed, but he never imagined it would happen to them. He had waited to hear his parents: unsure about what to do next. After what seemed forever, he saw the light in the passage go on and heard whispering. The stairs creaked as his parents made their way carefully down. Jack sat up in bed, torn between curiosity and the safety of his room. Then he heard his mother scream. He had no choice. He jumped out of bed and ran downstairs, the dogs racing excitedly in front of him. It wasn't until he got into the kitchen proper that he was able to see the utter destruction. There was mess from one end of the kitchen to the other; it was terrible, but the thing that upset him most was seeing his mother sitting on a kitchen chair sobbing. It took a lot to make her cry, but all this must have been overwhelming.

His father called out to him. 'Don't go any further, Jack, there's glass and china amongst all this mess. Keep the dogs away too. I'm about to ring the police. How about you go over and comfort your mother. She could do with a hug right now.'

Jack put his arm around her and looked in dismay at the kitchen. He couldn't help noticing the paw prints on the tiles and on some of the cupboards. He could see little footprints on the bench-top and on parts of the floor. Taking a closer look at the bench-top, he spotted a long red hair. He reached out and picked it up, then carefully put it into his pocket. Jack felt an overwhelming urge to throw-up. The only person he knew with long red hair was Felicity. He couldn't believe that she would be involved in something so stupid. It seemed impossible to believe that any of the folk would do this; he trusted them. He had stressed time and time again that they were only ever allowed in the family room, and even then, only in an emergency. What would make them disobey him?

He not only felt angry, but hurt that they had betrayed his trust in them. Jack looked around the room. Why would they come inside and create all this mess? It didn't make any sense. He held his mother more tightly and turned to face his father.

'How did this happen?' asked Jack, slowly. His father looked tired, and seemed reluctant to answer.

'I don't know. It's all a bit strange. The only things that I can see have been stolen are ten cakes, and the only prints are like animal footprints. So your guess is as good as mine. The prints do lead to the pet door so I'm wondering if some sort of creature got through and started looking for food. I guess we'll just have to wait and see what the police say. Now, you go off back to bed. We'll sort it all out in the morning.'

But in the morning Jack had his own sorting out to do. He felt Daisy was definitely involved. She had been determined to get back into the house, and had obviously brought along some willing helpers, one of them being Felicity. Jack sighed. He felt hurt that she had deliberately disobeyed him, and he would certainly be talking to her later on. He would talk to everyone.

By early evening the sky had become dark and threatening. It looked as if it could rain. Daisy felt miserable. It was her fault last night happened, but she just couldn't bring herself to tell Jack the truth. She would make out that she saw the cat. Jack couldn't get cross with them if they were only in the house to keep safe. She wasn't quite sure how she was going to explain the mess; that was going to be a bit more difficult.

Annie was horrified when she found out what they had done, and hadn't spoken to them since. She called them 'naughty little brats with bad manners', and would not speak to them until her anger had subsided. She was even more upset when she found out about the biscuits, and told Daisy to put them back immediately. Daisy could still hear the mushroom's voice ringing in her ears.

'Give them back to Jack straight away, my girl, and you tell him every naughty thing you and your so-called friends did last night, and don't bother talking to me until I'm ready.'

Daisy sighed. She didn't like Annie being cross with her, and she knew she was naughty, but did she really have to give back the biscuits?

Felicity was particularly upset; she had never seen Annie in such a state. 'She must be cross,' said Felicity, unhappily. 'She hasn't called us "pet," once.'

Neither of the girls was looking forward to facing Jack. Felicity shivered when she heard the back door slam, and Daisy cringed at the sound of loud footsteps stomping up the garden path. Jack sounded mad.

Everything went quiet when Jack finally stood on

the slate block next to Theresa. He wasn't smiling, and his face was pale. The folk had never seen him so serious; it wasn't like Jack at all. Not everyone knew exactly what had happened last night, but they had heard that something bad had gone on up at the big house. Maggie was dying to know what had happened. She loved a bit of gossip.

Katie and Herbert were also anxious to find out. All Herbert knew was that Reggie had got home very late last night, and was in a particularly bad mood. His feet were covered in something yellow, and he smelt odd. When Herbert kindly asked if he was all right he was promptly told to 'go to sleep'. It was all very strange.

Jack stood there silently, contemplating how to begin. He could feel light raindrops falling on his head and knew he would have to be brief before it started to rain properly. After a gentle nod from Theresa, he commenced.

'Last night someone or something broke into our home and made a terrible mess in the kitchen. It was so bad that it had my mother in tears and forced my dad to ring the police. They also stole things: ten chocolate cakes and my favourite chocolate biscuits.

The garden folk looked both shocked and bemused. Surely this wasn't true. Felicity looked across at Daisy. She couldn't believe that her friend still took the biscuits, after everything that had happened. She just couldn't believe it.

'Excuse me, Jack,' interrupted Theresa. 'Who or what are "police"?' Theresa knew a lot of things, but had never heard the word 'police.' She always wanted the correct meaning of a new word so that she knew what it meant next time.

'Police are people who wear special clothes called uniforms, and are trained to catch people who do bad things,' said Jack, watching Daisy out of the corner of his eye. 'The police believe,' continued Jack, 'that some sort of animal got in through the pet door because there were paw prints all through the mess, and we know the prints don't belong to Maxine or Scarlet. Anyway,' he said, looking down on the group, 'I know my dogs would never do anything like that. So what I want to know is, and I want the truth, did any of you come into the house last night? And, if so, was it one or more of you who made the mess? Remember, I want the truth, and I want it now.'

13

The Folk Seek Sanctuary

There was a deathly silence as the folk looked pleadingly up at Jack. The innocent ones couldn't believe one of their own would do such a thing, and the guilty folk had become mute. At last a barely audible voice spoke up through the stillness.

'I'm to blame, Jack.' said Daisy. 'I thought I heard the cat, so I suggested to Reggie, Ben and Felicity that we go to the house for safety reasons.' There was a murmur amongst the folk as she stepped forward, followed by Felicity, Ben and a reluctant Reggie.

'You never said there was a cat', interrupted Reggie. 'You never mentioned a cat. You told us we were going into the house for practice. That's what you told us.'

Daisy blushed. 'Well, actually there was a cat. I just didn't want to scare you all.'

'Thanks for telling us,' cried Maggie, glancing at Katie. 'Didn't we count? Weren't we important enough? I've always wanted to get eaten by a cat!'

Daisy turned to Maggie. 'Well, of course you are important, but you and Katie were too far away to warn.'

Maggie kept remonstrating. 'We weren't too far away to get eaten, were we?'

Annie shook her head in disbelief. Daisy was lying; there hadn't been a cat in the garden all week. This girl needed a serious talking to, and taught the difference between right and wrong.

Jack looked at Daisy. He wasn't angry any more, just sad that she had done this thing. 'I trusted you all, and even if there was a cat and you sought safety, why did you make so much mess?'

This time Felicity spoke up. 'It was my fault. I just wanted to see the cake tin, and look at the cakes. When we saw them we couldn't resist tasting them and then when we put the tin back a bowl of eggs fell on the floor. I'm so sorry. We didn't mean to do it; honestly Jack, we didn't.'

Jack frowned. 'What about the tea and the coffee, and the flour and sugar? How did they end up all over the floor?'

'I must mention,' blurted out Reggie, 'I had nothing to do with that part of the mess. Apparently the canisters fell down when Felicity tried to get the chocolate biscuits from the cupboard. I was gone by then, so don't blame me for that one.'

'I didn't steal the biscuits though,' piped up Felicity. I left them on the floor. I never wanted to go into the house. I never wanted to.' The little girl's pale face was streaked with tears as she began to shake uncontrollably.

Jack turned to Theresa. 'I'm not sure what I should do.' For the first time in his life he had an understanding of how difficult it must be for parents having to deal with naughty children. 'As some of the folk can't be trusted, do you think I should lock the pet door? I don't ever want this to happen again.'

Theresa looked down at her friends, huddled together trying to stay warm. 'I agree Jack. What Daisy, Felicity, Ben and Reggie have done is terrible. I'm very ashamed, but I don't know if you should lock the pet door. Then they will have nowhere to go. What if something did happen that put them in danger? They need to know they have a safe place to go, but I would like to think that this never happens again. What do you think Daisy, Felicity, Ben and Reggie?' The four nodded their heads slowly.

'I promise never to let this happen again, old boy,' said a dejected Ben, turning to Jack, 'and I know I speak for all of us.'

Daisy stood there, not saying a word. The biscuits felt heavy in her pocket. She didn't know what to do. It was so tempting to keep them, but she felt so guilty. They were Jack's favourite biscuits, and she had taken them. How could she tell him? Jack might hate her forever. She couldn't bear it if he did. Suddenly it was all too much for the little mouse; she had to tell him.

'I've done something really awful,' blurted out Daisy, too scared to look at Jack properly. 'I've borrowed your chocolate biscuits and it was all my fault. Felicity had no idea I had taken them, nor did Ben.' Daisy began to sob, as she dug into her pockets and handed him the biscuits. 'I only did it because Annie likes them. I didn't mean to be naughty.'

'I'm sorry too,' wailed Felicity. 'I'll never do anything like this again, ever.'

Jack took the biscuits from the remorseful mouse. 'Now, Daisy and Felicity, I want you both to stop crying and come up here,' he said, firmly. 'As you have both told me the truth, and feel bad about what you have done, I'm going to give you the biscuits to share with the others. Daisy, I want you to give Annie some extra ones. Do you think you can do that?' Still sobbing, the little mouse stepped onto the slab with Felicity.

'Y.. yes,' said Daisy, trying to get her words out. 'I p.. promise I'll share. I'll e..even give A..Annie extra. I p.. promise.'

Jack felt Daisy's hand reach out for his, and couldn't help but squeeze it. Felicity was still crying, preferring not to get too close. He looked down at the wet, sad faces of the rest of the folk. They all looked so miserable. How could he possibly stay cross with them. 'Okay,' said Jack, quietly. 'I won't say any more about it. I'll try to keep the pet door open, but I must warn you, my father is threatening to lock it to keep animals out, so be careful.'

Jack shivered. The rain was getting really heavy, and he was dying to get inside to have some tea and get warm. 'Now, everyone, I really have to go, but promise me you will all be good.' Jack had to grin at the sight of the little heads nodding madly, and he was satisfied that they had all learnt an important lesson, but looking at their small bodies hunched over in the pouring rain somehow made him feel sad. They were a big part of his life now, and all he wanted was for them to be happy, but that seemed so hard to achieve, even for the folk.

A week later, Daisy, Felicity and Annie stood together in the dark trying to keep out of the rain. It was a bleak night, and for the beginning of autumn was quite cold. Annie still wasn't talking to them, even though Daisy had begrudgingly given the mushroom two extra biscuits. She was sick of Annie still being cross, and had decided never to share anything special with her again.

Daisy sighed. She heard the clock chiming from the big house. She counted twelve bells, but there was something else; a rustling, scratching sound had caught her attention. Somewhere in the garden there was movement; she could hear twigs snapping and the sound of heavy breathing. Daisy sniffed. There was definitely something there. Her whiskers were quivering, and her tail began to swish from side to side. Daisy's heart was racing. There was something behind the lavender bush, something awful; she just knew it. The mouse felt sick in the stomach. It was that cat coming to get her. She was going to get eaten in punishment for lying. Daisy put her hands over her eyes. She didn't want to see it. If it was going to eat her, she just didn't want to see it.

'I'm sorry old girl, I didn't mean to scare you,' whispered Ben, stepping out from the shadows, 'but I think we have a large black cat in our garden, and I didn't want to attract any attention by yelling out to you. Are you okay? '

Daisy nodded, unable to speak. It was bad enough Ben scaring her like this, but now she really did have a cat to worry about. What was happening? Why had everything become so horrible?

'Good,' said Ben, patting her arm. I have already told Felicity, Maggie and Katie, and I think it would be entirely appropriate to make our way as quietly as we can to the pet door. Can you do it, old girl?'

'I think so,' said Daisy, shivering. 'I just need to hold onto someone. I feel a bit unsteady on my feet.'

Ben looked at the frightened mouse. It was hard to believe that this was the same Daisy who had bossed them around in the big house only a week earlier. 'Well,' said Ben, patiently, 'you and Felicity will have to hold hands. You must walk quickly, and try to be as quiet as you can getting through the bushes. Katie and Maggie should already be there.'

'What about Annie?' said Felicity. 'We can't leave her here all alone. She needs to come with us. She might get eaten by the cat. I couldn't bear it if she got eaten.'

'Neither could I,' whispered Daisy, totally forgetting how cross she was with the mushroom. 'I would die. Just die.'

'Don't you two worry about me,' said Annie, crossly. 'I can look after myself. Besides, I'd much rather stay here and take my chances than try to outrun that cat. Anyway, I can't imagine the animal being interested in an old mushroom, so I want you and Felicity to go without me.'

Daisy hesitated, but she knew Ben was anxious to get going, and Annie could be very stubborn: maybe she would be safest staying put. Felicity and Daisy kissed the top of the mushroom's head and said goodbye. Then they each took a deep breath, joined hands, and turned to Ben.

The little dog smiled at Annie. 'Take care, old thing. I'll keep these two safe. I promise. Now girls, I'll take up the rear so I can fend off the cat, and give you all a chance to get inside. Are you ready?'

'We are,' gulped Felicity, 'but we're scared. What if

the cat gets us? We're scared, Ben.'

He gently squeezed her hand. 'Nobody's going to get you; now go quietly.'

The rain was heavy by now and getting through the undergrowth was difficult. Daisy began to shake uncontrollably as her mind went back to the storm; it brought back memories of that terrible night. Felicity held the little mouse's hand tighter as if sensing her fear, hoping and praying that the cat had not heard or seen them. She could just see the house through the sheets of rain, but there was very little moon tonight, making everything look hazy. Felicity shuddered. The next hurdle was going to be climbing up the slate bricks, particularly as they would be wet and slippery. The main thing was to get to the verandah safely and once there they could make a run for it. Exhausted, the girls finally reached the edge and started to scramble up the bricks. The rain had made it dangerous and hard to get a grip.

Daisy started to panic. 'What are we going to do? I keep sliding, Felicity, I keep sliding. We need Ben. Where can he be? Where is he?'

Shh,' said Felicity, 'I just heard something. Stay perfectly still.' It was hard to hear over the rain drumming on the roof, but the girls sensed that they were not alone. Daisy took a deep breath while holding on tighter to the bricks. The suspense was awful.

'Well, there you both are,' said a familiar voice. 'Can I be of any assistance?' The girls almost hugged him; they had never been so happy to see Reggie in their whole life.

'Yes,' said Daisy. 'Push us onto the verandah; and hurry Reggie, the cat is somewhere in the garden.'

'The cat?' cried Reggie. 'That huge black animal that goes around eating things? That one?'

'Yes! Yes! That one,' said Daisy. She was getting exasperated at Reggie's continual chatter when they needed his help, and quickly.

'Is this the truth, young lady, or is it just another lie?' persisted Reggie. 'I can never tell with you.'

'It's true,' squawked a new voice behind him. Reggie spun around. Maggie and Katie were sitting close together by the pet door. 'Ben told us about the cat,' continued Maggie. 'We've been here for ages!'

'It's all rather distressing,' added Katie, quietly. 'Very distressing indeed.'

'See, I told you we weren't lying!' cried Daisy. 'Now please help us, Reggie. We haven't got time for this, we must hurry.'

But Reggie was far from happy. 'Why didn't somebody warn me, or even Herbert, for that matter? It's just not good enough; we're always the last to know: always.'

'For heavens sake, Reggie, shut up and push,' shouted Daisy and Felicity together over the noise of the rain. 'We have to get to the pet door and we don't know how close the cat is. Now just push us as hard as you can.'

Finally, huffing and puffing, Reggie propelled them onto the verandah. They were all exhausted but relieved to be closer to the door. Reggie was still gasping for breath when he heard Ben shouting to them from the garden.

'Get through the door.' cried the dog. 'Hurry, get through the door.'

Felicity struggled forward and pushed like Jack had

shown her, but nothing happened. Daisy tried to help, but the door remained shut.

'Push harder,' bellowed Reggie.' 'Push harder. Use some force. Ben is nearly here, which means the cat is getting closer.'

Felicity and Daisy were a mass of perspiration as they tried their hardest to open the door.

'We can't!' they screamed. 'We can't push any harder. Come and help us. The door's locked Reggie, the door's locked!'

14

The Black Cat

Reggie rushed over to help the girls, just as Ben came racing onto the verandah.

'The cat's behind me,' cried the little dog, wide-eyed. 'Get inside quickly.' Ben looked into their terrified faces. Something was wrong; why weren't they hurrying to safety?

'We can't!' squawked Maggie and Katie together. 'The door's locked! The door's locked!' Panic set in, as everyone tried frantically to push, but it was hopeless. Maggie began to flap her wings in frustration as Katie sat cowering next to the door. The kookaburra had never felt this frightened; there was a terrible sense of foreboding. Something bad was about to happen, she was sure of it.

Ben knew he must do something and quickly. He looked at the frightened faces of his friends. They had to do something; they just couldn't sit here and wait for the cat.

'I know it will be hard for Jack to hear us over the rain, but we have to make as much noise as we can, so he does. He is our only hope. Do you think you can try?' They all nodded. 'Well done, let's go!'

Daisy and Felicity screamed out Jack's name as loud as they could, and Reggie pounded the door with such force, it was a wonder it didn't break. Ben sat by the large window howling, hoping the dogs would hear his cries for help, but the house remained silent. They couldn't believe the pet door was locked. Jack had promised them he would keep it open. He had promised.

'What are we going to do?' wailed Daisy. 'Jack can't hear us, and Maxine and Scarlet can't hear us. We're all going to get eaten. If we can't open the door, we're all going to get eaten.'

'Just keep pushing and screaming,' yelled Ben. 'We just have to keep trying. Jack's got to hear us soon. He has to.'

Everyone was so intent at getting the door open that they didn't see the danger. They didn't see the dark shape climb stealthily onto the verandah, stomach flattened, growling menacingly as it crept forward. They didn't hear the low guttural sound coming from the creature's throat. They didn't hear anything, until a long, loud, screech ripped through the air. Felicity and Daisy spun round to see where the noise was coming from. Reggie and Ben stopped banging on the door.

Daisy gasped. She could see it now: two yellow eyes moving slowly towards them. They seemed to glow in the moonlight. They looked evil. Reggie, Felicity and Ben didn't make a sound. All they could do was watch; watch those eyes, those horrible haunting eyes.

Maggie was the only one doing anything. She was going crazy. Her wings were spread wide, flapping in rage at the intruder, and she was screaming at top note. 'Why isn't somebody helping Katie? Can't you all see the cat? Can't you all see that it's heading towards Katie? What's wrong with you all? Please help her!'

Daisy froze. She hadn't realised the cat was so

close. She could see its outline, and it was enormous. There was nothing she could do. It was too big and horrible. There was nothing anyone could do.

'Get out of the way, Maggie,' yelled Ben. 'You can't help her, old thing, and the animal will get you too. It's too big and strong Maggie,' persisted Ben, as he pushed in front of her. 'You just can't help her. Cats are meant to be scared of dogs; let me have a go.'

Daisy could hear Felicity sobbing, as the animal loomed before them. She shivered as she watched Ben creep towards it, but the dog looked so small and vulnerable. She held her breath as Ben lunged at the cat's huge frame, but it was hopeless. He didn't stand a chance. A massive black paw reached out, and struck him so hard he was flung to the other side of the verandah. Ben yelped with pain as his back leg hit one of the posts. Daisy cried out, but they were helpless: totally helpless.

Katie sat motionless, as the cat continued to crawl towards her. She didn't feel afraid anymore, she just felt numb. It was as if she was in a dream: a terrible dream. Soon she would wake up and everything would be all right, but those horrible yellow eyes kept staring down at her. They were hypnotic. She wanted to scream and fly away, but she couldn't move. As hard as she tried, she couldn't move.

Somewhere in her mind she could hear Maggie screeching, but maybe that was just a dream too. The little bird knew deep down that her life was nearly over. No one could help her now. Not even Maggie.

The cat was so close. She could hear it breathing, its hot breath almost upon her. She cringed as the monster slowly opened its mouth, showing two rows of sharp white teeth. She heard its long claws scraping on the slate as it edged closer and closer.

Katie sighed, a deep resigned sigh. She thought of her friends. She thought of Maggie. Then closed her eyes and waited...

'No!' roared Reggie, as the huge paw reached out. 'No!' When suddenly, without warning, two furry bodies rushed out through the pet door as the verandah filled with the brightest light they had ever seen. The cat stopped in its tracks, mesmerised by the brightness. Now it knew the meaning of fear as the two barking dogs hurtled towards it.

Like lightning, the cat turned from its prey and raced for the back fence, tail down and black fur bristling. All its thoughts of hunting had clearly disappeared as the dogs chased it across the lawn. The last sound those on the verandah heard was a screech from the animal as it scrambled through the blackberry bush and over the fence to safety.

Jack stood at the back door, unable to speak. He was shaking so much he could barely open the door. He couldn't believe what he had just seen. Katie had nearly been taken by the cat. How could this happen? He looked down at the folk's frightened wet faces. They just stood there. Nobody moved. Nobody spoke. They just stood there, as if frozen in time. They needed him and he wasn't there. How was he going to protect them from dangers like this? How? He seemed to be there for ages before Daisy spotted him.

'Jack, you've come to save us.' She could feel her eyes welling up with tears, as she ran towards the back door. Her little arms reached out, as Jack gently picked her up. 'We all thought Katie was going to die,' sobbed

Daisy. We couldn't help her, and the door was closed. Jack, the door was closed. It was horrible: so horrible.'

Before Jack could answer, Felicity and Reggie came running over, Ben limping behind them. He bent down and hugged each one of them, then made his way over to Katie.

'She's in shock,' said Maggie, gently placing her wing over her friend. 'She needs to keep warm.' She looked up at Jack, a tear trickling down her cheek, and landing on the end of her beak. 'I nearly lost her, Jack. I nearly lost my best friend.' Jack bent down and sat beside the magpie. She was hard to love sometimes, but right now he just wanted to hug her. He had never seen her cry. He had never seen her like this.

'Poor Katie,' said Jack, as he tenderly picked up the little bird and held her to his chest. Her heart was beating quickly, and she felt soft against his body. He could feel her shivering, as he tucked her under his jumper. 'Poor Katie,' whispered Jack. 'Poor dear Katie.' He looked down at the rest of them, and for the first time in his life knew what it was like to love like a parent. It was overwhelming.

'Okay everyone,' whispered Jack. 'I've opened the pet door, and I want you all to go through as quietly as possible. I'll meet you inside and dry you off; you're all soaked.'

One by one the folk entered the room, trying not to make a sound. Reggie was the last one in when, out of the blue, the door burst open with an almighty bang as Scarlet and Maxine raced through. Their tails were held high, and they couldn't get the obvious joy off their faces. They loved chasing cats; next to having a walk it was their favourite hobby. Jack saw the light go on upstairs, and waited. He knew someone would have heard the noise.

'Are you all right, Jack?' His mother sounded anxious.

'I'm fine, Mum. I'm just looking after the dogs. They heard something outside and now they're soaking wet. I promise I'll be up soon.' He heard the light go off. Thankfully his mother must have been too tired to investigate. He had to move quickly though, as it was getting late and it was a school day tomorrow.

'I must say, old chap,' spoke up Ben, 'I take back what I said before about Maxine and Scarlet. They saved our lives.'

'Yes, if it wasn't for them,' said Jack. 'I never would have heard you. So you can thank them. They are good little dogs.'

'I agree,' piped up Daisy, patting Scarlet's wet head. They can bark in our garden any time.'

'Three cheers for Maxine and Scarlet,' blurted out Reggie. 'Three cheers.' The two dogs sat amongst the folk, panting and happy in the knowledge of a job well done.

Reggie was the last of the folk to be dried off, and as Jack placed him next to the others, he could see their eyes slowly closing. It had been a harrowing night and one Jack never wanted to go through again. After saying 'Goodnight' to each of the folk, and making sure Katie was warm, he switched off the light. Exhausted, he climbed up the stairs, Maxine and Scarlet padding behind him. He couldn't believe what had just happened. He just couldn't believe it.

Once in bed, Jack couldn't sleep. He kept thinking of the cat. He kept thinking how terrible it would have been if he had lost Katie, and he felt guilty: guilty that he wasn't there to protect them, and guilty that the pet door was locked.

Jack sighed as he listened to the rain. It was heavy now. He could hear the dogs snoring at the bottom of his bed, and he could hear the chimes of the grandfather clock. He counted the chimes. It was four o'clock in the morning.

15

Meeting Mr Tom

'Jack,' yelled Mary. 'Come down here this instant.' Jack was half asleep. Surely it wasn't morning already. He felt exhausted, but his mother's voice sounded like she meant business. He stumbled down the stairs, shaking himself out of his lethargy as he went.

'What do you call this?' she continued angrily as he stood before her.

Jack looked into the family room. The sun streamed through the large windows and there, standing in the morning light, were Reggie, Ben, Maggie, Katie and the girls, still in the same positions he had left them last night. Jack gasped. The four o'clock curfew! We all forgot about the curfew. I don't believe it. He looked at his mother through bleary eyes. 'Well, it was raining outside, so I brought them in to get dry.'

Mary couldn't believe what she was hearing. This obsession Jack had with the ornaments was ridiculous. He spent so much time with them at night, and last evening she saw him reading to the wombat.

'Jack, you know the ornaments are only make-believe, don't you? You know they're not real. Getting wet was never going to hurt them. Sometimes I think your imagination goes wild and you really think the ornaments are alive.'

Jack was horrified. How much had his mother seen? 'Of course I know they're not real,' he said. 'I just enjoy their company.' Jack realised that from now on he would have to be very careful. He certainly didn't want his mother getting suspicious.

'Anyway', continued Mary, 'your grandparents will be moving up here on Monday, so there will be a lot to do. You won't be able to spend much time outside until they are settled. Now, can you please take these ornaments back to the garden and get ready for school.'

Jack moved his friends back to their homes, but he was worried. What if his mother found out about their secret lives? What if she found out about the golden-key? He shuddered at the thought. He couldn't let it happen, he just couldn't.

He did feel a bit excited though that his grandparents were finally moving up. Just imagine; when he got home from school they would be living right across the road. He could visit them any time he wanted to. It was going to be fantastic. He had waited for a whole year for this day, and on Monday it was really happening. His mum and dad were even taking the day off work to help them move in.

Jack wondered how the folk would feel when he told them that he couldn't visit for a while. They knew his grandparents were moving up to live across the road. Daisy was particularly excited because she loved Grandpa, and more importantly, she loved Grandma's chocolate cakes, but he wasn't sure about the others. They had come to rely on his nightly visits, and of course there was the cat. How would he solve the problem of the cat?

'I don't understand, pet,' said Annie, when Jack finally got up the nerve to tell them. 'I don't understand what your grandparents moving across the road has got to do with us? Why should it stop you visiting us? I really don't understand.'

'And what about the cat, old boy?' enquired Ben anxiously. 'We are still very worried about the cat. The garden doesn't feel safe anymore. It isn't like it used to be. It's a scary place.'

'I'll still be around,' said Jack, quietly. 'Just not as much. I have to help Grandma and Grandpa move in. They're old, and they can't do it themselves. I can't help it.'

'They are old,' agreed Daisy. 'They are really old. So I can see why Jack has to help them.'

'I'm still worried about the cat, old chap,' continued Ben, 'but I do understand. I really do.'

'Thanks Ben, ' said Jack, sincerely, and I promise I'll work out something to protect you all from the cat.' He looked around at the rest of the group. 'You do understand, don't you?' Everyone slowly nodded, but out of the corner of his eye Jack could see Maggie muttering something to Reggie. He could only imagine what she was saying. It hurt a bit. He could never please Maggie.

'We'll be fine,' said Theresa, grasping his hand. 'We'll miss you, but we will cope.'

'Good,' said Jack, giving Theresa a quick hug. 'I'll be a little happier knowing you are all okay with this. Anyway, it's only a week. I'll be back before you know it, and then everything will be back to normal.' Hesitating slightly, Jack finally made a move. He hugged them all, even Reggie, and then suddenly he was gone.

Daisy felt sad as she saw him disappear amongst the shrubbery. She shuddered as she heard the back door slam. The little mouse felt like he had deserted her. Jack, the one she always thought she could count on. He had deserted them all.

Jack's week was frantic. In between helping his grandparents unpack, he played his first final in soccer, and the team won. He had been playing for eight weeks before that and was really enjoying it. Then, much to his father's joy, his team had reached the finals, but Jack was nervous. The pressure to do well was huge, and he was afraid of stuffing it up, but as it turned out, Jack played his best game ever. His dad couldn't stop grinning and told him he had improved out of sight since his first game. That wouldn't have been hard, thought Jack: the first game he played was terrible. He had gone home in tears, vowing never to play soccer again, and now, thought Jack, he loved it. He actually loved playing a sport.

But the best part of all was how well Sam was doing. Jack was really pleased for his friend. He had been named best player and had won free tickets to the movies. Sam had turned out to be a very good soccer player, much to his mother's delight. He had not only lost ten kilograms, but also spent a lot of his spare time running and swimming to keep fit. Sam had dreams of playing for Australia one day, and getting fit was just part of achieving that dream.

Brian Madison had joined the team too, but was pretty hopeless. He was too big and ungainly for soccer. Jack felt sorry for him, especially when Brian's father came to watch. He would yell at him the whole time, calling him an idiot and a big girl. Now Jack knew where Brian got his bullying ways from.

'I hate playing soccer,' confessed a despondent Brian to Jack one Thursday morning. He always seemed to tell Jack his problems during their special education classes. Which was fine, thought Jack, but it didn't really help them with their maths, as one of them usually got caught and sent back to their regular class.

'Why do you play then?' said Jack, trying to concentrate on the teacher.

'Cos my old man wants me to. I'd rather play Aussie Rules. You know, a bit of rough and tumble, and it is very skilful. I mean, look how high they leap, and all that tackling. I think I'd be good at it. What do you think, Crane?'

Jack looked at Brian's big frame and miserable face. He really did feel sorry for him. 'Yeah, I think that would be the perfect game for you. I think you should try it.' Suddenly Brian's whole face lit up.

'You know what, Crane, I think I will. Who cares what my old man thinks. I'm going to give it a go. Now let's get on with this multiplication rubbish. I'm feeling in the mood for maths.' And so, as hard as it was for Jack to come to terms with, the weird friendship between himself and his former tormentor, Brian Madison, continued to grow. Even Sam admitted to liking Brian. Honestly, thought Jack, between befriending the ornaments and now Brian, he wondered what on earth would happen to him next.

Helping his grandparents move in was fun for Jack, but very tiring. They only had the balcony left to organise now, and Jack and his dad were going over on Saturday to help shift things. Jack would be glad when it was all done, so he could get back to his evening visits to the garden. He had only managed one so far, and the folk hadn't seemed too impressed.

'Nice of you to put in an appearance,' Maggie had quipped. 'We could all be eaten by now and you wouldn't even know.' Maggie was obsessed with getting eaten, thought Jack. It was all she ever talked about. He did feel a little hurt though, and began to think they were all being a bit selfish. After all, he had been the one who saved them from the cat.

Saturday morning was bright and sunny, but there was a definite chill in the air. Autumn was finally here. No longer would he have to put up with the stifling heat of summer. Everything came to life in autumn as the rain became more constant. He loved the way the leaves changed colour, and the countryside began to green up. It always looked so much better. He especially loved the food. No more salads; instead, things like pumpkin soup, roast beef and Grandma's lemon puddings. He loved it all.

From the minute Jack set foot in his grandparents' new house he knew he was going to love it. Already they had got it looking homely and cosy. He particularly liked the big gas fire at the end of the large family room, making the room so bright and welcoming. He longed to sit down on one of the new leather chairs and sit by the fire, but today he was here to work.

'Okay, young Jack,' said Grandpa, interrupting his thoughts, 'you can help your dad carry this cat ornament out onto the balcony. We want to see what it looks like.' Jack turned around. He was stunned. He'd never seen anything like it.

It was a large stone cat dressed in a checked waistcoat and with a black bow tie neatly wound around his thick neck. He was magnificent. Jack was fascinated by his long fine whiskers, and very big hands. They certainly weren't paws as such, but had thin tapered fingers with long fingernails attached. Jack giggled as he spied the perfectly moulded top hat that sat on his head. It really was a cool outfit. He had never seen an ornament like it.

'He's a beauty, isn't he,' said Grandpa, reading the boy's thoughts. 'His name is Mr Tom, and your grandmother bought him especially for this house, but I'm wondering if he's a bit big for the balcony.

The three of them took fifteen minutes to get Mr Tom into position. He was very heavy and hard to manoeuvre. 'I have to say, Ted,' said Jack's father, wiping his forehead, 'this cat looks ridiculous. He almost fills the balcony. Couldn't you have got something a bit smaller?'

Grandpa looked downcast, but he had to agree. 'I don't know what Grace is going to say. She loves the cat and has her heart set on it being out here.' He looked around him. 'But there's hardly room for anything else, so I guess that's out of the question.' Grandpa sighed. Which one of us is going to tell her? Personally, I would rather it wasn't me. I'm not that brave.'

Jack was oblivious to the chatter around him. All he could think of was Mr Tom. He couldn't get his eyes off him. Here was the perfect solution to the cat problem in the garden. Mr Tom could protect the folk in exchange for food and shelter. He just had to have him.

'Grandpa, if Dad says it's all right, maybe we could look after Mr Tom in our garden, and Grandma would be able to visit him whenever she wants. What would

Grandma think of that?' Both his father and grandfather looked a little unsure.

But when Jack's grandmother came out to see how Mr Tom looked, she was horrified. 'He can't stay here,' she said, angrily. 'He looks ridiculous! The garden centre assured me he would fit when I gave them the dimensions of the balcony. They can jolly well come and collect him; and for free!'

Jack was amused. He had never seen his grandma so angry, but she did calm down when Grandpa told her of Jack's proposal for Mr Tom. She even offered to plant some flowers around him.

Jack breathed a sigh of relief. Mr Tom would be a great addition to the garden. Finally, things were starting to fall into place. It was all good.

When Mary met Mr Tom she loved him straight away and laughed when she spotted the fob watch carved into the pocket of his waistcoat. She suggested that they all go up to the garden centre and buy Grandma something a bit more sensible to put on the balcony. Grandma ended up buying a stone frog and swore she could hear it croaking late at night. Grandpa said she was going mad.

It was with much difficulty, and with the help of Jack's uncle's trailer, that Mr Tom was deposited into the side garden next to Reggie and Herbert. It was the 8th of April: a day they would always remember.

The arrival of Mr Tom was very interesting for the folk, as none of them had ever met anyone quite like him. On the evening that Jack decided to make formal introductions, the weather had turned very chilly, and everyone, including Mr Tom, just wanted Jack to get on with it. Jack explained that Mr Tom was a friendly cat and was there to protect the garden from intruders. In return, Mr Tom would appreciate it if all his food could be gathered for him each evening.

'You must be joking!' piped up Reggie. 'We all take turns to gather food, and we all share. I'm not treating anyone differently.' The folk all nodded.

Mr Tom calmly looked on, brushing lint off his beautifully tailored waistcoat with his long, fine fingers. He straightened his hat and adjusted his black bow tie before speaking.

'Friends, friends, friends,' he purred in a very strange accent, 'it's like this. You have a problem with a nasty critter who likes eating things with warm little bodies. I, personally, am a lover of vegetables: carrots, beans, corn and the like. Little creatures covered in feathers and fur are not to my liking. I also detest getting my fingernails dirty or my waistcoat soiled, so as you can imagine, toiling in the garden is just not my thing.' He adjusted his bow tie again. 'I also abhor being kept standing out here in the freezing cold, so, I suggest, my friends, that we deal with this matter as quickly as possible.'

The folk were silent as they tried to digest Mr Tom's speech. Herbert was struggling with the word 'critter,' but didn't want to appear stupid, so refrained from mentioning it.

'Does this mean you will protect us from the cat, or any other animal that enters our garden?' said Felicity.

Mr Tom looked down on her with warm brown eyes. 'It does indeed, young lady. I will always be at your service.'

'Well, in that case,' said Felicity, looking around, 'I think gathering some food for Mr Tom each night is a small price to pay for our safety, so I don't mind doing it.'

One by one the folk murmured in agreement with Felicity that their welfare was the most important thing. Mr Tom looked as proud as could be. He was pleased that the whole thing had been dealt with quickly, so he could go to bed. Looking down at his watch, he decided to make a move. Everything appeared to be settled to his satisfaction.

'Well, friends,' he said, 'as enjoyable as this gathering has been, it's getting late and my newly acquired bamboo chaise longue, complete with plump green check mattress, awaits.' He looked down at Felicity, and tipped his hat at her. 'Tomorrow, child, I will write you a list of my likes and dislikes. Until then, I bid you all goodnight.' With that, Mr Tom glided through the bushes towards the side garden where his new bed awaited.

The folk were in shock: a chaise longue with a mattress! That sort of comfort was unheard of. 'Well I never,' said Annie, in disbelief. 'Have you ever heard or seen anything like it, and what on earth was that ridiculous hat all about? Have you ever seen such a hat? The cheek; coming into this garden, demanding this and demanding that. A list, for heaven's sake! What does he take us for: his servants? You mark my words, young Felicity; our Mr Tom is going to be more trouble than he's worth.' Annie shivered. 'Now let's go home. I don't know about you two, but I'm freezing.'

Daisy and Felicity walked on either side of Annie, holding onto the mushroom's tiny hands. The friends were deep in thought, worried about what the future might hold with Mr Tom in it. Life was a bit like that lately: all ups and downs. Nothing seemed to stay the same.

The first week of Mr Tom's presence in the garden was an interesting one. Daisy and Felicity had drawn the short straw and had to front up to the cat for his first food orders. The girls decided he was very good at giving orders, but appeared to do little of anything else. Another problem was that food was starting to dry up as they moved further into autumn. The vegetables were now becoming scarce and the winter crop had not even been planted. There was no fruit to speak of except for some dried up apricots and figs, and the apples and mandarins were still not ripe enough to eat. Mr Tom screwed up his face in horror as the girls' latest offerings were presented to him.

'Ladies, ladies,' bemoaned Mr Tom, as he held up two small figs, one apricot and two small green apples in his long fingers. 'What on earth do you call this? As you can see I am a fine specimen of cat, and as such I expect fine food. I can't possibly exist on this rubbish. These apples aren't even ripe! Now, ladies, I want you to really try hard, and keep reminding yourselves that Mr Tom is a fine specimen, and therefore needs fine food.' With that, he straightened his bow tie, pulled down his waistcoat, and eased himself into a comfortable position on the chaise longue. The conversation was now over.

By the end of the week Daisy and Felicity had had enough and complained bitterly to Theresa about how hard it was to please Mr Tom. 'We just can't find the food he likes. It's okay for us, but he hates it. We don't know what to do,' wailed Daisy.

Reggie overheard the conversation, and quickly came to Mr Tom's defence. 'Why, he's a fine fellow, young Daisy, and so intelligent. He keeps Herbert and myself amused for hours with all his interesting stories. You do know that he comes from a completely different country, don't you? He comes from America. Can you believe that? America!'

The folk looked decidedly unimpressed. 'What's "America", old boy?' spoke up Ben. 'Is it a garden, or a place? I mean really, old boy, what does it mean to us?'

Reggie continued to defend Mr Tom. 'It's a wonderful place according to Mr Tom, and if he says it is, then it must be. I won't hear a thing said against him, and neither will Herbert.'

When, however, it was Reggie's and Herbert's turn to collect Mr Tom's food, the folk were amused to see how quickly their attitude changed. The quiet evenings were interrupted by the sound of Reggie and Mr Tom having words.

Reggie would yell at Mr Tom for his arrogant behaviour and total disregard of all the effort that he and Herbert went to when looking for special food for him. Reggie even told him to go back to that place called 'America', as he wasn't welcome here any more. Mr Tom, on the other hand, would wave his long fingers at Reggie, reminding him in his smooth deep voice what a 'fine specimen' he was, and how he needed the special food to keep his beautiful fur in pristine condition, and for his information he wasn't going anywhere. He was staying put.

After a month of Mr Tom doing nothing but complaining, the folk had had enough, and Jack was summoned to an urgent meeting. All in the garden was not happy. Something had to be done and soon.

16

Mr Tom Gets Dirty

In answer to Theresa's call for an important meeting, Jack made his way through the darkness towards the cubby house. He knew his mother was at the kitchen window, and even though it would be almost impossible to see him, he sensed her watching his every move. For some reason she seemed to resent his visits into the garden and kept going on and on about the amount of time he spent outside. He found his mother's attitude baffling, particularly as he hadn't visited the folk properly for at least a month. Also, she seemed happy that things at school were improving. It didn't make any sense.

Everything seemed to be falling into place. He had even had Sam and Brian Madison around for tea on Saturday night. His mum thought Brian was a very nice boy. His dad was in his element comparing the good and bad points of soccer and Aussie Rules football with Brian and Sam. They had a great night.

'You're lucky, Crane,' said Brian, loudly, in their special education class the following Thursday morning. 'You'd have to have the coolest dad on the planet. I wouldn't introduce my old man to an ape. In fact,' said Brian, getting even louder, 'I'd rather the ape was my old man.' Jack cringed as the teacher glared at them from the front of the room, but once again, there was something about Brian that he couldn't help liking. He just hoped he was never invited to his place for tea, never!'

Jack was the happiest he had ever been, so why did his mother still feel the need to worry about him? His grandmother said that that's what mothers do, and his mother would still worry about him when he was fifty. Jack thought that would be dreadful. Imagine being fussed over when you were old. That's why he loved having his grandparents so close. They treated him like an adult and never fussed over him like his mother did. His grandfather was even helping him with his maths, especially some of the stuff from his special education class. He did wonder how poor Brian got on. The two of them never seemed to get anywhere.

Jack had to chuckle when he thought about maths. Herbert had reminded him only last week that he was there to help him. Jack felt awful having to decline his offer. He told him about his grandpa helping him, and how he went to special maths classes, and that maybe that was enough.

'Oh! It is, my boy,' said Herbert, quite happily. 'It is definitely enough. You don't want maths overload. I only said that to Theresa the other day, when she told me it was about time I learnt to count past ten. I told her I didn't want maths overload, so we left it at that.' Jack smiled. That was one thing about Herbert he loved: the way he saw things. He might want to learn, but he never got stressed out doing it, in fact he didn't get stressed out at all. If only I could be like that, thought Jack. If only!

It had been a long time since Jack had visited the folk and he couldn't wait to catch up with them all. He particularly missed Daisy, Felicity and Annie, and his nightly visits to Herbert. The past month had been so busy, and the days had become shorter and colder. Winter was here. Tonight he made sure he rugged up. It was freezing.

There was an excited squeal as Daisy and Felicity ran to greet him. 'We've missed you, Jack,' said Felicity, shyly, 'and so much has happened. Everyone is fed up with Mr Tom. We need you to help us work out what to do. Even poor Theresa has had enough.'

When Jack arrived at the slate block, he thought Theresa looked very pale and tired. She smiled weakly, reaching out and gently squeezing his cold hands.

'Oh! Jack, thank goodness,' she said, almost in tears. 'We have all had a terrible time in your absence, and I really don't think I can cope much longer.' The garden folk were stunned. They couldn't remember the last time they had seen Theresa cry; she always seemed so calm and in control.

'It's that confounded Mr Tom,' piped up Reggie. 'He's running us all ragged with his expectations and finicky ways. Nothing we seem to do is good enough. Poor old Theresa has spent the past month just trying to keep the peace!'

'Also, there is hardly any food left in the garden,' said Daisy, sadly. 'We are getting quite hungry, and it's harder and harder to find anything much to eat in the vegetable patch.'

'I say, old chap,' said Ben, 'you couldn't sneak out some more of that food Scarlet and Maxine eat? I found it absolutely delicious the other night when I had some of their leftovers, particularly the chicken in gravy: very tasty indeed. What do you think, old boy?'

Jack looked down into Ben's big brown eyes and grinned. 'I'm sure I can manage that for you, but not every night. My mother might get suspicious. She's been watching me lately. She even saw me reading to Herbert one night. So we all have to be careful.'

'I like your mum,' piped up Daisy. 'She's nice, and very pretty.'

'I like her too,' said Jack, laughing, 'but I don't want her to find out our secret. She can't. Anyway, let's get back to the problem of your food. I feel terrible that you have been going hungry: really terrible.' Especially, thought Jack, as he was having roast chicken for tea with gravy and baked potatoes. Maybe he could sneak some out later.

'Not as terrible as us, young man,' squawked Maggie. 'We could all be dead from starvation for all you care. Where have you been this past month? For your information, Katie and myself have been existing on worms. Yes, you heard me, worms!' There was absolute silence. Nobody wanted to side with Maggie, but it was true; Jack had been neglecting them.

Daisy shivered as she put up her hand to get Jack's attention. 'It's also getting cold, Jack. Feel my hands: they are freezing. Can't you find us somewhere cosy to sleep, like your house?'

Jack felt awful. He had been so busy with his own needs, and helping his grandparents, that he had totally forgotten about the needs of the folk. He hadn't even thought about their food supply. He just imagined that there would always be something there for them to eat. How stupid he was.

'I must ask, pet,' inquired Annie. 'Has your mother decided on what winter vegetables are to be planted this year? It's just that they should be sown soon, if we are to eat this winter. I just thought I would ask, pet.'

Dear old Annie, thought Jack. Only she could word it in such a way that meant 'get moving with the planting', without sounding bossy.

'I couldn't agree more,' rang out a deep smooth voice. 'We need to plant our winter crop.' The folk silently groaned as Mr Tom glided up onto the block of slate. 'I have many ideas, young Mr Jack, and I'm sure the folk here will happily help till the soil and sow the seed. I personally will gladly offer my services as supervisor.'

'Supervisor?' yelled Reggie. 'Why can't you do some tilling and sowing, like the rest of us? What makes you so different?'

Mr Tom sighed. 'I have already told you, good people, I don't like dirty hands or fingernails, and I certainly don't like my attire getting soiled. How many times must this be said?' With that, Mr Tom straightened his bow tie and checked his watch.

Jack could well understand why Mr Tom was causing a few problems. He wondered if he could reason with him, or at least get him to pull his weight a bit more. As far as he knew, he hadn't even had to deal with the black cat. Oh well, thought Jack, I can at least get the vegetable patch started. I'll work out what to do with Mr Tom and find somewhere better for the folk to sleep later on. There really was so much to think about. Sometimes Jack wished he had someone to confide in; just sometimes he wished he could tell his grandpa.

The meeting ended with not a lot being resolved, but Jack did promise to get the vegetable garden started as soon as he could. He just needed a bit of time. In truth, the hard bit was to get his mother to take him up to the garden centre.

She seemed out of sorts lately, and was definitely unhappy about something. As far as he could tell, his mother had never been the same since the storm. Jack just hoped that he hadn't done something to upset her. He loved his mother, and wanted her to be happy. When he mentioned this to his grandparents, they were at pains to tell him that he wasn't the problem and that his mother just got tired from all the things she had to do. They even offered to take Jack up to the garden centre and buy the seeds for him.

'I won't be planting the seeds, young Jack,' said his grandfather, as they wandered between the rows of lush green seedlings. 'I've hurt my back, but I know you will do a great job, and it could be a nice surprise for your mum.'

Jack couldn't wait to get home and start planning his garden. His grandfather had bought him seeds to grow broccoli, Brussels sprouts, cauliflower, peas, spinach and turnips. He knew Mr Tom liked most of these vegetables, so hopefully there would be no more complaints from the big cat.

Fruit would also soon be available. The apples near the fence were beginning to ripen to a nice bright red, and the mandarins were also nearly ready to eat. Maggie and Katie had found a walnut tree two houses down, so they had spent the week collecting nuts to store. There would be enough food to see them through the winter, but Jack would still smuggle food down to them. The folk particularly loved the food he brought them.

'I love it, love it, love it,' said Felicity, one night, as she was tucking into some pumpkin soup. 'I want to eat your food always. It's the best.'

'Me too,' cried Daisy, licking the remains of the soup off her whiskers, 'me too.'

'Well you can't,' said Annie, crossly. 'You can't have young Jack running down here at night bringing you food. Just enjoy it when he does, but be grateful for what you have.' Jack loved Annie. She was always right, and she somehow managed to keep the girls under control, but the one thing she couldn't control was Mr Tom. That was Jack's next problem. Getting Mr Tom to do some work and really become part of the garden.

He had been thinking about this all week, and finally he and Theresa had come up with a plan which they hoped would change the cat's selfish ways. Jack chuckled. 'I think it's time for the "fine specimen" to get down and dirty!'

The sun was slowly setting behind the distant trees like a big red ball as Jack made his way down to the vegetable patch. It was very cold and the wind was sharp, forcing him to plunge one hand deep into his coat pocket while using the other to carry his tools. He had agreed to meet everyone at five bells and had managed to smuggle out the smallest of trowels and spades for Daisy, Felicity, Theresa and Annie to use. He promised himself that if the plan worked he and the folk would only be out in the chilly air for a short while. 'Fingers crossed,' he said to himself, as he arrived at the garden gate.

'It's Jack,' squealed Daisy and Felicity together as

they raced over for a warming hug. 'It's so cold out here we can hardly feel our hands. Please find us a home so that we can stay nice and warm, please Jack. Squeeze our hands; feel our goosebumps; it's horrible, Jack, horrible. Promise us this won't take long.'

Jack shook his head. 'I have no idea, girls, how long it will take. It's all going to depend on Mr Tom; but the sooner we get started the better.'

Daisy and Felicity grabbed the smallest of the trowels and Annie took the tiny spade.

'What are we meant to do, Jack?' inquired Felicity. 'Do we start digging yet?'

Jack looked up the garden path for Mr Tom. 'No, girls, don't do anything until you hear me cough, then start digging holes anywhere you like. Maggie and Katie, you can both aerate the soil with your beaks.'

It seemed an age before they heard Jack cough. Immediately, the four of them started throwing soil around, not even bothering to dig proper holes. Then came the sound of heavy footsteps as an indignant cry rang out from the top of the path.

'Ladies! Ladies! What do you think you are doing?' Mr Tom was actually running towards them, arms waving and large hands outstretched. 'I'm supervising, remember, and we must begin with some sort of order; a garden bed has to be worked out properly. You can't just go in there willy-nilly throwing seed around and not digging proper holes. How can you possibly expect things to grow? A garden needs planning, and I am the person for the job!'

'Well I never, pets,' chuckled Annie, 'the great cat actually runs. Give me strength if he brings out one of those lists of his. So help me, ducks, I'll tear it up in front of him.'

Mr Tom finally arrived, huffing and puffing and waving something in his long fingers. Annie and Maggie groaned as the white sheet was placed in front of them.

'Where are the rest of the helpers?' said Mr Tom. 'I have written a list giving everyone a task. Felicity, go and round them up before it gets too dark.' With that, Mr Tom sank gratefully into the chair provided for him. Running always exhausted him, but now all he had to do was wait for his reluctant helpers.

It wasn't long before Felicity returned, but she was on her own. 'Reggie and Herbert can't come,' she said, quietly. 'Ben is unable to use a trowel, but sends his deepest apologies; and Theresa said she won't be able to help until later.'

Mr Tom pulled at his waistcoat with sharp tugs. He didn't like people to defy him, and he had his lists all ready to go! How on earth was he going to get the job done now?

'You still have us, ducks,' said an amused Annie. 'We can still plant seeds. You don't need a list with us to help you. Just tell us what to do.'

Mr Tom sighed, as he looked at his so called helpers: an old mushroom who could hardly hold a spade in those ridiculous hands of hers, a tiny mouse who kept tripping over her skirts, and a young girl who didn't appear terribly interested in the task at hand. To top it off he had two birds who didn't seem to understand the concept of digging a hole at all. What on earth were they doing with those beaks of theirs? But thank goodness the boy was here. At least he would be able to pull his weight.

With great patience, Mr Tom explained how deep

to dig the holes, how far apart they should be, and how each hole would need to be filled in once the seed was planted. He decided that Daisy and Felicity should dig the holes; Annie plant the seed; Maggie and Katie cover the holes; and Jack fill the watering can, and water the seedlings. Everything had to be done in order. He also explained that once it was dark they would keep planting by the moonlight.

'You're kidding!' squawked Maggie. 'Katie and I don't work very well by the moon. Can't we do some of the planting now and the rest tomorrow night?'

Mr Tom sighed. Why was everyone around him so ignorant? It was very tiresome. Taking a deep breath, he began to explain. 'Because the very best way to get beautiful vegetables,' said Mr Tom, waving his slim fingers around him and ignoring Maggie, 'is to plant by moonlight, and tomorrow night there will be no moon. Don't you folk know anything about gardening? Now, let's get to work.' With that Mr Tom huddled down into his chair, and pushed his hat further over his face, trying to keep out the cold air as much as possible. He decided that supervising was a thankless task.

Annie sighed. She didn't have the heart to tell Mr Tom that you didn't plant in the moonlight. You planted at certain phases of the moon: like when the moon 'waxed' or 'waned'. Annie had read it in a gardening book Mary had thrown out. It was a beautiful book. She looked across at the big cat resting comfortably, and just wished this whole planting thing would finish.

It was starting to get dark now and bitterly cold as the workers went about their business. Daisy and Felicity couldn't stop shaking; even their teeth were chattering. They heard the clock chime six bells and they all wondered when Mr Tom was going to realise what they were doing to his garden. Daisy just hoped it was soon; she couldn't remember the last time she felt so cold. She knew Jack was about to leave them and return to his warm house. He always left the garden by six o'clock. She wished that the folk had somewhere warm and cosy to stay in. She wished that more than anything in this whole world.

'Oh well,' said Jack, rubbing his cold hands together, 'I'm afraid I have to go now, everyone. I'm sure Mr Tom has got things in hand, and I look forward to seeing your completed vegetable garden tomorrow morning.'

Mr Tom jumped up with a start. 'Wait, young Jack. You can't leave yet. Who is going to cart the water? I can't possibly do it. I have the important task of supervising. You can't just up and leave when you feel like it.'

'I'm sorry, Mr Tom, I really have to go. My parents will come looking for me if I don't get home soon. With that, Jack winked at the others and made his way back to the house. He was chilled to the bone, and couldn't wait to get next to the warm fire, and eat some of his mother's delicious roast chicken. His heart went out to Daisy, Felicity and Annie as they stood there shivering, holding their trowels in their cold little hands.

It was terrible that they had to be out all night in these freezing temperatures. He really must find a suitable place for them to sleep during these winter nights, and soon.

Jack made his way through the maze of solar lights that his father had installed after the so-called burglary.

At least he could see, and they were sort of comforting. The folk couldn't stop talking about them when they were first put up.

'We love them,' squealed Daisy. 'We absolutely love them. They make us feel safe. Felicity, Ben and I play hide-and-seek amongst them. It's so much fun.' Jack smiled. It didn't take much to please Daisy. Just stick up a few solar lights and she was happy for weeks.

Shivering, Jack pulled his parka further over his ears. He wondered how Mr Tom was getting on. He just hoped that the plan would work. Surely the big cat would soon see how hopeless his helpers were, and take over. He loved taking over things. Jack chuckled. He could only imagine what Annie and Maggie were saying right now. Poor things: they must all be freezing.

Just as he was about to step onto the verandah, Jack had a terrible thought. What if the plan doesn't work? What if Daisy, Felicity and the rest of them are stuck in the vegetable patch all night? What if Mr Tom does nothing? But he needn't have worried, because just as he reached out for the door knob, he heard a strangled cry and a familiar loud deep voice penetrating the night air.

'Ladies! Ladies! Whatever have you done? My garden, ladies, my garden. Where is the order I told you about? This is not how it should be!'

Jack chuckled as he opened the back door and headed for the warmth of the kitchen. He could only imagine what was happening out in the garden.

Mr Tom was beside himself with anger. His so-called helpers had completely destroyed his garden. The holes weren't deep enough or far enough apart, and worst of all, Maggie and Katie had mixed up some of the seed when they were filling in the holes. He couldn't believe that his perfectly explained instructions had been so badly followed. Grabbing Daisy's trowel, he realised that if his garden was to be done properly he would have to do it himself!

'Now, ladies,' said Mr Tom, regaining some of his composure, 'I will do the first two rows and show you all exactly what needs to be done.' With that Mr Tom gave his waistcoat a tug, straightened his hat and bow tie and began to dig.

'I think this is our cue to leave, don't you, poppets?' said Annie, quietly to the rest of the helpers. Katie and Maggie nodded their heads in agreement and slowly made their way to their homes. Daisy and Felicity squeezed Annie's hands and tiptoed through the gate, leaving the moon to shine its glorious glow over the vegetable patch and a very industrious Mr Tom.

The next day was particularly bleak. Dark clouds hung gloomily over the garden, and a fine sprinkle of rain tried to penetrate the chilly air. Jack wrapped his scarf around his neck. Boy, was it cold! He wouldn't have bothered coming out this time of day, but he had promised the folk he would look at their vegetable patch. He didn't really expect too much, but he had promised.

Arriving at the garden gate, he peered around the corner, and was amazed to see that the vegetable patch was not only completed, but set out in beautifully organised rows. At the beginning of each was a tag indicating what seeds were in that particular row. They were even in alphabetical order. Jack couldn't believe his eyes. He spotted some torn bits of paper near the gate and grinned as he read the remains of Mr Tom's list. Poor old Mr Tom, he thought. It looked like the plan for the vegetable garden had worked perfectly.

Jack made his way around the side of the house to where Mr Tom lay stretched out on the chaise longue, his long feet hanging over the end. His waistcoat was undone and very dirty and his black bow tie lay limply around his neck. Mr Tom's arm hung over the side of the couch, and his precious hat sat precariously on the end of a bare branch of the bougainvillea.

The hat was covered in dirt, and Jack noticed a small tear. It looked like it had been carelessly flung there. How would Mr Tom ever recover from this? His appearance meant so much to him. Jack smiled, as he bent down and gently patted the top of the cat's mud splattered head. 'Now, Mr Tom,' said Jack, quietly. 'You really are a fine specimen of a cat, and you truly do belong in this garden.

17

Reggie has an Idea

As evening set in, Reggie stood huddled under the blue flower pot, grimacing as cold wet drops trickled down the back of his neck. It had rained all day and, although it had now stopped, remnants of the downpour were still dripping from the pansies onto the top of his red hat and running down his face onto his snow-white beard. It was most annoying. He could move of course, but he just couldn't be bothered. In fact, that's how he had been feeling for the past month. He seemed to have lost all his 'get up and go'. Everything was an effort.

Herbert thought that Mr Tom was the problem. 'He has a very strong personality,' the wombat said, that chilly evening, 'which has managed to squash your own strong personality. You are feeling left out and maybe just a little bit jealous of the attention Mr Tom gets from everyone.' Come to think of it, thought Herbert sadly, I always feel like that. I'm surrounded by people with strong personalities. Even Katie isn't afraid to speak her mind at times. Jack is the only one who truly understands me.

Reggie sighed. He knew Herbert was right. Ever since Mr Tom planted the vegetable patch on his own, everyone thought he was the best thing since sliced bread. It didn't matter what Reggie said these days; nobody seemed to take much notice.

It was a different story if Mr Tom suggested something; everybody listened with great interest, even Theresa. When Mr Tom announced recently that the broccoli and Brussels sprouts were ready to pick, he was given a standing ovation. Reggie couldn't believe it, particularly as Mr Tom had been in the garden for less than six months. As he said to Herbert one night, 'I was here years before that confounded cat, and now he seems to be taking over my role.'

Herbert nodded, 'And there really is only room for one overbearing, pompous and bossy person in this garden.'

'Yes,' said Reggie, stamping his foot, 'and I'm it!'

A cold wind blew across the garden, and Reggie shivered. Daisy was right; it really was far too cold to be out here all night. If only he could think of a comfortable dry spot where they could all keep warm over winter. He heard Herbert sneeze, and felt for the little wombat. He too, was struggling with the cold.

The only person who seemed to be coping was Mr Tom, but that wouldn't be too difficult, as Mr Tom curled up each evening on his chaise longue covered in an old rug that Jack had given him. The folk couldn't believe it. They had told Jack how cold they all were, but there didn't appear to be any rugs for them. Reggie shook his head, causing the rain drops to hasten their flow down his neck. 'Unbelievable', he mumbled crossly. 'Unbelievable.'

Standing there feeling sorry for himself, Reggie was unaware that Ben was standing quite close by, and nearly jumped out of his skin when he heard the dog's hearty voice.

'I say, chaps, have either of you ever felt so cold? It's quite bracing really, but it does prevent a chap from getting much sleep. Do either of you feel like a walk up to Theresa's slate block? We've decided to try and nut out some way we can all keep warm.'

Herbert shook his head, stating that his body was frozen solid and couldn't move anywhere, but he thanked Ben for his kind invitation, and wished him well in finding a solution.

'I'll come,' said Reggie, shaking the remaining drops from his hat. 'Anything is better than staying here.'

First they visited Mr Tom, but he was fast asleep. Reggie and Ben agreed it was best to leave him that way. They liked it when Mr Tom was asleep; things seemed to be less stressful.

The brisk walk to Theresa's was the best thing Reggie could have done. He could feel his feet now and his hands were slowly defrosting. By the time he and Ben arrived at the cubby house they were as warm as toast.

'Oh, Reggie, Ben,' squealed Daisy, 'it's so good to see you both. Come under the cubby with us; it's a little warmer.' She chuckled as she touched the top of Reggie's hat. 'Maybe you could make this your thinking cap, and find us a cosy home.'

Reggie smiled at Daisy's lame joke but he was secretly pleased at the warm welcome he had received. Maybe he should have a thinking cap. Imagine how popular he would be if he could find the folk a cosy home. What would Mr Tom do then, if Reggie was the smart one!

He thought about what was needed to make it the

perfect place to live in. It would have to be enclosed to keep out the cold and rain. It was important that it was spacious to accommodate everyone; and it needed to be safe. He still had nightmares about that black cat that nearly ate Katie. It was a frightening experience for everyone, not just Katie. Deep in thought, Reggie was unaware how crowded it was under the cubby until he bumped into Katie. Apart from Herbert and Mr Tom, everyone was here; even Theresa had joined them. It took a lot for her to leave her home.

'It's so much warmer under here,' said Theresa, rubbing her cold hands together. 'I can't understand why we haven't done this before. This is so much better than standing outside.'

'We agree,' said Maggie and Katie together, through quivering beaks. 'It makes things almost bearable.'

Reggie looked around him. Everyone did look a lot more comfortable, and most of the folk had stopped shaking. It was then that he had the most marvellous idea.

'Quiet. Quiet. Attention please,' said Reggie, returning to his normal bossy self. 'I have just thought of the perfect solution to our dilemma.'

There was silence as the folk eagerly turned to Reggie. He might even have something decent to say. Reggie had been known to have had the odd good idea.

'Nod your heads if you feel a lot more comfortable under this cubby.' They all nodded their heads. 'Well! If you feel happier and more comfortable under the cubby, imagine how you would all feel inside the cubby,' said Reggie, barely able to contain his excitement. 'It would be warm, it would keep out the cold and rain and, above all, we would feel safe. What do you all think?'

'I like that idea,' piped up Katie. 'I still lie awake waiting for that cat to return. It's quite harrowing, and sometimes I relive that whole terrible night.' She shuddered. 'Feeling safe sounds wonderful to me, absolutely wonderful.'

There was silence as the rest of the folk digested Reggie's idea. It really was a fantastic thought; but how was it going to work?

'Just a thought, old chap,' said Ben. 'How are we going to get inside the cubby without steps? It's okay for Maggie and Katie because they can fly, but what about the rest of us?'

Reggie hadn't thought about steps. 'I will talk to Jack about my idea, and hopefully he can think of a solution. Are there any other problems that you can think of?' Reggie was being nice to everyone and very willing to listen. He was just pleased to have their attention without Mr Tom constantly having his say.

The main complaints were about how dirty the cubby was and how ugly it looked, but everyone agreed that those things could be fixed.

'I think it's a wonderful idea,' cried out Daisy. 'Just imagine, we could paint the cubby pink and have green and blue polka dot curtains in the window. We might be able to have pots of brightly coloured geranium on the balcony and a bright blue door.' The more she thought about it, the more excited she became. 'Maybe, we could have lovely thick carpet on the floor like in the big house, and rugs to keep us warm. Oh! Felicity, isn't it exciting?'

'Settle down, pet,' said Annie, her soothing voice calming the exuberant little mouse. 'Reggie has to work it out with Jack, and until then we shouldn't get our hopes up. Also, poppet, I don't think pink is the right way to go, nor polka dot curtains, do you?' It never failed to amaze Annie how different Daisy and Felicity were from one another. Daisy was the excitable one: always after an adventure. Felicity on the other hand was a quiet reserved little girl who never really showed her feelings, yet the two of them were the best of friends and were always there for one another. Felicity said nothing about the cubby, but Annie was sure she was just as pleased as Daisy. It's so strange, thought Annie, how we are all so different.

Daisy frowned at Annie and reluctantly agreed that pink might be a bit much, but she was determined to have her say about the colour scheme when the time was right. It was so exciting to think that soon the folk might have their own winter home, and it was all thanks to Reggie. How amazing. It was rare for Reggie to get it right. Now what she had to do was work out how the cubby could be made to look better.

Daisy closed her eyes, oblivious to the chatter around her. Her head was just too full of colours, carpets and bright curtains, to listen. All she wanted to do was think, but she was so tired that all she could do was drift off into a peaceful happy sleep, only good thoughts filling her small head.

A hush descended over the garden as the clock chimed four bells. The only other sound to be heard was that of an old owl hooting to a friend through the cold still night. All the folk were now asleep, happy in the knowledge that their winter woes could soon be over. On his chaise longue, Mr Tom was snoring, blissfully unaware of Reggie's brilliant idea and his reinstatement to top spot in the garden. Only time would tell how Mr Tom would cope with that.

Jack walked towards the cubby, more than a little worried about facing the folk that evening. He hadn't been able to visit them all week because of the wet weather, and he still couldn't think of a good winter home for them. He dreaded looking into their hopeful faces and telling them that he still hadn't found somewhere comfortable for them to live. He had, however, managed to smuggle out some chocolate chip biscuits, the rest of Grandma's banana cake, apples and a flask of hot vegetable soup. Hopefully this would take away some of the pain they were feeling. At least it would take their minds off the cold.

As he approached the small gathering, he was surprised to hear a buzz of excited chattering. The folk certainly didn't seem upset tonight. Jack was again surprised when Theresa stepped forward from the middle of the group. She greeted him with a beautiful smile, her dark curls framing her pale face.

'Jack,' she said, 'Reggie has a wonderful proposal to put to you. We just hope you will agree with it. We are all so excited.'

Jack couldn't believe how happy Theresa looked. It certainly must be a good proposal. It was the first time he had seen her look happy for ages. She reminded him of his mother. Just lately they both seemed sad, and he didn't know how to help either of them.

'Ah! There you are, boy,' said Reggie, looking most commanding as he gazed down on everyone from Theresa's slate block. 'I have a very good idea to put to you regarding our winter home. We have all discussed it; well most of us have, and we are in agreement, but we need you to help us.' With that, Reggie launched into his idea, acknowledging all the good and bad points of his scheme. Finally, he drew breath, and waited for Jack's reaction.

Daisy was beside herself; it was all she could do to keep quiet. She had so many suggestions to put to Jack, and he was taking so long to answer Reggie. Also, thought Daisy, he had a box filled to the brim with food, and now she was starving. If only he would get on with it.

'I think it's a splendid idea, Reggie,' said Jack, patting the happy gnome on the head, 'and I'm sure my dad or Grandpa could make some steps. The only problem I can see is how Herbert and Ben are going to get up steps. We will also need to make them quite small so all your little legs can reach. It might be difficult explaining to my dad why I want smaller steps, but I will try. I'm sure we will be able to work all this out and you will get your home.

There was silence as the folk pondered this problem. They hadn't thought of poor Herbert and Ben, let alone their own small legs. In fact, they didn't realise they had short legs. Annie didn't much like her legs being referred to as little, but decided to keep quiet. The garden had never been so silent, as the folk racked their brains to try and solve the problem of the steps, when through the stillness a familiar voice could be heard from the back of the group.

'I have the solution, friends. I can solve the problem of the steps. I am here to help you all.'

Reggie groaned. He had forgotten about Mr Tom, and now the cat was going to ruin everything. Trust Mr Tom to be able to solve the problem of the steps. Just for once Reggie wanted to solve all the problems, but now Mr Tom was going to take over once again. Reggie couldn't stand it.

All heads turned as Mr Tom made his way to the front, gently pushing Reggie aside. Mr Tom didn't look quite as debonair since he had taken over the role of head gardener. His waistcoat was always smeared with bits of mud, and his hat never quite sat as nicely on his head since he had flung it into a bush. Daisy and Felicity liked him better since he became head gardener. Somehow he seemed more caring. He still had a presence however; one that made everyone sit up and listen and take notice, even Theresa.

'The way I see it, young Jack,' began Mr Tom, 'you need to build a ramp with safety rails. It should be strong enough for a human like yourself and also for a rotund wombat. A similar type of ramp was made for the children's miniature house in the last garden I was part of. It appeared to work very well and kept everyone happy. Just a thought, friends.' With that, Mr Tom tipped his hat, congratulated Reggie on his idea, and made his way cheerfully up the garden path to the vegetable patch.

Reggie watched the cat disappear. At least he had thought of the cubby house and not Mr Tom, but somehow Reggie felt he had been upstaged once again.

Jack felt an enormous sense of relief. He couldn't believe that he hadn't thought of the cubby before now. Good old Reggie. Now all he had to do was ask his father and grandfather to help him renovate it. Trying to explain why he wanted a ramp built instead of steps was going to be quite difficult. His father might not know how to make a ramp. The whole project was going to be very tricky.

Deep in thought, it took Jack a few minutes before he realised that something was tugging at his parka.

He looked down to see Felicity's sweet face gazing up at him, tears rolling down her freckly cheeks.

'Felicity, what on earth is the matter?' Jack bent down and gently wiped away her tears.

Felicity swallowed hard in an attempt to get her words out clearly. 'D..Daisy is m..making all the plans for the c..cubby, and she hasn't even asked m..me what I want.' Choking back her tears Felicity continued... 'I don't w..want p..polka dot curtains or a p..pink cubby. I w..want it to be g..green and cream, but Daisy never lets me have a say. She always gets her way, always. This t..time I w..want my s..say, too.'

Jack felt awful as the sobbing child wrapped her arms around him. He had to admit that Daisy did get her own way quite a lot, and he always seemed to give her more attention than Felicity. He didn't mean to, but Daisy was more outgoing. It didn't mean Jack loved Felicity any less. She was just harder to get to know than Daisy.

'You need to speak up for yourself, Felicity,' said Jack, kindly. 'You need to tell us when you are worried or unhappy or want to have a say in things, like decorating the cubby. You are an incredible little girl, and I promise that everyone will have a say about the cubby, especially you. Now,' he said, as a smile began to appear on Felicity's small face, 'I have something very special for you all and I would like you to help me. Do you think you could do that?'

Felicity nodded, wiping the last of her tears away and placing her cold hand into his warm one. Helping Jack give out the delicious hot soup and banana cake and biscuits made her feel the happiest she had been for a long time. It was usually Daisy who took over this sort of role but this time Jack had chosen her. For the first time since Jack's arrival in the garden Felicity felt very special, and very important.

It was a lovely hour that Jack spent with the folk. They all enjoyed their food, especially the soup. It was a bit of a laugh watching Maggie and Katie try to eat the soup. Even Mr Tom had a chuckle.

'Use a straw,' giggled Felicity. 'Please use a straw, Katie; otherwise I will laugh myself to death.' Surprisingly, the two birds took all the joking in good spirits; even Maggie.

'You should feel particularly proud,' Jack said, to Mr Tom. 'My mum made that soup from vegetables dug up in your vegetable patch. She praised me, but of course we all know who the real gardener is, don't we, Mr Tom?'

Mr Tom blushed. Although he always appeared very confident, even a cat like him liked to hear a bit of praise, particularly coming from the boy.

'All part of the service, young man,' said Mr Tom, over and over. 'All part of the service.' With that he tipped his hat, bid everyone a fond goodnight, and headed for his bed and much loved rug.

The rest of the group decided to spend some of the evening discussing the cubby and how it should look. There were arguments about colour schemes and furniture etc., but finally things were agreed upon.

The roof was going to be red; that was Felicity's suggestion. Theresa wanted the sides to be light brown wood paneling to blend in with the environment, and Reggie wanted the ramp to be light brown so that it wouldn't show the dirt. The balcony and posts were going to be cream, which was the colour Maggie and

Katie wanted, and finally, to add some 'oomph', it was decided that the door and curtains were going to be sky blue. Daisy clapped her hands with joy, as blue was the colour she wanted for the door. She rushed over and hugged Annie, as blue had been the mushroom's suggestion.

Theresa thought pots full of colourful flowers on the balcony would look beautiful. 'I would love to look after them,' said Theresa, happily. 'It would give me something to do. It would be a project of my very own. Look at the difference in Mr Tom since he has been in charge of the vegetable patch.'

Jack had to agree. Mr Tom was a far nicer cat since he had taken over the garden.

'I think flowers are a great idea, and I know my grandmother would enjoy planting them,' he said, enthusiastically. He was getting almost as excited as the folk, as more and more suggestions popped up.

Daisy asked Jack about carpet and rugs for inside the cubby. 'I want it to be warm and cosy like your house, Jack. I want it to be just like your house. I can't wait for it all to be done, I just can't wait,' squealed the excited little mouse.

Jack felt exhilarated as he ran back to the house. It had been a very successful evening. He had left the folk in a happy frame of mind, and that always made him feel good inside. Running into the warm family room, he was greeted by Maxine and Scarlet, eagerly wagging their tails. They seemed to sense his happiness and wanted to join in.

His father looked up from the evening paper and smiled as Jack breezed in. 'You look pleased with yourself, Son.' He couldn't get over the change in Jack these past six months. Gone was the morose sad little boy. In his place was a bright contented child who was excelling in his soccer, improving with his schoolwork and, most importantly, bringing home new friends. Alan sighed. It would be terrible if this was all taken away from Jack, but since Mary's hours at work had been cut by half, things were pretty tough. He dreaded the thought of selling the house, but they mightn't have a choice.

Mary had gone into a sort of depression at the thought of leaving the house and garden, and nothing he said was able to cheer her up. To make matters worse, her parents had only recently moved up to be close to them. He wished Mary would speak to her parents and ask them for help. It was all such a mess.

'Dad, can I talk to you about something?' said Jack. 'I have an idea that I want to run past you.'

Alan put down his paper and pushed his worrying thoughts to one side.

Taking his time, Jack continued. 'I want to do up the cubby and I want you and Grandpa to help me paint it and make a ramp to get to it. I could even get Sam and Brian to help. Poor Brian loves doing anything to get him out of the house. I really need some space of my own, Dad, and it would be perfect for my friends to come and visit. It could even be my birthday present. That's coming up soon. What do you think, Dad?'

Alan looked at his son's eager face. If they were going to sell the house, doing up the cubby would also improve the value of the property, but more importantly, thought Alan, it would be good to do something with Jack. It was strange though, that he wanted a ramp. 'Why do you want a ramp instead of steps?' inquired his father.

Jack swallowed. He knew his answer needed to be convincing. 'Because I want Maxine and Scarlet to be able to come up and keep me company when I'm on my own. They can't climb steps so it has to be a ramp. It would also be good for Grandma and Grandpa when they come to visit.'

It seemed ages before his father said anything, but finally he grinned and ruffled Jack's hair.

'Well, I can't argue with that reasoning, can I? I would love to help you renovate the cubby. It's about time we had a project that we can do together. I can't promise that I will be able to build a ramp, but we'll have a good go. In fact, tomorrow is Saturday, so we'll measure the cubby to see what size ramp we are going to need, and then go to the hardware store. I think it would be fun, and help get my mind off a few things.'

Jack couldn't believe his father was able to help him. Usually he was too busy, and things like renovating cubby houses came way down the list. 'I'll ring Grandpa,' said Jack, excitedly, 'and then I'll tell you what colours I want. Can I ring Sam and Brian and see if they want to help?'

Alan laughed; he had never seen his son so exuberant. 'You can ring the whole soccer side if that's what you want, but right now, get yourself ready for bed and we'll talk about it later.'

'By the way,' said Jack, wrestling with his pyjama top. 'Where's Mum? I haven't seen her since tea. Is she okay?' He could sense by his dad's body language that she wasn't okay, but as usual nothing was said to explain why his mum was acting so strangely.

'She's okay,' said his dad, rubbing his eyes. 'Just a bit tired. Work has been causing her some problems lately, but she's fine. Now, let's talk about your cubby.'

Jack smiled as he snuggled deep into his warm bed, making sure he didn't hit the dogs with his feet. He was feeling so happy right now except he was worried about his mother. Something was wrong with her. Surely Grandma and Grandpa could see she wasn't happy. If only his mother would tell him why she was so miserable: if only everything was like it used to be.

He stretched his hand out and gave the dogs a final pat while listening to their gentle breathing. They were in doggy dreamland. At last, thought Jack, at last everything is starting to fall into place. His mother was right. She told him that his life would get better, and now it had.

As he closed his eyes, and sleep started to take hold, he couldn't help wondering about his mother's life. Had her life got better? He couldn't tell, but for now, all he could think of was wood, paint, curtains and bits of carpet. All he wanted to do was sleep and dream about tomorrow and all the good things that it would bring.

18

Work Begins

Jack woke to a perfect winter's day. The watery sunshine was streaming through his bedroom window and specks of pale blue sky peeked between the grey clouds. Jack couldn't believe his luck. It had rained all week, but the day his dad and grandpa were going to start the cubby, the weather looked good. Jack's thoughts were interrupted when his father appeared quietly from behind the half closed door. He was dressed in working clothes and his dark hair hung untidily from under an old brown cap. Jack thought that his father looked strained and his normally bright eyes were dull and tired. In fact, he looked awful.

'Morning, Son', said his father, wearily, as he reached over and kissed the top of his curly head. 'I want you to get dressed in your old clothes and then go down and have some breakfast. Grandma is helping your mum make pancakes. After breakfast Grandma will show you what has to be done first, and Grandpa and I will pop up to the hardware store. Anything else you need besides paint?' Jack shook his head. 'Good,' said his father, making his way back to the door. 'Now get moving, Son. Your mum and grandmother are waiting for you.'

Jack had never eaten his breakfast so quickly. It

was delicious, but right now all he wanted to do was get started on the cubby. Nothing else mattered, not even pancakes. As soon as breakfast was over Jack made his way outside, laden with two buckets full to the brim with warm soapy water. His grandma said he would have to scrub down the cubby to get rid of the dirt before painting could begin. Jack shivered as a blast of cold air hit him. It was tiring carrying the buckets without spilling them, and when he finally reached the cubby he suddenly felt depressed. He didn't realise how awful it looked. It was so dirty and worn. How were they ever going to make it look good? To make matters worse, Brian and Sam couldn't come. Brian was going to soccer lessons, and Sam was going to a cousin's birthday party. Now it was left up to himself and Grandpa to get it clean. Jack didn't have much faith in Grandpa doing a very good job. He couldn't help grinning though, as he thought of some of the things Grandma had told him last night.

'Keep an eye on your grandpa, Jack. He's rather "slapdash" when he's doing jobs. Like the time he only painted half a tank and half a shed. The neighbours weren't very impressed; they had to look at the ugly half. Your grandfather doesn't believe in doing things he can't see. So make sure he does a proper job of your cubby.' Jack sighed. How was he going to do a good job of this?

He put down the buckets, grabbed the scrubbing brush, and began attacking the posts. Because it was such a boring job, his mind kept returning to his mother. She was very odd this morning. Apart from kissing him on the head, she hardly spoke. Something was definitely going on. He had this weird feeling that it was all to do with the statue, Rachel, who was smashed in the storm all those years ago. Surely, thought Jack in horror, surely, Rachel hadn't spoken to her. He couldn't imagine that she had. He felt sure Theresa would have known about it. No, it had to be something else, but what?

He wiped his brow with one of the old rags. He was getting hot. Even though the day was cold, the winter sun packed quite a punch, and he could feel himself breaking into a sweat. Imagine doing this in summer. Yuk! Jack chuckled to himself. He tried to imagine Mr Tom doing this. He would hate it. Mr Tom had told Jack once that hard work was not part of a cat's culture, so, as he was a fine example of the breed, he had tried to make sure the feline way of life continued in accordance with their work ethic.

Jack sighed. This cleaning thing was hard work. It would have been so much easier to just paint over the wood. Just like Grandpa would have done, but Grandma was different; everything had to be done properly.

Jack stood up and stretched. Every part of him hurt. He looked around, and out of the corner of his eye he noticed Reggie. He was standing next to Theresa. It was strange, thought Jack. Strange that he knew they were both watching him: that he knew they were real. He still found it so hard to believe. He couldn't help wondering what Reggie was doing here. Why wasn't he home?

He was deep in thought, when out of nowhere Maxine and Scarlet came racing towards him, barking excitedly. He heard the back door slam, followed by his dad and grandpa walking down the path. At last, thought Jack, at last the work could really begin.

The three workers spent a harmonious four hours working solidly on the cubby, only stopping now and then for a cool drink. Jack thought water had never tasted so good. He was very pleased with the progress they had made. He had managed to clean all the bits of the cubby he could reach, and Grandpa had even used the ladder to do the rest. When that was dry they would sand down the main parts and then begin painting. Jack did wonder how much of the cubby would get painted. He very much doubted that the back would get done.

His father was the complete opposite. Everything had to be done perfectly, which Jack was very happy about, as his father was building the ramp. Jack shuddered. Imagine if Grandpa was making it and left out some screws. It could be disastrous. He looked over at his dad who was patiently measuring bits of wood and then standing back and laying them side by side. He did this four or five times before he was satisfied. Yes! Jack was glad Grandpa was doing the painting; nothing could go wrong with that.

His father had managed to get some great wooden logs to make the ramp and reinforce the floor of the cubby. Jack was pleased that the cubby floor was getting reinforced, as he was a little worried that they wouldn't be strong enough for Mr Tom and Herbert. Imagine if poor old Herbert fell through the floor; he'd never set foot in the cubby again.

It seemed to take forever, but at last he and Grandpa had completed the washing and the sanding. His father had nearly finished putting the ramp together after hours of measuring and sawing. Hopefully they would all be able to take a break soon. Jack couldn't remember the last time he felt so tired. It was a happy 'tired', though, and when Jack and Grandpa stood back to look at the cubby, they were both pleasantly surprised to see how clean it was. It really looked quite smart.

'Well, Jack, it looks pretty good from here. I've been thinking about the painting,' said Grandpa, seriously, 'and we won't bother painting the back. I don't think there's much point really, with all those trees and things getting in the way. No one's going to see it, so it's a complete waste of time. Are you happy with that?'

Jack nodded, trying hard not to laugh. He knew Grandpa would find some excuse not to paint the back, and he wondered what Mr Tom would have to say about only half the house getting done. Everything had to be perfect for Mr Tom, and this was certainly not going to be perfect.

'Good,' said Grandpa. 'That's a relief. I didn't feel like fighting with all those trees and bushes. We'll start after lunch, which I hope,' said Grandpa, rubbing his stomach, 'comes very soon.'

Jack smiled as he thought of the folk. All this hard work was worth it if it meant them having somewhere good to live, but right now all he wanted was a rest and something to eat. He was starving.

Grandpa's loud voice interrupted his thoughts. 'Thank goodness, ladies. You've come to save us. This is jolly hard work.'

Jack looked up to see his grandma and mother making their way up to the cubby laden with food.

'Here we are, folks,' said Grandma, happily, 'we have ham and mustard sandwiches, chocolate cake, apples and pears. Your mum has the coffee and biscuits. It's time you all stopped for lunch.'

Jack sat there, enjoying the warmth of the sun on his face, and particularly enjoying the food. He could hear the others quietly talking as they sat there in the winter sunshine, eating and drinking and listening to the gentle hum of life in the garden. Although tired, everyone was chatty and excited about how the cubby was being transformed; even Mary. Today, thought Jack, as he looked around him, is one of those truly special days I will remember for the rest of my life.

It was freezing by the time they called it a day. Everyone was exhausted and glad to pack up, ready for an early night. Jack felt particularly sorry for Grandpa as he watched him slowly walk across the road. He had worked so hard and looked as if he could hardly move, but it had been worth it. Already the cubby looked great. With the same amount of effort put into the project tomorrow, Jack felt sure it could be completed by Sunday evening. Imagine what the folk must be thinking watching their little house take shape. He could almost hear Daisy's squeals of excitement. Jack let out a tired sigh. All he wanted to do was have something to eat, crash into a hot bath and then go straight to bed.

After dinner Jack reclined in the bath and let the hot water soak into every aching muscle in his body. As his mother would have said, 'this is bliss'. He couldn't stop thinking about the day. It had been fantastic: hard work, but fantastic. Working with his father and grandfather had been the best. He stretched out until his feet reached the end of the bath, and blew some foam into the air. He could stay here forever, but he felt so tired, so desperately tired. He tried to keep his eyes open, but they felt so heavy, so very heavy....

Alan and Mary looked down on their sleeping son. He was in his own bed now but they had found him nearly asleep in the bath. Alan chuckled.

'I have never known anyone to be dried, dressed in their pyjamas, and put into bed without so much as a murmur. Poor kid worked so hard today he must be exhausted.' He looked over at Mary and smiled. 'It will be okay you know; we will get through this. I'm here to talk about things whenever you want, and I'm here to listen if you need to talk about Rachel. Please Mary, we have to think of Jack,' pleaded Alan. 'We have to talk about it.'

Touching her husband's hand, Mary bent down and kissed her son's cheek.

'It's too late Alan,' said Mary, quietly. 'If you sell this house, I have not only lost my garden, but I have lost her forever. Nothing will ever be the same again.'

Alan shuddered as she left the room. He took one last look at his sleeping son, turned off the light and headed for the door. Despite Mary, it had been a wonderful day; working with Jack and Ted and listening to their endless chatter. Yes, smiled Alan, as he dragged his aching body to the bathroom and the welcoming bath. It had been a wonderful day, but he couldn't help thinking how glad he was that it was now over.

19

The Folk Settle In

'Wow, I can see the whole world,' cried Felicity, as she poked her head between the sky blue curtains that hung on each side of the cubby house window. She marvelled at the beauty of the distant hills as the sun began to sink behind them like a bright red ball. 'Oh Ben,' she cried, as the little dog padded his way up the wooden ramp, 'come quickly and have a look at the sun before it disappears. It's absolutely beautiful.'

Panting a little, Ben finally made it to the window, placing two furry paws over the edge just as the sun set. 'It certainly is magnificent,' he agreed, as he looked over the valley, which was still visible in the twilight. 'Look, old girl, I can even see the outline of the river winding its way in between those trees. I'd love to see the river properly and have a swim in it. Maggie and Katie told me that it is the best thing they have seen, especially in winter when it is full of water. Suddenly something else caught his attention. 'Felicity, can you see that wonderful-looking bird hovering over the valley. Look, Felicity, before it disappears; it's enormous,' cried Ben. 'I've never seen one like that before. It seems to be gliding. It's not flapping its wings at all. It's amazing!'

'That bird is a nasty piece of work,' said a raspy

voice behind them. Ben and Felicity jumped. They hadn't heard Maggie and her friend Katie come through the door. They certainly didn't see them come up the ramp.

'I'm sorry, dears,' said Katie, softly. 'We took the quick way up and flew here. It's a wonderful view, don't you think? Maggie and I never tire of it when we are out hunting for food.' Katie's eyes focused on the bird still circling over the valley. 'Maggie is right, you know; that bird is dangerous. It is looking for little furry creatures to catch and take back to its nest. You had better be careful, young Ben. That creature could mistake you for a mouse or something, and just swoop.'

Felicity shivered, her thoughts turning to Daisy. She was a little mouse, and Felicity couldn't bear it if that horrible bird swooped down and dragged her best friend off to its nest. As soon as Daisy was safely in the cubby she would warn her about that bird.

Daisy screamed with delight as she ran up and down the newly installed ramp. 'This is awesome,' she squealed, 'absolutely awesome. I can't believe we finally have our very own home. It's awesome.'

Mr Tom cringed as he watched the little mouse. If he heard that dreadful word 'awesome' one more time he would scream. As wonderful as young Jack was to the garden folk, he had introduced some diabolical words, which unfortunately the younger folk had cottoned onto and would repeat time and time again. It was most annoying. What on earth did 'cool' and 'wicked' mean, anyway? Dreadful words.

'I don't think the miniature house is particularly "awesome", young Daisy.' Mr Tom shuddered as he used that word. 'I don't consider a half painted house that looks absolutely ridiculous from the back, particularly "awesome," and I have made a point of telling young Jack just that.' Mr Tom's long fingers pointed towards the back fence, and every now and then he would tug at his waistcoat.

Daisy had not seen the cat this agitated since they messed up his vegetable garden.

'As I keep repeating,' said Mr Tom, his voice getting louder and louder, 'if a project is to be done properly there must be some sort of order, and I don't see much order here. I find it most unbecoming that I should be expected to live in a half completed house.'

'Well, I think it is very pretty from the front, and I really love the blue door and curtains,' said Felicity, from the cubby window. She knew how much work had gone into renovating the cubby and was anxious to defend Jack and his family. Along with Reggie and Theresa, Felicity had watched every single thing they did, and knew how tired they got. She had spent the whole time hiding behind a tree. She didn't want to be noticed; not like Reggie.

'Jack and his family worked very hard, Mr Tom, while you were snoozing, so I think you should be grateful for what they have done. Anyway, who cares what the back looks like? No one can see it because of all the trees and the stone wall behind it. Sometimes I think you are too fussy. I love it; so there!' She spoke with such conviction that even Mr Tom was forced to back down and keep any other negative thoughts about the cubby to himself.

'I love it too,' cried out Daisy. 'It's so cosy, and on cold nights it's going to be...'

Covering his ears with his large hands, Mr Tom muttered angrily to himself, 'Don't say that word. I can't stand to hear it one more time.'

'...awesome!' squealed the excitable little mouse.

Mr Tom could take no more. He muttered some sort of farewell and hurried as fast as he could down to the sanctuary of his beloved vegetable patch.

As darkness set in, the folk slowly made their way to their new home. There was an excited buzz in the air as the prospect of having a roof over their heads during these cold nights had finally sunk in.

Reggie was feeling particularly happy and couldn't wait to show Herbert. He was on a constant high, as everyone kept thanking him for his brilliant idea and telling him how wonderful he was. He was starting to feel his old self again.

As Maggie put it, 'Reggie has returned to being the obnoxious person we all know and love.'

One by one they walked up the ramp and stepped through the newly painted blue door to the most magical sight they had ever seen. Even Reggie was lost for words. Theresa had laid out the night's meal on a small plastic table that Jack had provided for them. It even had a blue and white check tablecloth. The light of a torch that Jack had attached in the ceiling gave a soft glow over the table, which was completely covered with food. It was the best food the folk had seen for a very long time.

Jack had smuggled out some banana cake, apricot muffins, chocolate biscuits and lemonade, as he thought their first night in the cubby should be a special one. Mr Tom had gathered some broccoli, turnips and Brussels sprouts from his garden and proudly placed them in between the muffins.

But Maggie and Katie had brought the best food of all: from the house four doors down. 'They seem to do barbecues any old time; even in winter,' said Maggie, happily, 'and fortunately for us, five delicious sausages had been left outside. Not so good for them of course,' she added, chuckling. The folk had never seen Maggie in such a good mood: never.

'It was stressful bringing them back here,' said Katie, quietly, 'but we managed. Theresa has even cut them up for everyone to enjoy. I'm so pleased.' With that said, the little bird unobtrusively went to sit down, never one for wanting to make a fuss.

Standing transfixed, the rest of the folk didn't know what to do next. Nobody wanted to look greedy. Even Theresa was hesitant as to how to start proceedings. There was just so much food. No one seemed game to make the first move. Until one little mouse, unable to wait any longer, jumped forward.

'I'm starving, everyone! Let's go for it ... two four, six, eight, bog in, don't wait,' cried Daisy. 'Don't be shy, take a plate!' With that she grabbed a paper plate and filled it with a muffin, a chocolate cake, two pieces of sausage, a piece of broccoli and a tiny Brussels sprout. Daisy had never felt happier. Whenever there was plenty of food she was in another world.

Annie was kindly handing out small cups of lemonade, as the folk collected their food and settled down around the walls of the room ready to enjoy their meal. Ben smiled as he looked around him. Nothing could be better than this: everyone together in a warm house with plenty of food in their stomachs.

He gave a contented sigh as he heard the sound of the late night owl, and wondered where that other bird he saw this evening went for the night. 'Back to his nest, I expect,' said Ben, quietly to himself. He gave a little shudder as he remembered what Katie had said about the bird. Not to worry though, thought Ben, closing his tired eyes. Nothing can go wrong now we are safe in our new house. Nothing can ever go wrong again.

Jack found it hard to get to sleep. All he could think about was the garden folk, and wishing he could be with them for their special dinner in their new house. He knew Theresa was going to do something special, so he had made sure they had plenty of food. It was becoming much harder to smuggle food to them lately, as his mother seemed to be getting a bit suspicious.

'You surely haven't eaten all that banana cake, Jack.' She had said, crossly on one occasion. 'I only cooked it two days ago. At this rate I will have to give you rations. I can't find the muffins either. What on earth are you doing eating all this food? If I didn't know better I'd think you were feeding an army.'

Jack couldn't help smiling. If his mother only knew where the food was really going. He told her that a new friend from soccer had come around with Sam and Brian while she was out, and they had had a party in the new cubby. He felt awful lying to his mother, but he didn't have a choice. His mother must never find out about the ornaments. As keeper of the golden key, he was the only human who could ever know the secrets of the garden. He must be very careful in the future. He must never give her reason to be suspicious again.

Snuggling further down into his warm bed, he wondered what the folk were doing. At least they were out of the cold, and had plenty to eat. Surely nothing could go wrong now, surely only good things would happen now. Jack yawned, as he listened to the clock chiming in the hall. He could feel his eyes begin to close as thoughts of the folk slowly disappeared into the night.

Before school, Jack quickly got all the folk out of the cubby and placed them back in their proper spots. Mr Tom thankfully hadn't stayed in the cubby overnight; he preferred his own bed and, from what Jack could make out, his own company. Jack called out a hurried 'goodbye' to everyone, and was off, leaving the folk to stand in the cold for the rest of the day.

They hated this time and counted down the hours until they were properly active again. They envied Theresa her view from the top of the garden. She was the only one who still had an interesting time as, from her pedestal, she could look at anything in the valley that took her fancy.

Daisy sat shivering. She couldn't help thinking how lucky Theresa was to be able to see so much. It must help the day go quickly, thought the mouse; it must be exciting looking at different things. Theresa always has something new and interesting to tell us over tea. One day, I'm going to stand on a pedestal, just like Theresa, then maybe I'll see exciting things and my days won't be so long and so boring. She looked up enviously at the girl staring into the distance.

But if Daisy only knew what Theresa was looking at so intently! If she only knew the danger that existed high above the garden. Because Theresa did, she was staring right at it. High above her, gliding ominously across the late afternoon sky, was a large bird. She couldn't take her eyes off it. It looked so powerful and so beautiful, and yet, she sensed something evil. Something about the creature made her uneasy. Something about the bird made her feel afraid. Then suddenly, it swooped down into the valley below, and was gone. Theresa shivered and closed her eyes. She hoped she would never see the bird again, but somehow she knew she would. She just knew.

20

Ben's Night of Terror

The evening routine began with Jack returning some of the folk to the cubby. He always helped Annie and Herbert, as it took them so long to get there, and occasionally he would carry the girls as a special treat. They loved it and would squeal with delight as he swung them high up in the air. Tonight, Jack was even more excited than usual, because the next day he was going to Sam's house for his birthday and would be staying there overnight.

It would be his first time away from home and he was feeling a little nervous. He had never slept in someone else's room before, and he was a little bit worried about Sam's mother. His friend was always going on about how strict she was. So when Jack suggested they had a midnight feast, Sam went very quiet. He didn't look at all comfortable with Jack's suggestion.

'I don't know, Jack,' said his friend, slowly. 'Ever since I lost all that weight, Mum almost keeps the cupboard under lock and key. She knows every single bit of junk food in there. Even my sister isn't game to take anything. She's even got a written record of what's in there. I tell you Jack, she's obsessed. I think it's too risky.' But Jack persisted. It was his first sleepover, and he wanted to make the most of it.

'Well, I could bring the food. I could bring chips, chocolate and some biscuits. Then your mum would be none the wiser. It will be fun. Come on Sam. Please say yes.'

'What if I put on heaps of weight?' said Sam, reluctantly. 'Mum still weighs me you know. But,' he conceded, 'it would be fun, and I still love chips and chocolate. Okay! We'll do it.'

So a plan was hatched. Jack couldn't wait. Imagine talking to someone all night. He'd never done that. Sometimes he really wished he had a brother or a sister, and could do crazy things like that with them; stuff that he couldn't do on his own. Although, once he told Brian how he wished he had a brother, and was soon set straight. Brian hated having brothers and sisters. He had four brothers and one sister.

'You're so lucky, Crane,' said Brian, miserably, one Thursday morning. 'You're so lucky to be an only child. I didn't even have any breakfast today. My pain of a sister had the last piece of toast, and my youngest brother had the last bit of cereal. All my old lady said, was "stop whining and get ready for school". I tell you Crane, I sometimes think my parents couldn't care less about my welfare, and now, I'm starving!'

Looking at Brian's large frame, Jack didn't think he was exactly fading away, but he and Sam did wonder what sort of home life he had. Needless to say, they shared their food with him at recess. Mainly, thought Jack, to prevent Brian from taking some poor year-two's food. Brian still had a slight tendency to intimidate. He still didn't quite get it.

Jack's only concern now was telling the folk. They weren't very good with change, particularly Maggie and

Reggie, and didn't mind telling him how they felt.

'Who's going to take us out of the cubby in the morning if you're not here?' complained Reggie, once Jack had told them the news. 'We'll freeze if we're outside all night, absolutely freeze. It's not fair, young Jack. I think you should take our needs into consideration.'

'That's enough, Reggie,' said Theresa, firmly. 'The boy deserves some fun, and we shouldn't be so selfish. One night won't kill us. Anyway, if you don't want to freeze, stay in the cubby until Jack gets home the next day.'

'I agree,' said Herbert. 'The boy needs to enjoy himself occasionally. I say, go out and have some fun my boy, and if the others were here, I'm sure they'd agree; even Maggie.'

'Thanks, Herbert,' said Jack, giving the wombat a hug. 'I'll let you personally tell the others, especially Maggie.'

Oblivious to what was happening outside, Daisy, Felicity and Annie stood inside the cubby watching the sunset through the large window.

'It certainly is beautiful, pets,' said Annie, screwing up her eyes so that she could see as much as possible. Sometimes she wished she could wear glasses like Jack, and then she would be able to see everything. Maybe she could ask Jack for glasses when she allowed him to paint her. She was still undecided about that; the boy handling her all the time. It didn't seem proper. Glasses, on the other hand, would certainly solve her squinting problem. Right now, though, there was something that Annie had no trouble seeing, and it made her feel very uncomfortable.

'It's so strange seeing things beyond our garden,' continued Annie, as she watched the creature high in the sky. 'I can even see a big bird heading this way. Goodness me! It's getting very close though, pets; I don't think I like it. I don't like it at all.'

At that moment Ben was heading up the garden path on his evening stroll. He was still quite a distance from the cubby, and taking his time to get there, when, glancing up, he noticed Felicity, Daisy and Annie all standing at the window, pointing at the sky, and Jack down below waving his arms. Just for a second Ben wondered what they were all doing: but just for a second. He quickly decided it was none of his business, and anyway, he was far more interested in what his walk had to offer.

Ben loved this time of night. He would sniff nearly every bush that he came to, breathing in all the different smells. He never got the same smell twice. He didn't like to be hurried either, as one bush could contain a number of aromas, and from these he knew if Maxine and Scarlet had been there during the day. It was as if they had left him their own personal message. Sometimes it took nearly an hour to complete this task. He just loved it.

The folk knew not to interrupt Ben during this time, so he wondered why Daisy, Felicity and Annie were all now waving madly at him from the cubby, and yelling out his name. Felicity seemed especially enthusiastic: he had never seen her jump so high, and as for Jack, he was now screaming at top note, 'Run! Run! Run!' Everyone seemed very excited, but why? Ben frowned. There wasn't a meeting to attend. He wasn't late for anything. Now Theresa had jumped from her pedestal and, holding up her skirts, was running in his direction. What on earth was going on!

Ben sniffed. The air smelt strange. It sort of smelt like Katie, but stronger, and why did he suddenly feel so cold? He listened, but he couldn't hear a sound. Not even his friends. It was too quiet, thought Ben. It was a scary sort of quiet. He needed to get back to the cubby. He didn't feel safe.

Then from out of nowhere Ben felt a cold rush of air accompanied by a loud whooshing sound. It was so loud it hurt his ears. He had never heard or felt anything like it. It was coming from above him. He looked up. There, hovering over him, was the largest bird he had ever seen. It was that bird. Ben couldn't believe it. It was the same bird he had seen the other night. He felt sick. This monster was about to take him, just like Maggie said, and nobody, not even Jack, could help him now.

He stood transfixed as the massive wings loomed over him, blocking out everything else. His heart was thumping against his chest as long sharp claws bore down in the direction of his small furry body. He could hear the folk screaming to him to run but his legs felt like lead; he just couldn't move. No matter how hard he tried, he just couldn't move.

He was in a state of shock as the claws got closer and closer. Ben stared into the cold yellow eyes, wincing in pain as the huge talons grabbed his neck in a vice-like grip. It left Ben helpless; hot burning sensations rushing through his limp body. He felt light-headed; everything seemed to be spinning. All he could do was watch in terror as he became captive to this creature. His garden swirled around him; the folk were floating in all directions; it was such a blur that it seemed unreal.

Suddenly, there was another huge rush of wind and burst of speed as the bird began to soar. Ben's beautiful garden disappeared out of sight below, as the bird's powerful wings pushed them higher and higher, leaving the only world he knew far behind him.

The garden was silent. Nobody moved. Nobody spoke. All that could be heard was quiet sobbing as the folk tried to take in what had just happened. Felicity could hardly breathe, she was so distraught. Jack just sat there; head in his hands.

'I don't understand,' said Theresa, finally. 'What kind of bird was that? What kind of bird would take one of us? And why Ben? Why Ben, Jack? Why?'

Jack looked up. His eyes were red, and tears ran down his pale face. 'It was an eagle, Theresa, and I don't know why it took Ben. I really don't know.' He wanted to tell them that it would be all right, and he would find Ben, but he didn't have a clue where to start looking. The eagle could have taken him anywhere. The only way that Ben could survive was if he turned to stone before the eagle reached its nest, but then he would probably drop him and Ben would be smashed to bits. Jack swallowed hard. He had never felt so helpless and so empty in his whole life.

Ben didn't know whether it was the freezing wind rushing around his face keeping him alert or his desperate need to stay alive, but what he did know was that this bird was never going to get him to its nest; never! He realised that he had to act, and fast. The trouble was he couldn't move because the talons were embedded so tightly into his neck, but he did have one thing in his favour: two rows of sharp strong teeth. The bird's right talon was very close. All he had to do was stretch a couple of centimetres above the bird's claw to the tender part of its leg.

Ben tried to move his neck, but it was impossible, the bird's grip was just so tight. His front legs could just reach the creature. Maybe if he hit it hard enough, the bird would let him go. With all his strength he stretched his sturdy legs as far as they could go, until he felt the soft underbelly of the eagle. Pushing as hard as he could, he kept hitting the bird's stomach; hoping against hope that something would happen.

Finally, the bird's grip loosened slightly, allowing Ben to move his head that bit closer. Ben had never bitten anyone before and hated the thought of doing it now, but he had to; his life depended on it. He swallowed hard as he looked across at the bird's huge leg. He had no choice; he had to hurt the creature if it meant saving his own life. With a deep sigh, he opened his mouth as wide as he could, reached over and sank his strong teeth into the bird's soft flesh.

With an almighty screech the eagle released its prey, blood pouring from the wound. Ben felt a heavy thud as the angry bird pushed him away, leaving him to face the elements. The cold wind lashed around him as he began to fall. It was a strange sensation; like floating in a big black room, with nothing but silence all around him. Ben found it exhilarating in a scary sort of way. He could feel his heart pounding, as he fell through the black emptiness. There was no one to help him; no one to comfort him. There was absolutely nothing.

He had escaped, but what now? How could he possibly survive once he hit the ground? Ben closed his eyes, and thought about his short life. He thought about his wonderful friends that he was leaving behind, and he thought about his home. The home he would never see again. He took a deep breath, sniffed the cold moist air, and waited; waited for the inevitable.

Jack had never felt so distressed. The emptiness was unbearable. His heart ached. The folk had been in a state of shock when he left, and he could think of nothing to say to them that was the least bit positive. Through her loud sobs Daisy pleaded for Jack to go and find Ben.

'Please Jack,' begged Daisy, 'please go and find Ben. We love him and we can't live without him. Jack, please.' The mouse was inconsolable, but Ben was gone; they had seen him taken by the eagle, so what could he possibly say or do to make them feel better. It was hopeless.

Thankfully, Mr Tom had rallied, and was doing his best to get some food into everyone, but it was a lost cause. Even Daisy refused to eat anything. He had never seen Daisy and Felicity so upset. He wondered if they would ever get over this tragedy. He knew he wouldn't; ever.

Walking back to the house, Jack's shock suddenly turned to anger. How could this happen? Why couldn't he save Ben? Why? He hated himself for not doing more, and he hated that eagle with a vengeance, for taking his best friend. Daisy was right. He had to do something: anything. What was the point of being holder of the golden key if he couldn't protect them. What did that key actually do anyway? He knew he needed the key to be part of the folk's lives, but what else was it for? As far as he could see it just sat in his drawer doing nothing. The key didn't save Katie from the cat. He and the dogs did, and it certainly hadn't helped him save Ben. Jack kicked the ground angrily. As far as he could tell nothing would get Ben back, not even the golden key.

Jack took a deep breath and looked up to see his mother preparing tea. The bright light in the kitchen streamed through the window onto the lawn. It wouldn't be too long before darkness set in. Without giving it a second thought, Jack grabbed his bike, put on his beanie, and made his way out the side gate. The wheels of his bike were making a horrible sound. They badly needed oiling. He wished Sam was with him. He hated this. He hated having this secret.

And he couldn't help feeling guilty as he raced carelessly down the hill towards the river. He knew his mother would be furious if she knew what he was doing, but right now, nothing else mattered. He didn't care about anything, except finding Ben.

He hesitated before crossing the road. There was a steady stream of traffic, making it hard to cross. Light rain had begun to fall and the car lights reflecting on the wet roads made everything look sinister. Jack shivered, as he pushed his bike quickly to the other side while there was a break in the traffic. He made his way to where the bike track started. It ran alongside the river and went all the way into the village, but tonight he would be lucky to get far at all. It would be dark very soon.

Gingerly, Jack got onto his bike and made his way down the track. It felt eerie, and everything looked so different. He could only just make out the trees along the bank, and the river looked murky and cold. He could hear the gentle lapping of the water, and the occasional splash of a fish, but apart from that it was quiet; just the annoying sound of his bike wheels squeaking. The whole thing gave him the creeps. He half expected some sort of river monster to leap out and grab him, nearly falling off his bike in fright when an owl hooted in the tree above him. He had never felt so scared in his life.

Jack stopped suddenly. He could have sworn he heard a dog whimpering. It sounded so close, but it couldn't be. It just couldn't. He must be imagining things. He just wanted it to be Ben so badly, but deep down Jack knew he was gone. The little dog was gone forever.

Shining the light from his bike down onto the river, Jack tried desperately to see, but it was hopeless; he could barely recognise anything, and the continual squeaking of the wheels of his bike was driving him mad. There was nothing for it; he would have to turn back. The whole thing had been a complete waste of time. Ben was never coming back. Never!

Slowly he made his way back to the entrance. Somewhere along the river he could hear a clock chiming. Shivering, he counted six chimes. A dog could be heard howling into the night, as the rain got heavier and heavier. Jack pulled his beanie further over his ears, put his feet on the pedals, and headed for home.

Jack's parents were very aware that something major had upset their son. Nothing was said, as the three of them sat around the kitchen table. They didn't even mention the fact that it was after six thirty before he came inside, or the fact that he looked almost blue with cold and was soaking wet. His shoes and pants were covered in mud, and he looked as if he had been crying. Nothing was said because he was home safe, and they had learnt that asking questions was usually unrewarding. Jack would tell them eventually. As hard as it was, they would just have to wait.

Mary watched her son pushing his food around his plate. Her heart ached for him, but she was so caught up in her own misery she couldn't think of anything to say. What sort of mother was she? This was her son, and she just sat there.

Finally, his father broke the silence. 'Are you all right, Son, or is there something you want to tell us? Remember the pact we made; to tell each other any problems we may have. I told you how worried I was about meeting my new boss. Now I think it is your turn to tell me what is troubling you.'

Jack kept staring at his plate, unable to look his father in the eye. How could they possibly understand his distress at losing a stone dog? How could they possibly understand that he had spent the last half-hour looking for him in the dark? It would be all they could do not to laugh at him. He looked across the table at his mother. Maybe she would understand. After all, his mother admitted to being upset about losing the statue Rachel. Still, thought Jack, she never volunteered any information about why she was upset or who Rachel was named after, so why should he tell them anything. Anyway, his mum acted as if she couldn't care less about him lately, so why should he bother.

'Does this pact include Mum?' grumbled Jack, turning his attention to his father. 'She's been unhappy lately, but she hasn't bothered to tell me why. She hasn't been the same since the storm, in fact it's like I don't even exist any more, so why should I tell you anything; why?'

Mary was shocked. Jack was right. Since the storm she had gone into a deep depression. It had brought back all those terrible memories, but she never ever meant it to affect her relationship with her son. She loved him so much. It was just that everything had got on top of her. Her hours at work had been cut to almost nothing, and worse still, Alan was talking about having to sell the house. It was all too much, and she knew she wasn't coping. She hated it. Right now she felt like she was at the bottom of a very dark hole.

'This isn't about your mother, Jack,' said his father, firmly, 'and there's no need to use that tone. We are worried about you, both of us. We want to know what has made you so miserable.'

Jack took a deep breath. How would they ever understand what he was about to tell them? 'Promise you won't laugh at me.' He looked from one parent to the other. 'You know my stone dog, the one we call Ben? Well,' said Jack, trying to hold back the emotion, 'well, he's been stolen, and I might never see him again. I love him so much, and now he's gone.' Jack couldn't hold it in any longer. Large tears ran down his face. 'I want you to find him, Dad; I want my dog back.'

21

The Rescue

Ben woke up cold and sore. His body ached from head to foot, and he felt blood dripping from the wound on his neck where the bird had taken him. He was alive, but where was he? He tentatively moved his front paws. The right one was very painful, and he yelped as it touched something cold and wet. As he listened he could hear gentle lapping. It was the same sound that Maxine and Scarlet made when they drank from their water bowls. Maybe he had landed in someone's pond, or in a lake, or maybe even in the river. Ben lifted his head as high as he could and sniffed the air, but there was nothing that smelt familiar: absolutely nothing. He tried to move, but his lower body was wedged between two hard stick-like things, and the front of him was in freezing water. It felt horrible.

He could hear strange sounds all around him, some loud, some soft, and there was a croaking noise. That did sound familiar. Ben screwed up his eyes tight to stop himself from crying. Where was he? He was exhausted and panting uncontrollably. He felt frightened in this strange place.

It was then he heard it. A different sound, but somehow familiar. Was it a bad sound? He couldn't remember. It was a sort of squeaking sound, and was getting louder and louder. Ben kept perfectly still just in case it was a bad sound, but he just knew he had heard it before. Maybe it was in the garden. He couldn't remember.

Ben strained his eyes. He could just make out the faintest of lights through the misty rain. It looked like this squeaking thing was gliding along the bank. It gave him the creeps. He anxiously watched the light moving up and down the bank, until finally the strange squeaking thing disappeared through the mist, and he was once again left on his own.

He bent down and licked his sore paw. He had never felt so alone in his whole life. He wanted Theresa. He wanted Jack, but more than anything else he wanted his home. The miserable dog lifted his face to the night sky, the watery moon just peeking out from behind the trees. He opened his mouth as wide as he could and let out a mournful howl as the sound of a distant clock rang through the dark cold night. It was six o'clock.

'Hurry up Grace,' said Ted, the next morning. 'We're only going for a walk to the river, not climbing Mount Everest. What on earth are you doing?'

Grace sighed. She hated going out in the cold and would much rather stay by the warm fire. Ted had this thing about a daily walk, regardless of the weather, and expected her to enjoy it as much as he did. Maybe she should see if Jack and the dogs would like to come before he left for Sam's house. She was pleased he was staying at Sam's place overnight. It would take his mind off Ben. The poor boy had been inconsolable last night, after the little dog had been stolen. Mary was terribly upset and had told Grace that Jack had reacted as badly as if it was Maxine or Scarlet that had been stolen.

'He's only a stone dog, Mum,' said Mary, almost in tears. 'Jack treats those ornaments as if they are real. I don't know what to do. I even saw him reading to the wombat one night, and last night I saw him put all the smaller ornaments in the cubby. He told me he was keeping them safe. What am I going to do?'

As Grace put on her shabby old walking coat, she shook her head sadly. When she reminded her daughter at how upset she had been when the ornament she loved had been broken, the subject was quickly changed. Rachel was never to be spoken of, but Grace did feel that Jack was lonely. The ornaments had become his friends. Just like her dolls had when she was a child. Anyway, after her walk she'd make the poor child some chocolate cakes. That always brightened his spirits.

With that in mind she grabbed her hat, then her scarf, and finally a large black umbrella. 'All this trouble,' she moaned, 'just to freeze to death.'

But the walk along the river was surprisingly enjoyable. Grace realised how much she needed to get out and clear her head. Things had been so tense lately. She knew Mary was depressed, but she wouldn't talk about it. She never talked about things that worried her. The whole situation was so upsetting, and there was absolutely nothing she could do.

Her mind was suddenly brought back to the present, as something sharp touched her leg. 'Oh! Scarlet, you clever girl. You've brought me a present.'

Grandma gently removed the stick, picked up the dog, and kissed the black woolly head. 'You really are a tonic, Scarlet. Now, when I put you down, go and show Grandpa.' Grace had to laugh as the little dog dragged the stick along the path. She was trying desperately to get to Grandpa before her big sister did. Maxine was on her way to Ted with an equally big stick. Grace smiled. They were dear little things.

'I must admit,' said Ted, as he removed the stick from Maxine's mouth, 'I can't really understand the boy's fixation with these ornaments. First it was Daisy and now the little dog. I thought things were going well for him. He's even going to a birthday party this morning and staying over. I didn't think he needed to rely on make-believe objects anymore.'

Grace wrapped her coat tighter as a blast of wind caught her off guard. 'Things are better for him. He's just a sensitive little boy, and a lot of things are going on in that household at the moment. The boy's not stupid. He knows things aren't right. I just wish they would sort themselves out. Anyway, if the dog's not found, we'll buy him another stone one for his birthday; that's only a month away.' She looked at Ted. 'He'll be eleven. Can you believe it? Our little boy will be eleven.'

The rest of the walk along the river bank was in silence, as both Ted and Grace admired the beautiful houses that could be seen through the bare trees. Winter was the only time the houses were visible. Grace loved the river when it had been swollen by winter rains. When she and Ted used to come up and visit she always loved to take a walk along the river. She found it soothing.

The dogs were happily sniffing along the river bank, tails up and heads down, enjoying the different smells. It was so new and exciting.

All of a sudden they both stopped, frozen solid in their tracks. Grace watched them, intrigued by their behaviour. The two animals just sat there. They didn't move a muscle. They didn't make a sound. It made her uneasy. She felt the need to race over and comfort them, they were acting so strangely, but instead, she quietly walked over to where they were sitting, and put on their leads. The last thing she wanted was for the dogs to take off. If she lost Maxine and Scarlet, it didn't bear thinking about. Jack would never forgive her.

Grace held on tight to their leads, as she followed their gaze to the other side of the river. All she could see were two large tree branches sticking out from the bank and lying partly submerged in the water, but the dogs had definitely seen something else, as they continued to stare, still not making a sound. That in itself was unusual, thought Grace. Maxine and Scarlet were so loud for such small dogs, but today was different, today they weren't making a sound.

She tried to drag them away, anxious to get moving, but they both dug their claws into the side of the bank, refusing to budge. Then, through the quiet, Scarlet let out a high-pitched wail. It was chilling. Grace had never heard anything like it. She could feel Maxine shaking, the dog's sturdy body pushing closer into her. It was extraordinary. What had they seen? What was making them act this way? She moved as close as possible to the river's edge, but still couldn't see anything. It was frustrating.

'Well! I don't believe it,' yelled a voice, so loud that

it almost caused her to lose her footing. 'I don't believe what I'm seeing,' continued the voice. 'Have a look Grace. Have a look at what's wedged between those branches.' The next minute Ted was standing alongside her, pointing to something. 'Can't you see it? It's absolutely unbelievable. You'll have to get Alan. I can't do this on my own. I'll stay here and guard it, but you must go back and get Alan.'

Alan sighed as he stood in the shower, the warm water bringing his frozen body back to life. It had taken some effort, but he and his neighbour had finally managed to rescue the stone dog from the river without falling in themselves. It was lucky that he was at home when Grace had arrived at the house to get help. It was also fortunate that his neighbour, Bill, owned a long piece of rope that they wrapped tightly around Alan's waist as he gingerly made his way into the freezing river to retrieve the forlorn creature.

Alan had felt quite foolish dragging Bill out to rescue a stone dog, but once he had explained the circumstances, Bill was more than happy to help, and Ted was more than happy to fix it. As for Grace, chuckled Alan, she hated walking up and down the hill at the best of times. After doing it four times today, she informed Ted he could go on his walks by himself. She wasn't going near that hill ever again!

Once back in the warmth of his house, Ted surveyed the little dog. It had certainly taken a battering. There were deep scratch marks on the side of its neck and one of the front paws had nearly broken off. The poor little thing was covered in leaves and mud and one of its ears hung limply.

'Oh well,' said Ted, brushing the dirt off the top of the dog's head, 'a good clean and touch up will help you, little fella, and before you know it you'll be back with young Jack, guarding the garden.' Ted smiled. It did have a cute face. Its brown eyes were so big and round he could swear it was looking at him. He even thought he detected a smile as he fixed the dog's poor little ear. If he used his imagination he could almost believe it was real. Ted shook his head. 'I'm getting as bad as my grandson. Of course it's not real.'

Gently patting the dog on the head, he placed it carefully on top of the cupboard to dry. He glanced out of his kitchen window just as the sun was setting over the misty hills. Ted loved this view. He never tired of it.

Sighing, he turned off the light and said a final goodnight to the small dog. If he had gone a little closer though, he would have noticed that the big brown eyes were full of grateful tears and the long fluffy tail was wagging so hard that he would have heard it banging against the cupboard. If Ted had only known. He was that close to discovering Jack's secret.

22

The Reunion

Jack watched his father reading the evening newspaper. He seemed particularly interested in the property section. He'd been reading it for ages.

'Why are you looking at the houses for sale?' said Jack, grumpily. He couldn't really be bothered asking, but it was odd.

'No reason,' said his dad, looking over the top of the paper. 'I'm just filling in time until tea. Which reminds me, don't forget that you are going to Grandma's and Grandpa's for tea. They're looking forward to hearing about your sleep-over. How was it, anyway? You haven't told us a thing.'

'Fine,' mumbled Jack, as he listened to the clattering of plates in the kitchen. He had enjoyed Sam's party, but he had no desire to talk about it, especially to his parents. 'Anyway,' continued Jack, 'why do I have to go over to Grandma's and Grandpa's tonight? They are having tea so early, and I don't even feel hungry. Why can't I stay here? I don't feel like going. In fact I don't feel like doing anything. It's not fair.'

Alan dropped his paper onto the floor, and looked at his son. 'When do you think you will lose this attitude, Jack? Both your mother and I are sorry that your dog was stolen, but it's not the end of the world. We'll get you another one. You have to learn that things don't always go the way you want. That's called "life". And, in answer to your question, you are going over to see your grandparents because they want to see you. And maybe, just maybe, they can help you better than we can.'

Alan sighed as he picked up the paper. Trying to communicate with Jack was so difficult. He would never speak about things that worried him. He reminded him so much of Mary. If she was upset about anything, usually Alan had to guess what it was. She never volunteered any information, and could sit for hours without speaking.

For example, she had never spoken of her early life in England. She was Jack's age when her family had emigrated to Australia, and for some reason she had never wanted to discuss it, and she certainly never wanted to discuss Rachel, even if he did. It didn't seem to matter what he wanted, and Jack was exactly the same.

Jack looked down at the brightly coloured rug. He was a bit stunned. His father had never got quite that cross with him before. He kept staring at the rug. Funny how he'd never noticed those large red and orange circles before. It was a cheerful rug, and the flames from the fire seemed to dance all over it. He didn't want to move; he just wanted to sit there looking at the circles. He hadn't even been out in the garden, and felt no desire to do so. All the folk were so sad that he felt they needed some time alone to come to terms with their loss.

Jack sighed. His father was right, he had been a pain these last few days, but his parents didn't understand his loss. How could they?

Daisy sat huddled in the corner of the cubby wrapped in one of the old blankets Jack had provided for their home. She shivered as a sharp wind blew through the window. She had never felt this sad and lonely before, and try as she might, could not stop the tears that rolled down her cheeks. It was the first time she had ever lost a friend, and she never wanted to feel this empty again. Why was life so cruel? She loved Ben so much. He had always been there for her, like in the storm, and when Katie nearly got taken by the cat. It was Ben who ran down to the back of the garden to try and scare it off, even though the cat was bigger than him. It was Ben who helped her with Herbert during the storm, and it was Ben who always made her laugh. How was she ever going to survive without him?

Felicity stood silently on Theresa's slate block, staring out to the horizon. The last time she had done that she saw the horrible bird take Ben and fly off towards the distant hills. She could feel the tears welling up in her eyes. She just couldn't stop crying. It was awful. She watched the hills, night after night, hoping that something would happen, but it never did. Apart from the odd croaking crow it had remained the same, quiet and still. Perhaps if she kept looking hard enough, just maybe she would see the bird bringing Ben back. What if the creature realised its mistake? What if it realised just in time that it didn't have a mouse, but some other furry creature? Maybe it would bring Ben home. What if Ben could somehow escape and find his way back to them? There were so many questions, but after three days there was still no Ben. 'Oh! Where are you Ben?

Please come back to us, please,' sobbed the little girl, wishing with all her heart that she could have done more to save her friend on that fateful day.

Theresa and Annie watched on, trying to be strong for everyone, but it was very hard. All they could do was stay positive, and be there if anyone needed to talk; that was all they could do.

Jack walked into his grandparents' bright warm family room. The fire was on, sending a rosy glow over the polished floor boards. Grandma was busy preparing tea, and Grandpa was reclining in his new chair. He looked extremely comfortable.

'Hello, mate,' said Grandpa, flying awkwardly out of his seat. 'I'll never get used to this newfangled chair,' he said, grinning. 'They don't have any instructions about how to get out of these things.'

Jack couldn't help smiling. His grandfather always managed to make him laugh, no matter what.

'Come and give me a hug, Jack,' said his grandma, affectionately, 'and tell me what you have been doing with yourself. I hear you stayed at a friend's place last night. I'll stir the soup while you tell me all about it. Your grandfather has to go and get something for you before we have tea. So tell me all about last night.'

Jack felt better as he chatted with his grandma and helped her butter some warm rolls. He was even starting to feel a little hungry. The smell of pea and ham soup, and the thought of lemon pudding bubbling away in the oven, was just too tempting. It was nice, thought Jack, being over here with his grandparents. Much nicer than home. Things didn't seem right there at the moment. He wished he could stay here forever.

His thoughts drifted back to Ben. He tried hard to put it out of his mind, but it was always there. The memory of Ben being taken was always there.

'Are you all right, mate?' Jack jumped. He hadn't heard his grandpa come back into the room. He was carrying something quite large, and it was covered with an old towel. 'I've been working on this for a couple of days,' continued Grandpa. 'We found it down by the river. Well actually, Maxine and Scarlet found it. So I've been fixing it up. Do you want to see it?'

Jack nodded and stared at the object. There was something about the shape that looked familiar. There was something about it that made him feel strange. He could feel himself shivering. Even though the fire was on, he felt cold. Jack found it difficult to think properly because he knew; he knew exactly what was under the cover.

Slowly the sheet was removed and a small brown head was revealed. Jack took a deep breath as two large round eyes stared straight at him. He couldn't believe this was happening.

The dog's neck was covered in scratches and his left ear and right paw looked a little crooked, but it was him: it was really him. He reached out, and gently touched the top of the dog's head. His hands were shaking and he struggled to get his breath. Jack took the dog and held him to his chest. He never wanted to let him go. A tear ran down his cheek, as he turned to face his grandfather.

'You've found Ben, Grandpa. I don't know how I can ever thank you. You've found my dog.'

His grandparents stood there in silence. They

couldn't believe what they had just witnessed. Jack loved this ornament. He really loved it. Grandpa smiled. 'I think it's time we ate, Jack, then we'll take you and the dog home. Are you okay with that?'

Jack nodded. 'I couldn't think of anything better,' he said, placing Ben next to him and grabbing a bread roll. 'I couldn't think of anything better in the whole wide world.'

Theresa heard the back door slam. It was Mary, followed by Jack. She hadn't seen Mary for ages and she missed her. She missed watching her potter around the garden and hang out the washing. She missed her sitting on the garden seat and drinking her tea. Theresa was fascinated by her, but lately she only ever came out briefly, and when she did, she looked so sad, thought Theresa. So desperately sad.

But today she was laughing, and so was Jack. He looked happy. Why was he so happy? wondered Theresa. She was disappointed that he could act this way. It was as if he didn't care about Ben being missing. It was as if he only cared about the thing he was carrying. Even from this distance she could tell that Jack was hugging it tightly to his chest. It must be something very special. Oh! If only she could get closer.

Theresa kept staring at the shape. There was something about it. There was something about it that looked familiar. She watched Jack intently. She watched him patting its head. She felt sad. He used to pat Ben like that. He used to... and then it struck her, but it couldn't be. It just couldn't. She felt sick in the stomach. It just wasn't possible, but it was him. She just knew it. She just knew that the shape she was looking at was Ben. Jack was holding Ben!

Daisy and Felicity could hardly control themselves. They couldn't believe what they were seeing. They thought they had lost him. They thought they would never see him again, but here he was staring right at them. Those big round eyes were staring right at them. They could see the scratch marks on his neck, and his ear that curled over slightly, but it didn't matter. He was alive. Beautiful Ben was alive. They watched in amazement as Jack gently placed him under the urn. Ben was back with his friends. He was back safe and sound, and most importantly he was back in the garden he loved.

23

Mary Meets Her Soul Mate

Mary sat alone, staring out into the bleak night. Her son had gone to bed exhausted. It had been a long emotional day for him, but he was happy. She smiled as she thought of Jack. He had been very anxious to get her back inside this evening; it was as if the garden was solely his after sunset. He loved it, just like she did, but somehow there was something else. As if to a magnet, every night Jack was drawn to the garden. It worried Mary sometimes; particularly this obsession he had with the ornaments. It was as if they were his friends. Look at the state he had been in when the little dog was stolen. Mary sighed a deep sad sigh. Somehow the situation reminded her of something, but she couldn't quite put her finger on it.

She shivered. Even the heat of the fire seemed unable to penetrate her frozen bones. It had been an exceptionally cold winter and a depressing one. She had been told last week that she no longer had a job. Her employer had been apologetic, but said that he couldn't keep Mary on; 'not even for a few hours a week'. On top of everything else, this had been the last straw.

She turned from the window and stared into the fire, mesmerised by the dancing flames. It helped her to forget. Now that she wasn't working, Alan was adamant that the house should be sold. In frustration, he had even yelled at her. He had never done that before. It was so hurtful. 'Ask your parents for help, Mary, or we sell this house. That's my final word on the matter.' She remembered yelling back at him and storming out of the room. It was terrible.

Mary could feel tears welling up in her tired eyes. Alan didn't understand how much she loved this place. It wasn't the house so much; it was her garden, her beloved garden. It was as if it were a part of her. It was the only thing over the years, besides her beautiful son, that had given her comfort.

Mary turned her face back to the window and looked out into the night. There was a glimmering dotted line where, last summer, Alan had placed solar lights between the bushes and along the garden path. It had been after the kitchen was vandalised. To this day, nobody, including the police, had ever worked out what really happened. It was the strangest thing. Since the lights had been put in she had never been out at night to see how they worked; maybe it was time she did. Maybe she could try out the new seat Alan had bought for her. She just needed time alone, and the garden was the perfect place.

Grabbing her coat and scarf, Mary quietly let herself out the back door. She was forced to wrap the scarf around her face as the cold night air stung her cheeks; it was absolutely freezing. She walked onto the verandah, shivering a little, and noticed the foggy haze that encircled the solar lights. In fact the whole garden was covered by a filmy mist, giving everything a ghostly, mystical appearance. Mary stepped down onto the lawn, and hesitated; should she go on, or go back inside? It was strange being out there in the dead of night. It wasn't like being in her garden at all; it was like a completely different place.

She wished she could stop shaking; even her teeth were chattering. Mary couldn't tell if it was from the cold or fear, because right now, she was scared. There was nothing to be heard, not a sound, but she felt like she was being watched; it was the strangest feeling. She had an eerie sense that she was not alone.

Continuing down the garden path, Mary was comforted by the warm glow of the solar lights. She noticed that Ben the dog, Daisy the mouse, and the little girl were not to be seen. Even Annie the mushroom was not in her usual place. Mary had seen Jack place the ornaments into the cubby some nights, so she presumed that's where they all were. He seemed to worry about them catching cold, thought Mary sadly. She wondered what he had done with Mr Tom. It was impossible for her son to move him. Maybe she'd go around to the side garden and see for herself.

With some difficulty, Mary slowly made her way around to the side, but it was hard to see. The lights were so dull, the garden was barely visible. She stopped briefly. Something didn't feel right. It wasn't just the darkness and the strange shadows. It was something else. Was it the complete silence? She wasn't sure. It was just a feeling she had: a very strong feeling.

She passed the big blue pots, but there was no Herbert or Reggie. She guessed Jack had put them with the others. She kept walking to where she knew Mr Tom stood, but the wall was bare. Mary was stunned. How could Jack have moved him? How? She glanced across to the chaise longue, and could scarcely believe her eyes. It was Mr Tom. There, stretched out in front of her, was Mr Tom.

The huge ornament took up the whole couch. His legs were curled up, and covered by one of her old pink blankets. There was no way her young son could have lifted the cat up there, and how had he bent his legs? Mary couldn't take her eyes off him. He looked so life-like. A light mist swirled around Mr Tom's head, as he quietly lay there in what appeared to be a deep comfortable sleep. He looked almost human. Mary shivered. She felt she had no business being here; it was like she was intruding in someone's house. She wanted to go, but she couldn't stop staring at him. She moved a little closer. She could only see his face under the rug, but it looked real, so very real. She reached out; her fingers nearly touching his long fine whiskers. She was so close. Then it happened. The impossible happened.

The cat moved! Right in front of her, the cat moved! Mary screamed, turned round and fled. She didn't look back. She just kept running. This couldn't be happening. It couldn't. She must have imagined it; maybe it was the mist playing tricks with her eyes. It just wasn't possible. How could a stone ornament move? How could it? She should go back inside, but she couldn't think straight. Something compelled her to keep going. She raced past the wrought iron seat and the huge yellow daisy bush. She wasn't going to stop until she reached the cubby and the little seat. She wasn't going to stop until she got there.

Alan looked through the bedroom window at his wife's shadowy figure walking away from the house. He watched her follow the line of solar lights along the garden path until she disappeared from view in the swirling mist that engulfed everything. It was a dreadful night; one of those cold winter nights when no one should be outside. He wondered if he should go and get her, but somehow he didn't think that that was a very good idea. He felt awful that he yelled at her: really awful, but she was so unreasonable. The problem could be solved if she only asked her parents for help. He knew they would gladly help. He just knew they would.

Alan sighed, but, the worst part of all this was Jack. He loved this house. Even more, he loved the garden. How on earth was he going to tell Jack that they were selling the house? How?

Short of breath, Mary finally made it to the top of the garden. She was exhausted. She couldn't believe what had just happened. She was glad to reach the small seat; it was comforting to see something solid; something real. What was it about this garden? Did Jack know something about it? Is that why he was out here night after night? If only she knew.

Shaking, Mary sat down and sucked in the freezing air. It was refreshing. She looked around her. The cubby was close by, and it made her wonder. It made her wonder about the ornaments.

The moon was peeking out from behind a cloud, its soft light spreading a glow through the mist giving the garden a more familiar appearance. Mary could even see her pots, full of newly planted pansies, and she could smell the strong scent of eucalyptus through the cold air. It made her feel calmer. The garden always made her feel calmer: even tonight: even after Mr Tom.

She placed her face into her cold hands, and

stretched out her long legs. Mary tried to imagine life without this garden, but she just couldn't. Maybe she could look for another job, or maybe she could ask her parents for help. Either way, she was never going to leave, never.

She suddenly felt tired and defeated, unable to hold the tears back any longer. She hadn't been game to cry before in case Jack heard her, but now, out here in this lonely garden, she couldn't keep them away. It was as if she was finally grieving for everything she had lost in her life. Her sobs were gentle at first, but gradually became louder and louder until she cried like a small child.

She remembered being ten years old, in England. She remembered playing with her new puppy. He was golden and fluffy, with soft brown eyes. She would hide from him amongst the lavender bushes, and giggle uncontrollably as she watched him bounce around the garden trying to find her. Oh! How she loved her puppy, and how she loved her garden.

Then one cold wet winter's day, her parents told her they were moving to a new country. They were moving to Australia for a better life. Mary couldn't understand it. She had a good life. She had her family, her friends, and her beautiful puppy. Above all she had her garden, her own magical garden. She had it all. Why did she have to leave?

From the day she left, she had pushed the memory of her puppy and the garden to the back of her mind. She never spoke of them again, and now, thought Mary, sobbing; now it was happening all over again. Everything she loved was always taken from her: everything.

Theresa quietly got up from where she lay in the

cubby. She had heard footsteps. No one came out into the garden this time of night. Not even Jack. She cautiously pulled back the curtains and peeked through the window. Someone was sitting on the seat. She couldn't see properly through the mist, but there was definitely someone on the seat. She quickly glanced around the room to check that everyone was asleep, and then quietly opened the blue door.

She crept down the ramp and moved silently towards the seat. She could hear sobbing. She got a little closer, and nearly cried out in shock. It was Mary. She was sitting with her head in her hands and sobbing. She was out here all alone; sobbing.

Theresa felt so sad for her. She wanted to race over and comfort her, but she knew it was wrong: so terribly wrong. She thought of Daisy, and all the trouble she got into for talking to Jack, but how could she just stand here and do nothing? Who would know if she spoke to her? They were all asleep. Nobody need ever know. She was so close to her. She reached out and gently touched Mary on the shoulder. She felt her shiver. She didn't want to frighten her. She just wanted to help her.

'Why are you crying, Mary,' said Theresa, softly. 'Why are you in so much pain? Please let me help you.'

Startled, Mary turned round quickly to see where the voice was coming from. She had felt something brush against her shoulder, and now someone was speaking to her. Was she going mad? First Mr Tom, and now this. Mary looked up. There, looking down at her was the loveliest young woman she had ever seen. She had the kindest eyes. Her long dark hair hung loose around her shoulders, and her pale skin was so fine it shone in the moonlight. She was beautiful.

'Who are you?' said Mary, nervously. 'What are you doing here?' She couldn't drag her eyes away. There was something about the young woman. Something that seemed familiar, but what? 'Do I know you?' continued Mary. 'Do you live close by?'

Theresa looked into Mary's tear-stained face, and took a deep breath. 'I live here, Mary. This garden is my home. You do know me, but we have never spoken. My name is Theresa.'

It seemed forever before Mary spoke. She had wiped away her tears, and kept staring straight ahead. Slowly, she turned her head to see if the statue was where she remembered it to be, but all she saw was a vacant pedestal. She cleared her throat.

'You're Theresa? The girl on the pedestal?'

Theresa nodded, and slowly sat down. She placed a warm hand over Mary's cold one, and spoke in a whisper. 'Does it frighten you that I can talk to you? Does it shock you that I look as human as you do? You see, it is perfectly normal to me, but as a human, you must find it unbelievable.'

Mary stared into the moonlit garden. 'You don't frighten me, but I do think it's unbelievable.' She turned to face Theresa. 'Although, in a way, it doesn't shock me. I have always had a funny feeling about this garden. I have always felt that I wasn't alone. As I watched Jack over these past months, and came to realise his need to be with you all, I did wonder what was going on, but it all makes sense now. It all makes perfect sense.'

She hesitated, trying to find the right words. She

hadn't told anyone this, but there was something about this young woman. She wanted to tell her everything.

'I had my own special garden once,' said Mary, quietly. 'Not like this. I didn't have any ornaments, but it was special. I even had my very own puppy. I was only Jack's age, but I still remember that terrible feeling of loss when I had to leave them. Now Alan wants me to leave this garden, with all its beautiful memories. I can't do it Theresa. I just can't do it.'

Theresa sat perfectly still, taking it all in. What Mary was telling her was awful. She couldn't imagine what life would be without Jack.

'What about Jack?' said Theresa, finally. 'How will he cope with this news? And, what about us? We love him very much, and we rely on him in so many ways. What about us, Mary?'

'I don't know,' said Mary, honestly. 'I really don't know. She was quiet for a moment before she spoke. 'Has Jack known about your secret for long?' Mary looked straight into the girl's eyes. 'I still find this so hard to comprehend.'

'It's only been a year this spring.' Theresa ran her fingers through her dark hair as she thought about that day. 'But it seems such a long time ago. We met him a week after the storm, when Daisy was injured and Grandpa fixed her. Jack saved Daisy's life, so she spoke to him. She shouldn't have, but we are so glad she did. I can't imagine our world without him. He's helped us through some terrible times. Really terrible.'

'What sort of terrible times?' said Mary, still wondering if she was going slightly mad.

'Oh, things like saving Katie the kookaburra from a horrible black cat. It was so close,' said Theresa, with a shudder. 'I wasn't there, but apparently Maxine and Scarlet heard their cries for help, and the next minute Jack was standing at the back door. The dogs chased the cat away. They saved Katie's life, and,' continued Theresa, 'there was the dreadful time that Ben the dog was taken. That was even worse.'

'I remember that time,' said Mary, interrupting. 'I had never seen Jack so upset. If only I'd known. Do you know who stole him?'

'Stole him?' said Theresa, puzzled. 'He wasn't stolen. He was taken by an eagle; right in front of us. I still feel sick thinking about it.'

'Taken by an eagle? But that's awful,' said Mary, shocked. 'No wonder Jack was so distraught, and I was no help at all. I feel so terrible for him.'

'Well, it worked out all right in the end, but it wouldn't have if it wasn't for Jack. We need him, Mary,' said Theresa, with pleading eyes. 'He's part of us now. He really is. Jack even helps us to sort out squabbles and problems.'

'Do they need sorting out?' said Mary, smiling for the first time. 'I mean, what are these 'squabbles and problems'? It just seems so hard to imagine what they are like.'

'Oh, they need sorting out all right, particularly young Daisy and Felicity. Those two can get up to all sorts of mischief.' Theresa chuckled. 'It's very hard to stay cross with them though; no matter how hard I try, and Reggie the gnome and Mr Tom are always trying to compete for top spot. Since the arrival of Mr Tom it has been an ongoing battle, but we all find it very amusing.'

'I saw Mr Tom tonight,' said Mary, shuddering at

the memory. 'I saw him move. I thought I was seeing things. I think I still do.

'I don't blame you. Seeing Mr Tom move would be confronting for anyone,' said Theresa, 'let alone a human. I like him though. He's a very interesting cat.'

'Tell me more,' said Mary, with a touch of excitement in her voice. Her misery had temporarily disappeared. This was just too incredible. She had to know more. 'Tell me about all of them.'

And so, with the mist swirling around them and the light of the moon shining upon them, Mary heard all about Herbert, Annie, Katie and Maggie. She hung on her every word. Theresa told her everything she could think of, pleased to see Mary in a happier state of mind.

Mary sat there in wonderment. It was hard to believe that this was happening. That suddenly she had found herself in this magical world; a world that previously only Jack knew existed. These folk were real; they did real things, good and bad, and the more Theresa spoke of them the more she felt she knew them.

It was then it came to her; a wild thought, but one that had to be investigated. She took a deep breath. 'Did Daisy and Felicity come into my house a few months ago and wreck my kitchen? It has been bothering me for ages; I badly need to know.'

Theresa felt awful. That was an incident the folk were not proud of; and one that Daisy and Felicity in particular had been punished for, but she had to tell her the truth. She couldn't lie. Reluctantly Theresa told her everything. She told her about the pet door, and how Jack said it could only be used in emergencies. She told her how Daisy had been determined to get inside, and had talked Felicity, Ben and Reggie into going.

'Apparently, Daisy had insisted on finding the cake tin. She and Felicity particularly love your little chocolate cakes; we all do. But,' said Theresa, trying not to laugh, 'whenever Daisy is involved something always goes wrong, and that night there was a series of accidents getting to the cakes. Daisy is very cute, but she can also be very naughty. I am so sorry.'

'Oh! I'm pleased,' said Mary. 'Not pleased that they wrecked my kitchen, just pleased that it wasn't humans who did it. There are some humans who aren't very nice. I'd much rather it was Daisy, Felicity, Ben and Reggie who were inside. 'I'm just so thankful I finally know who was responsible.'

'Speaking of humans,' said Theresa, with some urgency, 'please keep your meeting with me a secret. We are not allowed to speak to humans. Jack is the one exception. He even has a special golden key which allows him into our world. I should never have spoken to you. No one else should ever know about us. I don't even want Jack to know that we have met.'

'I would never tell a soul about you,' said Mary, a little hurt that Theresa thought she would, 'and I promise I will never tell Jack about tonight, never. This is his place, and I don't belong here. I will never breathe a word to anyone. I promise.'

'Shall I tell you more then?' said Theresa. 'She was comfortable now that their secret was safe. 'Or would you rather I stopped?' She could hear the chimes of the grandfather clock. It was three o'clock in the morning.

'Keep going,' said Mary. 'Please keep going.' She

listened in complete silence as Theresa told her about life in the garden. To her it sounded like the most wonderful place. She almost felt envious of Jack. She wanted to be part of it too.

'And finally,' said Theresa, her voice faltering, 'finally, there was my very best friend. But she's gone now. I haven't seen her since the last big storm we had. I haven't seen her for ten years.' Theresa wiped her eyes. 'She was so pretty, and so much fun. She would visit me every day, and tell me all the gossip. Sometimes she would bring me flowers. She always carried a basket full of beautiful flowers.' Theresa smiled. 'I can see her now, racing down the path, blonde hair flying. Even with her blue ribbon, her hair always seemed to be in a mess. Annie was always telling her to tidy it up. She didn't care though. She would just laugh and kiss the top of Annie's head. She said that life was too short to worry about things like that. She said life was for living.' Theresa stopped. She looked across at Mary. She had gone deathly pale. She looked awful.

'What was your friend's name?' Mary's voice sounded so cold.

'Her name was Rachel, and to this day I don't know what happened to her,' said Theresa, sadly. 'I still miss her, you know. I just wish I had something to remember her by. I haven't even got her blue ribbon. I just have my memories.'

'I put that ribbon in Rachel's hair,' said Mary, in the same cold voice, and every week, I would fill the little basket she carried with fresh flowers. It was important to me.'

Theresa stared at her in disbelief. Mary knew Rachel? She knew her friend? But why did she sound so angry? Why did Rachel's name make her angry?

Mary cleared her throat. Her voice became softer. 'I do know what it means to lose someone you love, and I know how it hurts. The thing is,' said Mary, lowering her voice, 'the thing is it was me who found your friend after the storm. It was me who had to pick up her broken body. I'm so sorry. I'm so sorry you lost your friend.'

Theresa wanted to cry, but nothing would come out. She just sat and listened; listened to the whole sad story.

'You know, I loved her too,' said Mary. 'There was a connection with Rachel for me as well.'

'A connection?' said Theresa. 'What connection? She hadn't spoken to you, had she? She surely hadn't spoken to you?'

Mary shook her head. 'No, it was nothing like that. Before Jack, there was someone very special in my life.'

Theresa waited patiently for Mary to find the right words.

'Before Jack, I had another child.' Mary turned to face Theresa. 'A beautiful daughter. She was so lovely ....'

'You had a daughter?' interrupted Theresa. 'Jack had a sister? I can't believe this is happening. First Rachel, and now this. What was she like? Oh, Mary, please tell me what she was like.'

Mary smiled. 'She was everything a mother could want. She had big blue eyes and a mass of golden curls. I used to put a blue ribbon in her hair to stop it getting in her eyes. She was always such a happy little girl.'

'Is that the ribbon you gave Rachel?' Theresa felt

ill. Her friend's ribbon belonged to Mary's daughter. It was all so sad.

Mary nodded. 'In the warmer months, we would come out into the garden together. We would sit on a rug and just play. Sometimes I would take her hand and we would walk around the garden and pick flowers. She loved the garden.' Mary wiped her eyes. She was trying so hard not to cry. 'A fortnight before her third birthday, our little girl became very ill. It was all so sudden. It was all so terrible. Then, on Friday the fifth of August, she quietly left us. Every year at this time I feel so sad.

'Why this time of the year? Why not other days?' Theresa couldn't imagine what losing a daughter would be like. She felt like she needed to know everything.

'Because,' said Mary, sadly, 'because today is the fifth of August. Today she would have been fourteen years old. My daughter Rachel would have been fourteen.'

'Is that why you called my friend Rachel?' said Theresa, almost in tears. 'After your daughter?'

'Yes. I felt as if the spirit of my daughter was in my garden with Rachel. When I found your friend in pieces, I felt that I had lost my daughter all over again. It's only here in my garden, surrounded by my flowers, that I feel my daughter's presence. She is everywhere. It's here I feel at peace, and I know if I have to leave, I will have lost her forever.'

There was complete silence as the two women sat together, thinking of those they had loved and lost. Thinking of what might have been.

'Thank you for telling me about Rachel,' said Theresa, breaking the silence. 'It has filled a hole in my heart, and given me a sense of closure.' She glanced at Mary. 'Now you need to tell Jack about baby Rachel. He needs to know he had a sister. He needs to know he isn't alone, and you need to move on, Mary. So that Jack can, too. He loves you, but he needs his mother back, to be completely happy. You know that, don't you?'

Mary took a deep breath. 'Yes, I do. Thank you for caring enough to listen. It will still take time, but I know unburdening myself to you will fill a hole in my heart too, and I promise, I will tell Jack.'

'All we have to do now,' said Theresa, feeling strangely at peace, 'is to work out a plan. A plan where you can stay here forever, and we will, Mary. I promise you we will.'

Meanwhile, in the cubby, the folk were snoring, oblivious to the heartfelt discussion taking place outside their door. They were warm and cosy, with full stomachs, happy in the knowledge that all their friends were safe. For them, everything was now right with the world, and they were all certain that nothing would ever trouble them again. All, that is, except one: one of them who was wide awake and listening to the chatter below. Little did Theresa know that one of them now knew her biggest secret. Little did she know that one little mouse now knew everything.

24

Jack's Special Night

From his bedroom Jack could hear the sound of talking and laughter ringing out from the kitchen. His parents were happily chatting, and he smiled at Grandpa's loud laugh and Grandma telling him to be quiet. Jack stretched his long thin legs to the end of his bed, feeling for the dogs, but he should have known that they would already be downstairs waiting to be fed. They reminded him of Daisy: always hungry. He yawned. For some reason he felt very tired and didn't feel like getting up, even though today was going to be very special.

He looked across at the photo his mother had recently placed on his bedside table. He looked at the blue eyes staring down at him, and the mass of golden curls that framed the pretty face. He wished he could hear his sister's voice and touch the blue ribbon in her hair, but he couldn't. All he could do was stare at the photo, and wonder what might have been. At least now he knew who the statue Rachel had been named after. He had known that it had to be someone special, and he was right.

Jack had been hurt and angry when his mother told him about Rachel. When she told him after all these years that he had a sister. He was hurt that his parents had never bothered to tell him before; angry that Rachel wasn't with him now; and angry that she wasn't here to celebrate his birthday. For today he was going to be eleven years old. Today, he was only two years away from being a teenager.

He leant over and opened the curtains, the sun nearly blinding him as it streamed through the bedroom window. It was a beautiful spring day, a perfect day for a birthday.

Jack's thoughts were interrupted by the grandfather clock chiming downstairs. It was seven o'clock, and his mother had told him to be down for breakfast by half past. Time to get moving. He pulled on his clothes and reached into the dressing table drawer for his watch, then stopped. Next to the watch, in its usual place, lay the golden key, gleaming in the sunlight. Carefully, he picked it up and turned it over in his hand. After that terrible time when he thought he had lost it, he had made sure that the key was always stored safely in the drawer, but today was different: today was a special day. He smiled and pushed it into his pocket.

He thought about that day. The day he met the folk. The day he was handed the golden key. He found it hard to believe that it was a whole year since he met Daisy and the rest of the folk; a whole year. He had to pinch himself sometimes. It was almost unbelievable that he had a garden full of ornaments that came to life, but here he was, on Saturday the sixth of September, about to celebrate his eleventh birthday with them. It was truly amazing. They were even giving him a party.

Sometimes he wondered what his life would have

been like if he had never met them. They had given him confidence to try new things, and always encouraged him. They loved him for just being himself, without expectations or criticism. 'Well, not much criticism,' laughed Jack, out loud, unless you took into account Maggie, Reggie, and Mr Tom. They could all be very critical.

Then he thought of Daisy, and chuckled. The little mouse was the very first ornament he had met, and she would always hold a special place in his heart. Daisy had cried and cried when he told her he was going to be eleven. She even tried to count the number of years on her fingers.

'You must be really old, Jack,' she said. 'I haven't got enough fingers.' Then her eyes opened wide. 'I don't want you to die,' she wailed. 'Humans die when they get old. I don't want you to die, Jack.' She was inconsolable until Jack assured her that he was still young and had no intentions of dying. Jack explained to the little mouse what birthdays meant, and that humans celebrated their birthdays no matter how old they were. He told her about the special birthday cake he had every year and all the delicious food that was there to eat. At the mention of food Daisy's eyes again opened as wide as saucers and the tears suddenly disappeared.

'Will we get yummy food this year?' she squealed, excitedly. 'Will we, Jack, will we?'

Gently touching her bonnet, Jack promised to bring plenty of food. He told her that the party would start at six bells the following day. It would begin as soon as the sun had set. Daisy clapped her hands with joy and rushed off immediately to tell the others. It seemed that Jack's dying of old age had been quickly forgotten. After all, this was the most exciting thing that had happened in the garden for a long while, and Daisy was going to make the most of it.

Jack couldn't help wondering what the next ten years would hold for him. He couldn't believe how his life had changed in just one year. Things that he would never have dreamt of or imagined possible had happened. He was now in a soccer team and was one of the best players. His father and grandfather were there every week urging him on. Jack loved them being there. It gave him a good feeling.

Lots of other things had changed too, like Brian Madison going from bully to being one of his best friends. Poor Brian, thought Jack. Last week his father got removed from watching him play soccer. The referee got sick of being called a 'cretin'. The referee was only fourteen years old.

'What a wimp,' said Brian, crossly. 'I'd give anything if all my old man called me was a "cretin." That's so lame.' Again Jack wondered what his father was really like.

So many other things had happened. Horrible things, like the time he nearly lost Ben to an eagle, and Katie to a black cat. It had taken the placid kookaburra a long time to get over that. She was so quiet, thought Jack. He never really knew what she was thinking.

Ben the dog, on the other hand, loved a chat. He was always searching Jack out to tell him the latest gossip. He seemed to get over being taken from the eagle fairly quickly. Even though it had been devastating at the time, Ben remained the same happy dog.

The folk were an interesting lot, thought Jack,

as he brushed his unruly hair. Look at Mr Tom and Reggie. They were quite impossible sometimes, but they did make life in the garden very enjoyable, and of course there was his beloved Herbert. The wombat seemed a bit happier these days since he explained to Maggie and Reggie that they were bullying him. Jack chuckled when he thought of Annie and Maggie. They both said what they thought, but were so different. Annie always made him laugh. Maggie on the other hand was a little more difficult. Still, he loved them all. Each one of them was special.

Jack made his way down the stairs, his thoughts turning to Felicity and Theresa. Felicity was a dear little girl with such a serious personality. Ages ago, Jack had talked to Felicity about her shyness and how she had to speak up if she wanted something, or wasn't happy. She had taken Jack's advice, but now, Daisy was always complaining that Felicity was 'getting too big for her boots' and wouldn't always do what Daisy wanted her to do. Jack sighed. It was so difficult to find a happy balance.

Finally there was Theresa. She was so beautiful and wise. If it wasn't for her he never would have been game to play soccer or stick up for himself against the bullies. Yes, thought Jack, I am a very lucky boy.

He reached the bottom of the stairs and headed towards the delicious smell of bacon frying. His mother had promised him a special birthday breakfast, and right now that was all he could think of. Thoughts of the folk disappeared as he was welcomed into the warm room with a very loud, 'Happy Birthday!' Grandpa and Grandma were sitting at the table each holding a large mug of tea. His grandma loved tea, and said if she was ever stuck on a desert island that's all she would need. She stopped drinking just long enough to blow him a birthday kiss.

'Happy birthday, Jack,' said his father, brightly. 'Hope you're feeling energetic. We've a lot planned for you today, so eat up.'

His mother gave him a huge birthday hug, after placing two large platters onto the table. One was piled high with bacon, tomatoes, French toast and pancakes. The other was full of all kinds of fruit. Jack didn't know where to start until he thought of Daisy's famous saying. 'Two, four, six, eight, bog in, don't wait.' He grinned to himself, and pushed a fork into the huge pile of food.

Jack could see his presents stacked up on the bench, and suddenly felt excited. Up until now, it had been much like any other day, but now he really did feel like he was having a birthday.

'I think it's time for presents, don't you?' said his mother, happily. She placed them on the table in front of him and gave Jack another kiss.

He looked at her carefully. Somehow she seemed different. Gone was the tired, stressed look. Her dark hair shone in the morning sun and her green eyes sparkled. He couldn't help thinking how pretty she looked.

She had told Jack how relieved she was that he knew about Rachel, and how happy she was that Grandpa and Grandma were helping them to buy the house, but there was something else, thought Jack. His mother almost had a glow about her.

His parents had told him last night that they had something special to talk to him about. Something good. Maybe that was it. Anyway, he really didn't care what the reason was; he had finally got his mother and father back, and that was all that mattered.

At the top of the garden, Daisy stood basking in the spring sunshine. It was wonderful to feel warm again. She sighed as she thought about the conversation between Mary and Theresa. She had heard everything that winter's night. She had heard Mary and Theresa talking. She knew about Rachel and she knew that Theresa had spoken to a human, but for now, it was just her secret. She wouldn't even tell Felicity or Annie. Poor Annie, thought Daisy, she had been so very cold this winter. Every evening the mushroom had complained that her hands and feet were frozen solid, and she couldn't move at all.

'This is worse than living in Siberia,' she had moaned. 'I'm sure I'd be better off there than here. I know I would.' Of course Annie had never been to Siberia, but Theresa had read in one of her books that Siberia was a very cold place. 'I feel like I can't go on another day,' Annie had wailed. 'I need some sun.'

Luckily for Annie, they now had the sun during the day and, thanks to Reggie, a warm place to stay at night. It had been Reggie's idea that the cubby be renovated for their use, and he never seemed to tire of reminding them of the fact.

Just thinking about their new house made Daisy feel excited. Tonight they were having a birthday party for Jack in the cubby and it was going to be so much fun. She just couldn't wait. Daisy couldn't wait for a lot of things; life had so much to offer, and she wanted to make the most of everything.

Even cleaning up the night before had been exciting. Under the instruction of Mr Tom, she and Felicity had worked for hours getting their new house clean, and then filling it with bright colourful flowers. She just hoped Jack loved it as much as they did. Mr Tom had done his best to make sure he would. The cat hadn't stopped nagging them until the job was done properly.

'It needs to be spotless, girls, spotless,' said Mr Tom, sternly, as he waved his long fine fingers at every corner of the cubby. 'Then when you have finished that task, I would like you both to collect as many apples as possible. Theresa wants us to have something healthy for dessert. Maggie and Katie will shake the tree for you and young Ben will help you carry the basket. I could write you a list of instructions if you would prefer?'

Without hesitating, the girls shook their heads. 'I think we can manage,' said Felicity, firmly. 'We are not stupid, Mr Tom, and we don't need any of your lists.'

'As you wish,' said the large cat, slightly hurt at the young girl's tone. 'I will leave you to your tasks.' With that, he tipped his hat and abruptly left for the vegetable garden. Sometimes Mr Tom felt he was misunderstood by the other folk, and tonight was one of those times.

Felicity could be quite sharp sometimes, thought Daisy, as she swept the cubby house floor. Poor Mr Tom; he never meant any harm. The little mouse couldn't work Felicity out. She seemed more aggressive than normal; more determined to be heard. She never used to be like that. Annie said it was because she was growing up, and Daisy had to start being less bossy to her. Daisy didn't even realise she was bossy.

Felicity would always be her best friend though, she knew that, and they would still have a lot of fun together, but her friend was different. Daisy chuckled to herself as she thought of someone else who had been bossy last night.

It happened after they had all completed their tasks, and Ben and Felicity decided to race each other up and down the ramp. Even Mr Tom, who had returned from his garden duties, happily helped out, using his fob watch to see who was the fastest. Daisy had joined in, squealing with excitement and almost turning cartwheels as her legs ran as fast as they could. It was so much fun.

The more the folk ran, the more excited they got, and even Herbert and Annie got in on the act. They did look a funny pair. Herbert hardly moved at all, and Annie's little legs seemed to take ages to get going. They were all having a great time, until they heard Reggie's booming voice.

'Are you all mad? If you keep doing this you are going to break the ramp. I want you all to stop this foolishness now. When are you people going to grow up and act your ages?' Reggie was huffing and puffing and his cheeks were bright red.

'How can we act our ages, pet?' laughed Annie. 'We don't know how old we are!'

Reggie stared at the old mushroom. Her face was beginning to peel, leaving big grey blotches. As far as he was concerned she looked hideous: absolutely hideous.

'Take a look in the mirror, then,' yelled Reggie. 'Then you will see that you're not just old, you're ancient! You're a silly old mushroom; that's what you are: silly!'

Suddenly the running stopped and there was a hushed silence. No one spoke to Annie like that, no one, and they certainly didn't call her silly.

The old mushroom stopped laughing. Tears appeared in her eyes and trickled down her weathered face. In all her years she had never been spoken to in such a manner. It was so hurtful.

Daisy and Felicity rushed to Annie's side and held her tight. Maggie and Katie clucked around her while Ben and Herbert each held one of her funny-shaped hands. Even Mr Tom was miffed that Reggie had treated the old mushroom in such a manner, and from that moment Reggie was on the outer. Nobody could be bothered with him, and they made it quite clear he would not be welcome at Jack's party.

Daisy grinned to herself. Yes! What an evening it had been, but this morning heralded the start of a brand new day: Jack's birthday! She sniffed the air and could almost smell the jasmine. Soon everything would be blooming, and the garden would be a riot of colour. The bees and colourful birds would be back and the garden would come alive again, but now, uppermost in Daisy's mind was Jack's party and all that food. It was going to be awesome. 'I can't wait for tonight,' squealed the little mouse out loud. 'I just can't wait!'

Jack stood at the kitchen table, overwhelmed with his presents. He was holding a brand new soccer ball in one hand and new soccer boots in the other. He buried his face into the leather, breathing in its newness. 'I'm rapt;' said Jack, putting on his boots, 'absolutely rapt. Thanks heaps, Mum and Dad.'

'You deserve it, Son. You really deserve it. Your mum and I are both proud of you.'

Jack felt an inner glow. His father wasn't one for giving a lot of praise, and to be told he was proud of him was the best gift Jack could ever receive. With two presents opened, he tore the paper off a parcel given to him by his grandparents. He laughed. It was the biggest chocolate frog he had ever seen. He couldn't even begin to imagine what the folk would do with this.

'Thank you so much, Grandma and Grandpa,' said Jack. 'I love it, and I can't wait to get stuck into it.'

'Oh,' said Grace, 'that isn't the only present we've got for you. That's just something to open now. The real present is being delivered for you later on today.' Grandma kissed the top of his head. 'We think you will adore that one.'

From up in the cubby, Felicity heard the back door slam, and was delighted to see Jack stride into the garden bouncing what looked like a brand new ball. He does look happy, thought Felicity. He looks really happy. She couldn't help thinking what a different boy Jack was now. For years the folk had watched him mope about the garden looking very miserable, and just about always on his own, but now, he was a different boy. Now, he enjoyed life, even with its ups and downs, and there had been lots of down times for Jack since becoming part of the garden. Like the time she, along with Daisy, Ben and Reggie accidentally wrecked his mother's kitchen. 'That was terrible,' chuckled Felicity. Jack had been so cross, and Annie was so angry, she hadn't spoken to them for a week.

Then there was the time Daisy nearly got crushed by a tree during the storm, and of course, there was Ben and Katie. Felicity shuddered as she remembered the night the little dog was taken by the eagle, and the time the kookaburra nearly got eaten by the cat. Without Jack, Daisy wouldn't have been fixed, and Ben and Katie wouldn't have been saved. So tonight they were going to have a birthday party for Jack. To thank him for all the things he had done for them. It was going to be wonderful, thought Felicity. It was going to be the best night in her whole life.

Theresa watched Jack make his way up the garden path. She smiled at him playing with his new ball. This time last year Jack wouldn't have given soccer a second thought, let alone wanting a ball for his birthday. Theresa looked at Jack through loving eyes. The boy had proved to them how loyal and trustworthy he was. Theresa was proud of him. As far as she was concerned he was one of them now. He was one of the folk.

She smiled to herself when she saw Mary come out into the garden. They hadn't spoken since their heart-to-heart a few months ago, but Theresa had found little notes hidden amongst the daisy bushes. One note in particular made her very happy. It was on such pretty pink paper, and it read:

Dear Theresa,

We can't believe it. The angels have blessed us with something so very special: something I have been praying about for a very long time. We are going to have a baby. If it's a girl, would you mind if we call her Theresa?

Love, Mary

PS I have left something that I think you will like, under the big yellow daisy bush.

That evening Theresa had found a beautifully bound leather poetry book on birds. When she opened it she was stunned, absolutely stunned. Folded neatly between the pages were a bright blue ribbon and a note:

Now you have Rachel with you forever. All my love, Mary.

Theresa had already read the book three times. She just loved it. There was a particularly sad poem about two little birds locked in a cage. One day the door was left open and they had their chance to be free, but only one of the birds could fly, and instead of escaping into the blue sky, he decided to stay with his friend, and closed the door. The poem had upset Theresa terribly. She didn't know why, but it had. Felicity had found her weeping behind the daisy bush.

'Why are you crying, Theresa?' The little girl looked worried. 'Why are you crying?'

Theresa didn't want to tell her. It was so silly, but when she read her the poem, Felicity understood.

'I know why it has made you sad,' said Felicity, in her serious tone. 'The little bird wanted its freedom, but because he loved his friend so much, he was willing to stay trapped in his cage. He loved his friend more than he loved being free.' She looked at Theresa. 'Like us really. We are all trapped too you know. We are trapped in our bodies, and in this garden. That's why you feel sad. I feel sad too, sometimes,' said Felicity, softly, 'but, like those little birds, we have each other, and that's all that matters. Don't you think?'

Theresa had kissed the top of her friend's red curly

head, and told her how clever she was. She was right, they did have each other, and that was all that mattered.

Theresa's thoughts returned to the present as she looked back into the garden. She watched Mary walk up to Jack and hug him.

'It's time to get ready, Jack,' said his mother, quietly. 'We have a big day ahead of us, and you have also got your own party in the cubby later on, so let's make a move.' Mary gently took hold of Jack's hand, and to Theresa's delight, slowly turned her head and smiled at her. She gave a slight wave, and then they were gone.

Theresa smiled. Mary would be her window to the world, and that would have to be enough. She was lucky. She had some wonderful friends and she had Jack and Mary, and now, all she had to do was wait; wait for the best party ever.

Herbert was also watching Jack and his mother. The boy had gone ahead in leaps and bounds since the days he would come and read to him. He missed those long chats. He still saw Jack sometimes, but the boy was always so busy. Still, thought Herbert sadly, he was happy for him, and he still had Mr Tom and Reggie. Best of all he was going to his first ever birthday party, and he wouldn't miss that for the world.

Reggie was still feeling very put out by the folk's attitude to him. Just because he spoke his mind sometimes, the whole world got upset. He hadn't meant to hurt the old mushroom's feelings, but she really should have had more sense. Anyway, the good thing to come out of the whole situation was that running up and down the ramp was now banned.

Theresa had come down hard on everybody, particularly him. She had torn strips off him for upsetting Annie, and made him go and apologise. Annie had been quite good about it, but the others, particularly that silly little mouse and the young girl were still not talking to him. Ridiculous, thought Reggie; utterly ridiculous.

At least he was now allowed to go to the party: that was a start. Good old Herbert said he could sit with him, but only on condition that Reggie had to try and rise above the situation. Herbert was often right. He was a wise old thing sometimes, so tonight Reggie decided he would try and be as civil as possible to everyone: even that annoying mouse. After all, it was the boy's special night, and nothing must go wrong; absolutely nothing.

Ben could hardly contain himself. Tonight they were going to celebrate Jack's eleventh birthday. Mr Tom had been chief organiser, and Theresa was in charge of the food. The little dog could hardly wait. After the horrible year he had had, this was going to be the best. Yes, thought Ben, as he watched Jack carting a huge box full of food to the cubby. This is definitely going to be the best.

Jack looked at his mother stuffing all the food into the large hamper. He couldn't believe how much she was putting in. 'Why are you giving me all this food? There's only going to be me and the dogs, and they won't be eating much.' It puzzled him. He was expecting to have to smuggle food out, not have it given to him without any fuss. This was too weird.

'I know,' said his mother, sweetly, 'but I want this to look like a real party. Maybe you could put some of your ornaments in the cubby to make it look like you have people with you. When you have had enough, ring this bell and Dad and I will join you. I'd love to see the cubby, and your father will soon help you get rid of some of the food.'

Jack shook his head in amazement. He looked at his mother as she packed all the food and drink into the hamper. There were small sausage rolls, little pies and pasties, lollies, birthday cake, a plate of fruit and cordial. Daisy and Felicity will go bonkers, thought Jack; absolutely bonkers.

'Now, Jack, take this up to the cubby and I'll go and get Grandma and Grandpa. Remember they have a special present to give you.' His mother gave him a quick kiss and sent him on his way.

Jack walked thoughtfully up to the cubby. His mother's attitude to the garden and the ornaments was certainly different, but he mustn't let them come inside the cubby. That would be disastrous.

He lugged the hamper up the ramp, puffing a little as he dragged it in through the door. Once inside, he was bowled over by how good the room looked. It was usually a bit of a mess, unless Mr Tom came to visit. He had never seen it so clean and inviting.

There were flowers everywhere, a new tablecloth on the table, and all the plates and cups had been neatly stacked on top of the window ledge. Their blankets were in a neat pile in the corner, and the cushions were placed along the wall for people to sit on. The room was spotless: not a speck of dust or a cobweb to be seen. Jack was impressed.

Looking around the room, he felt a bit choked up. Apart from his parents, nobody had ever bothered to go to so much trouble just for him. As Daisy would say, 'it's awesome: absolutely awesome.'

Jack sat down on the small plastic chair. Even though he was excited about tonight, something was nagging at him. So far everything about his birthday had been perfect, but he couldn't help feeling that that was all about to change. Something out of his control was about to happen. But, as he heard the back door bang and his name being called, he pushed that thought to the back of his mind.

There was a flurry of fur as the dogs raced into the cubby, licking him all over. They led him down the ramp and onto the lawn. His grandparents and mother and father were waiting for him. For some reason, that feeling of doom swept over him again.

'I told you we had a special present for you,' called out Grandpa proudly. 'We walked the city for this, so we hope you like it.' Grandma was beaming, but his parents looked apprehensive. Suddenly Grandpa stepped to one side and there, standing behind him, was the largest present Jack had ever seen. It was wrapped from top to bottom in bright yellow paper with red spots. He couldn't stop staring at it. The thing was massive, and there was something about it: something that gave him the creeps.

'Come on Jack,' yelled Grandpa. 'Come on and open it. The thing won't bite!' Grandpa was getting impatient. 'You'll love it. I know you will.'

Annie watched the proceedings taking place. She was still feeling a bit fragile after Reggie's outburst the night before. He had apologised, but it had left her feeling very low. She knew she was old-looking, but it didn't feel good to be told. She was just so thankful to have the girls. They had been so good to her. They had comforted her and told her how much they loved her. It made Annie feel needed.

'Why don't you let Jack paint you?' Felicity had suggested. 'You would feel so much better.'

'Yes,' Daisy had cried, excitedly, 'he could paint you blue. Please let him paint you; please let him, Annie.'

The old mushroom smiled at the memory. Maybe one day she would let him paint her, but for the moment she had far more important things to think about; such as Jack's party tonight and this strange gift-giving ceremony taking place in front of her right now.

Jack, urged on by Grandpa, hesitantly approached the present. He was close enough to touch the wrapping, but where to start: it was just so big! He began to tear at the paper.

'Smile, dear,' called out Grandma from behind him. He turned round to face the camera. He heard his mother cry out. She was looking over his shoulder, covering her mouth with her hands, her eyes bulging like saucers. What was going on?

'Oh, come on, Jack,' yelled Grandpa. 'Have a look. He's a beauty!'

Jack spun round. The paper had fallen to the ground. He stared at the unwrapped present in disbelief. A hush fell over the gathering.

Grandpa's hearty voice continued. 'Well, Jack, we'll leave you to it, but you enjoy your new ornament. Not everyone can claim to have a North American Indian living in their garden!'

Jack swallowed hard as he stared in amazement at the young Indian boy before him. Not only was he complete with bow and arrow and headband and feather, but emblazoned on his right upper arm were three black circles in a perfect column. Jack pushed his hand deep into his pocket allowing his fingers to tighten around the golden key. He couldn't believe that this boy had the same circles as Theresa. Was he the next chosen one? Could he tell them about the power of the circles. Could he tell them their connection to the golden key? There were so many questions. Questions that not even Theresa knew the answers.

'I wish I did know what my powers were,' said Theresa, one day when the subject of the key and the black circles had come up. 'My friend Rachel knew, but she never had the chance to tell me. She just told me to guard the key with my life, and that the circles meant I was the next chosen one, but that's all Jack. That's all I know.' She had looked at him with kind brown eyes while gently touching his shoulder. ' Don't worry, Jack, we will find out. When the next chosen one enters the garden, we will find out.'

It was unbelievable. If only Grandpa knew, he thought. If only Grandpa knew the consequences of bringing this new ornament into the garden. A young Indian boy, complete with weapons: the thought was horrifying.

He shook his head and looked across to the distant hills. The sun was sinking like a beautiful red ball as his world promised to change once again, and Jack wondered whether it would be for the better, or then again..., but he couldn't worry about that now; he had a party to attend.

Epilogue

Jack slowly closed the book. There wasn't a sound. He knew it was late, but he hadn't been able to stop reading. All those memories coming to life on the page. A big part of his childhood was locked up in this book, and most importantly, they were in the book. Everything they did. Everything they said. Everything they felt. He smiled. It was there for everyone to read, but only he, Bella, and his sister, Tess, knew the truth. Except, thought Jack, suddenly. Except for Sam and Brian. At the time he had no choice. He had to tell them. He had to tell them the truth about the garden.

He looked down at his sleeping son. Jack was worried for him. If only he could tell him the truth. If only Peter could really step into that world. Just like he and Tess had, but it wasn't possible. It just wasn't possible.

'Daddy, is the book finished? I fell asleep.' Mia sat up rubbing her eyes.

'It is, precious.' Jack gently squeezed his daughter's hand.

'Daddy,' said Mia. 'Come closer. I don't want Peter to hear. I have to tell you something. It's very special, and you are the only person I can trust.'

'Am I?' said Jack, intrigued. 'This sounds mysterious.'

'It is,' said Mia, whispering into his ear, 'but you have to promise you won't get cross with me. I did something you told us not to do. So don't get cross.'

'Hmm,' said her father. 'I can't promise anything until I know what you've done. Can I?'

'Well,' said his daughter, fiddling with her hair. 'Well, the thing is, I crept outside after tea, and I waited.' She hesitated, watching her father. He said nothing. 'I waited for the sun to set,' continued Mia, 'and then I went looking for them.' She saw her father stiffen. 'I called out to them. I know I shouldn't have, but I did.'

'And ...,' said Jack, knowing exactly what his daughter was going to tell him, 'did they answer you?'

'No,' said Mia, slowly. She sensed that her father was a bit cross. 'No, but I kept calling out. I could hear something in the bushes. I felt a bit scared at first, and then I saw her. She was standing right in front of me. It was one of them Daddy. I know it was.'

'Are you sure it wasn't your imagination?' said Jack, clearing his throat. What else could he say. What else could he say to his daughter.

'No,' said Mia, crossly. 'It was the little girl. I know it was. She had a blue dress on, with yellow flowers, and she had red curly hair. Just like in your book ....'

Jack frowned. But it wasn't like the book. He had never described the colour of her dress. He and Bella knew it was blue with yellow flowers, but he had never written it in the book. He looked into his daughter's face, her dark eyes now struggling to stay open.

'She spoke to me, Daddy. She asked me what my name was. She asked me what I was doing in the garden.' Her eyes felt heavy, but she had to tell her father.

It was important. 'I told her my name was Mia,' she said, quietly. 'I told her I belonged to you. I told her your name was Jack.'

Mia lay back down. She closed her eyes. 'She ran away, Daddy, when I said your name. She didn't even say goodbye. But she was real. I know she was real.'

There was a moment's silence before her father spoke. 'What was her name, darling? What was the little girl's name?'

'Felicity. The little girl was Felicity. Just like...,' said Mia, 'just like....'

Jack gently pulled the covers up, and kissed the top of his daughter's curly head. What was he going to do? What was he going to say? It was so complicated. He slowly stood up as he heard the clock chime in the hallway. He turned off the light, as the clock kept chiming. It was midnight, and he was exhausted. Both physically and mentally. He would work out what to say tomorrow, but right now, all he wanted was his bed. Right now, all he wanted to do was sleep. He would tell them tomorrow. He and Bella would tell them tomorrow.